# BRIAN FLYNN

# THE TRIPLE BITE

With an introduction by
Steve Barge

DEAN STREET PRESS

Published by Dean Street Press 2019



Introduction © 2019 Steve Barge



First published in 1931 by John Long

Cover by DSP

ISBN 978 1 913054 53 3

www.deanstreetpress.co.uk

# BRIAN FLYNN
## THE TRIPLE BITE

BRIAN FLYNN was born in 1885 in Leyton, Essex. He won a scholarship to the City Of London School, and from there went into the civil service. In World War I he served as Special Constable on the Home Front, also teaching "Accountancy, Languages, Maths and Elocution to men, women, boys and girls" in the evenings, and acting in his spare time.

It was a seaside family holiday that inspired Brian Flynn to turn his hand to writing in the mid-twenties. Finding most mystery novels of the time "mediocre in the extreme", he decided to compose his own. Edith, the author's wife, encouraged its completion, and after a protracted period finding a publisher, it was eventually released in 1927 by John Hamilton in the UK and Macrae Smith in the U.S. as *The Billiard-Room Mystery*.

The author died in 1958. In all, he wrote and published 57 mysteries, the vast majority featuring the super-sleuth Antony Bathurst.

# INTRODUCTION

"I believe that the primary function of the mystery story is to entertain; to stimulate the imagination and even, at times, to supply humour. But it pleases the connoisseur most when it presents – and reveals – genuine mystery. To reach its full height, it has to offer an intellectual problem for the reader to consider, measure and solve."

THUS WROTE Brian Flynn in the *Crime Book Magazine* in 1948, setting out his ethos on writing detective fiction. At that point in his career, Flynn had published thirty-six mystery novels, beginning with *The Billiard-Room Mystery* in 1927 – he went on, before his death in 1958, to write twenty-one more, three under the pseudonym Charles Wogan. So how is it that the general reading populace – indeed, even some of the most ardent collectors of mystery fiction – were until recently unaware of his existence? The reputation of writers such as John Rhode survived their work being out of print, so what made Flynn and his books vanish so completely?

There are many factors that could have contributed to Flynn's disappearance. For reasons unknown, he was not a member of either The Detection Club or the Crime Writers' Association, two of the best ways for a writer to network with others. As such, his work never appeared in the various collaborations that those groups published. The occasional short story in such a collection can be a way of maintaining awareness of an author's name, but it seems that Brian Flynn wrote no short stories at all, something rare amongst crime writers.

There are a few mentions of him in various studies of the genre over the years. Sutherland Scott, in *Blood in Their Ink* (1953), states that Flynn, who was still writing at the time, "has long been popular". He goes on to praise *The Mystery of the Peacock's Eye* (1928) as containing "one of the ablest pieces of misdirection one could wish to meet". Anyone reading that particular review who feels like picking up the novel – out now from Dean Street Press – should stop reading at that point, as later in the book, Scott proceeds to casually spoil the ending, although as if he assumes that everyone will have read the novel already.

It is a later review, though, that may have done much to end – temporarily, I hope – Flynn's popularity.

> "Straight tripe and savorless. It is doubtful, on the evidence, if any of his others would be different."

Thus wrote Jacques Barzun and Wendell Hertig Taylor in their celebrated work, *A Catalog of Crime* (1971). The book was an ambitious attempt to collate and review every crime fiction author, past and present. They presented brief reviews of some titles, a bibliography of some authors and a short biography of others. It is by no means complete – E & M.A. Radford had written thirty-six novels at this point in time but garner no mention – but it might have helped Flynn's reputation if he too had been overlooked. Instead one of the contributors picked up *Conspiracy at Angel* (1947), the thirty-second Anthony Bathurst title. I believe that title has a number of things to enjoy about it, but as a mystery, it doesn't match the quality of the majority of Flynn's output. Dismissing a writer's entire work on the basis of a single volume is questionable, but with the amount of crime writers they were trying to catalogue, one can, just about, understand the decision. But that decision meant that they missed out on a large number of truly entertaining mysteries that fully embrace the spirit of the Golden Age of Detection, and, moreover, many readers using the book as a reference work may have missed out as well.

So who was Brian Flynn? Born in 1885 in Leyton, Essex, Flynn won a scholarship to the City Of London School, and while he went into the civil service (ranking fourth in the whole country on the entrance examination) rather than go to university, the classical education that he received there clearly stayed with him. Protracted bouts of rheumatic fever prevented him fighting in the Great War, but instead he served as a Special Constable on the Home Front – one particular job involved warning the populace about Zeppelin raids armed only with a bicycle, a whistle and a placard reading "TAKE COVER". Flynn worked for the local government while teaching "Accountancy, Languages, Maths and Elocution to men, women, boys and girls" in the evening, and acting as part of the Trevalyan Players in his spare time.

It was a seaside family holiday that inspired him to turn his hand to writing. He asked his librarian to supply him a collection of mystery novels for "deck-chair reading" only to find himself disappointed. In his own words, they were "mediocre in the extreme." There is no record of what those books were, unfortunately, but on arriving home, the following conversation, again in Brian's own words, occurred:

> "ME (unpacking the books): If I couldn't write better stuff than any of these, I'd eat my own hat.
>
> Mrs ME (after the manner of women and particularly after the manner of wives): It's a great pity you don't do a bit more and talk a bit less.
>
> The shaft struck home. I accepted the challenge, laboured like the mountain and produced *The Billiard-Room Mystery*."

"Mrs ME", or Edith as most people referred to her, deserves our gratitude. While there were some delays with that first book, including Edith finding the neglected half-finished manuscript in a drawer where it had been "resting" for six months, and a protracted period finding a publisher, it was eventually released in 1927 by John Hamilton in the UK and Macrae Smith in the U.S. According to Flynn, John Hamilton asked for five more, but in fact they only published five in total, all as part of the Sundial Mystery Library imprint. Starting with *The Five Red Fingers* (1929), Flynn was published by John Long, who would go on to publish all of his remaining novels, bar his single non-series title, *Tragedy At Trinket* (1934). About ten of his early books were reprinted in the US before the war, either by Macrae Smith, Grosset & Dunlap or Mill, and a few titles also appeared in France, Denmark, Germany and Sweden, but the majority of his output only saw print in the United Kingdom. Some titles were reprinted during his lifetime – the John Long Four-Square Thrillers paperback range featured some Flynn titles, for example – but John Long's primary focus was the library market, and some titles had relatively low print runs. Currently, the majority of Flynn's work, in particular that only published in the U.K., is extremely rare – not just expensive, but seemingly non-existent even in the second-hand book market.

In the aforementioned article, Flynn states that the tales of Sherlock Holmes were a primary inspiration for his writing, having read them at a young age. A conversation in *The Billiard-Room Mystery* hints at other influences on his writing style. A character, presumably voicing Flynn's own thoughts, states that he is a fan of "the pre-war Holmes". When pushed further, he states that:

> "Mason's M. Hanaud, Bentley's Trent, Milne's Mr Gillingham and to a lesser extent, Agatha Christie's M. Poirot are all excellent in their way, but oh! – the many dozens that aren't."

He goes on to acknowledge the strengths of Bernard Capes' "Baron" from *The Mystery of The Skeleton Key* and H.C. Bailey's Reggie Fortune, but refuses to accept Chesterton's Father Brown.

> "He's entirely too Chestertonian. He deduces that the dustman was the murderer because of the shape of the piece that had been cut from the apple-pie."

Perhaps this might be the reason that the invitation to join the Detection Club never arrived . . .

Flynn created a sleuth that shared a number of traits with Holmes, but was hardly a carbon-copy. Enter Anthony Bathurst, a polymath and gentleman sleuth, a man of contradictions whose background is never made clear to the reader. He clearly has money, as he has his own rooms in London with a pair of servants on call and went to public school (Uppingham) and university (Oxford). He is a follower of all things that fall under the banner of sport, in particular horse racing and cricket, the latter being a sport that he could, allegedly, have represented England at. He is also a bit of a show-off, littering his speech (at times) with classical quotes, the obscurer the better, provided by the copies of the *Oxford Dictionary of Quotations* and *Brewer's Dictionary of Phrase & Fable* that Flynn kept by his writing desk, although Bathurst generally restrains himself to only doing this with people who would appreciate it or to annoy the local constabulary. He is fond of amateur dramatics (as was Flynn, a well-regarded amateur thespian who appeared in at least one self-penned play, *Blue Murder*), having been a member of OUDS, the Oxford University Dramatic Society. Like Holmes, Bathurst isn't averse to the occasional disguise, and as with Watson and Holmes, sometimes even his close allies don't recognise him. General information about his background is light on the ground. His parents were Irish, but he doesn't have an accent – see *The Spiked Lion* (1933) – and his eyes are grey. We learn in *The Orange Axe* that he doesn't pursue romantic relationships due to a bad experience in his first romance. That doesn't remain the case throughout the series – he falls head over heels in love in *Fear and Trembling*, for example – but in this opening tranche of titles, we don't see Anthony distracted by the fairer sex, not even one who will only entertain gentlemen who can beat her at golf!

Unlike a number of the Holmes' stories, Flynn's Bathurst tales are all fairly clued mysteries, perhaps a nod to his admiration of Christie, but first and foremost, Flynn was out to entertain the reader. The problems posed to Bathurst have a flair about them – the simultaneous murders, miles apart, in *The Case of the Black Twenty-Two* (1928) for example, or the scheme to draw lots to commit masked murder in *The Orange Axe* – and there is a momentum to the narrative. Some mystery writers have trouble with the pace slowing between the reveal of the problem and the reveal of the murderer, but Flynn's books sidestep that, with Bathurst's investigations never seeming to sag. He writes with a wit and intellect that can make even the most prosaic of interviews with suspects enjoyable to read about, and usually provides an action-packed finale before the murderer is finally revealed. Some of those revelations, I think it is fair to say, are surprises that can rank with some of the best in crime fiction.

We are fortunate that we can finally reintroduce Brian Flynn and Anthony Lotherington Bathurst to the many fans of classic crime fiction out there.

## *The Triple Bite* (1931)

*"First find the Bulb, that flowers more bright,*
*than Daffodil or Crocus white.*
*Look ne'er for Sun, but seek the shade.*
*From Sky they came, on the Death Parade."*

BRIAN FLYNN made no secret of his admiration for the Sherlock Holmes stories that he read in his childhood, but there is perhaps no clearer love-letter to the work of Sir Arthur Conan Doyle than his tenth Anthony Bathurst novel, *The Triple Bite.*

The sidekick of the sleuth narrating the tale. A coded message leading, perhaps, to hidden treasure. A master criminal for our hero to pit his wits against. A mysterious method of murder that defies detection. And, as evidenced by Flynn's own introduction, one aspect of the story was inspired directly from a throwaway line in a Sherlock Holmes story. There is no need to allude to which story it is here, as Anthony Bathurst will let you know that fact as the tale concludes – and a rather more surprising connection to Sherlock Holmes as well.

There are many mentions in the Holmes canon to cases that Holmes solved but are, for whatever reason, not to be discussed with the public, ideas that writers have seized upon in recent years to pen their own stories of the Great Detective. Before Sherlock Holmes entered the public domain, however, most writers had to be content with using the ideas with their own characters.

Flynn follows this approach, as it is Bathurst's knowledge of Holmes' obscure cases that puts him on the right track in this case, but he takes things a little further. Apparently Scotland Yard has detailed files on these undocumented cases – so Flynn is presumably saying that Holmes and his investigations took place in the same universe as Bathurst's investigations.

This approach is similar to the one taken by Derek Smith in *Whistle Up The Devil*, where he refers to the adventures of the Great Merlini, whose exploits (notably 1938's *Death From A Top Hat*) were written up by Clayton Rawson. One other example is the 1966 Ellery Queen title, *A Study In Terror*, where Ellery finds an unpublished manuscript by John Watson detailing Holmes' hunt for Jack The Ripper, although that manuscript may well have been the script for the film of that adventure, released the previous year.

This is a slightly odd choice by Flynn, as Bathurst mentions Holmes alongside other fictional detectives in his first appearance, *The Billiard Room Mystery*, and as far as I am aware, it is never mentioned again, but I think one can indulge the author in this instance. There is a possibility that this was meant as a tribute or thank you to Conan Doyle, given that the great man had died only a year before publication.

One other thing worth mentioning is Flynn's use of a narrator for the third time (following *The Billiard Room Mystery* and *Murder en Route*). His choice here is Cecilia Mary Cameron, the niece of Colonel Ian Cameron whose receipt of a cryptogram starts the chain of events, and he does a better job writing a woman's voice that some of his male contemporaries. As with *Murder en Route*, there are times when events necessitate Cecilia relating events that she wasn't present for, and I think it was for this reason that Flynn rarely used the first person again, but it gives a different focus to the story, showing again that the author was determined to try something different with each book. However, anyone who was hoping for a more realistic interpretation of Antony Bathurst through a woman's eyes will be left wanting, though, as he is described as "the most perfect combination of scholar and athlete that I have ever been privileged to see."

How one can tell that someone is a scholar by simply looking at them is anybody's guess, but apparently having "keen grey eyes and a sensitive, mobile mouth" helps. So now you know.

It is a particular delight to be able to bring *The Triple Bite* back into print, as out of all of the first ten Brian Flynn novels, it is by far the rarest. Never reprinted in any form, not reissued in the United States – in all of our research, we managed to find just one copy of the book outside the British Library. But one is all we needed to be able to bring it to you, and we hope you enjoy the highly entertaining mystery.

Steve Barge

# FOREWORD

I desire to place on record my debt to the late Sir Arthur Conan Doyle for the idea (contained in one line of a short story by him) from which this story of mine germinated.

BRIAN FLYNN.

# Chapter I
# THE MEN BEHIND THE "SCREEN"

I NEVER thought it would fall to my lot to write what is popularly known as a "thriller", but Lois insists that I am the right person to do it and when Lois sets her mind on anything—well, *"Dieu le veut"*. She was just the same at school right from the first day that she arrived. Ordered everybody about; took possession of everything that could be taken possession of, to the manner born; expressed her intention of defying school rules that had existed for centuries, and altogether "queened it", after a stay there approximating half an hour. Since then, she has grown up and quietened down, but the old habits flash out at times and Lois "gives orders". I remember one Sunday—but there, I am digressing, as I was afraid I should, when I started. First of all, as I shall figure prominently throughout the narrative, let me introduce myself.

I am Cecilia Mary Cameron. A year ago, when the events took place that I am about to relate, I was twenty-two. My father was the Lieutenant Graeme Cameron who won the V.C. at Ploeg Street, for what I have heard described by soldiers who were there, as one of the bravest deeds of the whole War. Winning it cost him his life, and losing him cost Mother hers. She never properly rallied from the shock of his death, and two years afterwards I was an orphan. Lois Fletcher was a real brick to me those days and I can never repay her adequately for what she did for me. When I left school I went to live with my uncle, Daddy's elder brother, Colonel Ian Cameron of the Queen's Own Cameron Highlanders. He was fourteen years Daddy's senior and a year ago he retired from the Army and we went to live at a place called Dallow Corner in Sussex. He little knew the horror that lurked there! Uncle Ian had one child of his own, my cousin Douglas, in the early thirties. Now I think I can get on, although I'm very much afraid that I haven't followed the first instructions that Lois drummed into me. "When you write the yarn, Cecilia Mary Cameron," she said, "be bright; be 'snappy'; people don't want to wade through pages and pages of descriptions nowadays and what's more, my cherub, they simply won't do it. Be advised by Timothy's grandmother and get down to the 'thrills' as quickly as you can." Although my fear is that I shall prove to be but *une méchante écrivaine*, I will do my best to follow her advice. As I tried to say before, Lois has never let me down yet and if it hadn't been for her kindness and the sympathetic assistance of Mr. Armstrong, the gentleman who lived in the next house to us, I should have probably crocked up on that first morning after the first tragedy occurred. You see, it was like this. When the time came for Uncle Ian to retire, he decided that he must live somewhere near the Sussex Downs. So, prompted by Nigel Strachan, he bought the bungalow known as Dallow Corner. It's a big, ten-roomed bungalow which takes its name from the place itself, and is about equidistant from Quoynings and Stretton. What is more, it is situated right in the middle of some really topping country. Uncle bought it as it stood, furniture and appointments, and at the price for which Uncle got it, it was a peach of a bargain. The people to whom it had belonged had packed up altogether during the first week in May and gone abroad. Douglas put him on to it. Douglas is a barrister and heard of it being in the market from an intimate friend of his, also at the bar, the Nigel Strachan whom I mentioned just now. Nigel Strachan was tremendously keen on us getting it and assured us that we might go a thousand miles farther and fare infinitely worse, which, as I pointed out to him, was very obvious. Negotiations took but a few days, and Uncle and I travelled down to Dallow Corner on the evening of the eleventh of November. Uncle had wanted to stay in Town for the morning to attend the Armistice Day celebrations, so we caught the 8.37 train out of Victoria. He had been poorly for some little time, backwards and forwards to his doctor, and before we went to the station he insisted on us feeding somewhere. So we went into a favourite restaurant of his in Soho. The events of that evening come back to me most vividly. He piloted me to his special table in the extreme left-hand corner and I can remember well the many pairs of eyes that were turned on him as we made our way to it. For he was a man of considerable distinction. His iron-grey hair, blue eyes and florid cheeks, added to his upright "military" carriage, were sufficient to single him out for attention in any company.

"This is my table, Cecilia," he said. "I 'phoned Moroni to reserve it for me. I've dined here for years. I shall miss this down in Sussex, I can tell you. You can guess why it appeals to me so especially. Look."

I looked as I took my seat at the table and realized what he meant by his last remark. The table to which he had brought me was separated from the others on the same side of the room by a screen; the tables on the other side of the apartment, however, were plainly visible to us from where we sat. The dinner was excellent as I knew it would be. Uncle saw to that. He had a most discriminating taste in almost every direction and at a quarter to eight we began to make preparations to go. But Uncle Ian asked me to wait for a moment.

"Just a moment, my dear," he said, "if you don't mind. We've bags of time. I want to use the 'phone in Moroni's private office. I want to get through to Ellison at the club. So hang on for a second or so, will you?"

I nodded agreement, of course, and Uncle walked away. I can remember that I had just placed a cigarette in my cigarette-holder, when a phrase spoken in a man's voice at the table directly behind me, caught my attention. For much to my astonishment, the words that reached my conscious mind were "Dallow Corner". Without pausing to think, I strained my ears in an attempt to catch more. But the voice had now sunk to a mere whisper. Then I heard a laugh. I should describe it as a coarse sort of laugh. More than that even. It was low throaty, and altogether horrible. Then I heard another voice say something about "salmon" to which the voice of the horrible laugh replied, "Good job he died. If he hadn't I'd have slit his throat for a tenth part of it." At that moment my uncle returned and gestured to me that he was ready for our departure. The demon of curiosity had caught me, however, and on an impulse, I motioned to Uncle Ian to sit down again at our table; somewhat surprised, he obeyed, and I scribbled something on the back of the menu and passed it over to him. "Change places with me and listen hard." They were the words that I wrote. Somewhat impatiently, and with a frown of perplexity on his brow he obeyed me again. For a few moments there was no indication on his face that he was able to hear anything. Then I saw his brows furrow as though he were excessively puzzled. "What have you heard?" I whispered across to him. He shook his head and at the same time put a finger to his lips for silence. For a moment or two we sat there. Then my uncle made a move, motioning me at the same time to rise from my seat. I joined him, in order that we might leave the table and pass down the apartment. We passed the screen and I'm afraid I looked very eagerly to see who were the occupants of the table behind us. To my utter chagrin and dismay there was nobody there, although the condition of the table spoke eloquently of very recent use and occupation. Whoever it was that had been there could have preceded our own exit by a matter of a few seconds only. Directly we reached the pavement outside I turned to Uncle Ian and repeated my question.

"What did you hear, Uncle?"

"Very little, my dear, and yet perhaps too much. I heard the words 'Dallow Corner' mentioned two or three times, but I couldn't catch the connection. While I was waiting to hear more, they must have got up very quietly and made their way out. You and I probably picked out those two words 'Dallow Corner' because they are so familiar to us. What puzzled me most, however, was the last sentence spoken by that gentleman with the charming chuckle. He said, 'let's call the little venture, salmon-fishing at Dallow Corner'." Uncle Ian turned to me and his face was hard and set. "My dear Cecilia, there isn't a big enough, or a suitable, stretch of water for such a thing as 'salmon-fishing' within ten miles of Dallow Corner. So what's the game?"

"He must have meant a fish-shop," I answered hopefully. Had I known, however, what lay in store for us, from the time of the coming of "Flame" Lampard to the night of horror in the darkened room when the last scene of all was enacted, I should never have answered my uncle as I did.

# Chapter II
# NIGEL FLINGS A BOMBSHELL

THE MORNING after our arrival at our new home we had a visitor. It was our nearest neighbour, a Mr. Ralph Armstrong. When I first saw him, I was irresistibly reminded of that exquisite portrait in the National Gallery, "The Doge of Venice". I do not think I have ever seen a more perfectly "scrumptious" looking old man. If you don't believe me, ask Lois. His silvery-white hair, clean-cut features of delicately-chiselled nose and sensitive mouth, made you think of cathedrals and Bishops' gaiters, paternal blessings and such things as monasteries and Vesper bells. From this description of mine you will gather that his atmosphere was ecclesiastical. When you heard his voice for the first time, you were reminded of these "churchy" things even more, for it was all of a piece with his appearance. He introduced himself to us in the most charming manner, and gallantly welcomed us to Dallow Corner. Without wishing to draw any odious comparisons, he said that he was glad that our predecessors had gone from the district and that we had taken their place.

"How long have you lived here yourself?" inquired Uncle Ian.

"For seventeen years, Colonel Cameron. I retired here during the Great War, when I was fortunate enough to inherit a considerable sum of money." He smiled. "I love the place. I hope that I shall never live anywhere else. I wouldn't want to. Any more than I could ever endure poverty."

In some ways, I am glad that this wish of his was eventually gratified for it was easy to see the sincerity that shone in his eyes.

"Another devotee of Sussex by the sea, eh?" demanded my uncle, jocularly.

Mr. Armstrong bowed. "I would never attempt to deny it," he replied. "I run a little car, and it has enabled me to explore every inch of the country."

When he left us, after drinking a toast to our coming, it was with a pressing invitation to come again soon, a gesture that he immediately reciprocated.

"Good-bye then, Mr. Armstrong," said my uncle. "That's understood between us, then. You're coming to dinner on Thursday. By the way, there's something I want to ask you. You're an old inhabitant of these parts and I've no doubt you can help me. Can I get any decent fishing round here? I don't mind a matter of a mile or two."

Our visitor smiled again and shook his head negatively. "I'm afraid that you are going to be disappointed in that, Colonel Cameron. There's nothing of that kind in the immediate neighbourhood. The only water we have is a tiny stream about half-way between your place and mine." He paused, to continue almost immediately. "I hope that doesn't mean that we shall lose you. Are you tremendously keen on—"

"Oh no, Mr. Armstrong. Not for a moment. I'm not such an ardent angler as all that. In fact, beyond a little 'dapping' in Ireland a couple of years ago, at my brother-in-law's place, I've done scarcely any for a considerable period now. I merely asked you in case there should have been an opportunity here. That was all. As there isn't, I must put up with it."

Mr. Armstrong waved his soft, grey hat as he departed. "Till Thursday evening, then, Colonel. *Au 'voir.*"

Douglas and Nigel Strachan came down the same evening— the evening of the day following upon our arrival, I mean. It seemed to me that there was a queer look in my cousin's eyes, but Nigel had the air of one who was simply bubbling over with wild excitement. He was like that, was Nigel. Like the boy who has bought a birthday present for his mother and who has the hardest job not to show it to her a week before the event. Who suggests its presence in the house to her by a series of oblique and indirect references.

That evening, Nigel Strachan seethed and bubbled and bubbled and seethed, so unmistakably, that within a very little time I began to watch him with a huge and secret enjoyment. After dinner, when we were having coffee, Douglas cleared his throat rather dramatically and broached the subject that was evidently occupying Nigel's mind.

"Old Nigel's got something to spill, guv'nor," he said, distinctly nervously, I thought. "Are you fit?"

"Oh," said Uncle, nonchalantly. "What about?"

"Well," responded Douglas, giving Nigel a sort of sideways look, "I don't know that I'm the right person to answer that. Beyond that it's something to do with this place, Dallow Corner, into which district you've just moved, I know no more about the affair than you do. Still, let old Nigel cough up what it's all about. Then you'll be able to say whether you're interested or not. Come on, Nigel. Cough it up, old hoss. And for the love of Mike remember your reputation in chambers as a champion liar. Fire away." Nigel hit back.

"A better construe of 'splendide mendax' than 'champion liar', Douglas, is 'lying in state'."

Directly Douglas had mentioned the place, Dallow Corner, Uncle Ian sent a look over to me that was very similar to the look that I had seen pass between Douglas and Nigel. The look that reveals to the participants a secret understanding. I said nothing, however, but gave myself the satisfaction of a sort of clandestine smile inside me somewhere, as I prepared to listen to what Nigel Strachan had to say to us. First of all, he went over to the door of the lounge in the approved manner, opened it, looked to see if there were anybody outside, closed it again, and then came down to seat himself at my side.

"Forgive me for being mysterious, Colonel," he explained, with a hint of apology in his tone, "but I don't feel in the mood for what, after all, may be risks." He leant over towards my uncle and spoke his next words very quietly—scarcely above a whisper. "The fact is, I believe I'm on the track of something pretty big, and it's to do with this little corner of the globe."

"There are only two people on the premises here besides ourselves," Uncle Ian reassured him. "Mrs. Veitch, my housekeeper of many years' standing, and Hardy, the chauffeur. And I expect he's in the village pub. He's a mug if he's not. You can get a 'pint' down here for about twopence halfpenny."

Douglas looked up gratefully at his father's words and gazed longingly at the door. I think the sentiment pleased him. But he saw that I was watching him, so he dissembled.

"Nigel Strachan," he repeated banteringly. "On the track! Scotland Yard an 'also-ran'. Tut-tut, Strachan, the facts! The facts! Be as explicit as you can and confine yourselves strictly—"

Nigel unceremoniously waved him aside. He was still the essence of good humour and my cousin's badinage flew by harmlessly. "When I said 'on the track' it was perhaps an inaccurate expression. It would have been better if I had said, 'I believe I've been put in the way of something pretty big'. My uncle looked at me, and nodded encouragingly. 'Get on, my boy. You're more interesting to me than perhaps you think. And I shouldn't be surprised if Cecilia isn't in the same boat with me."

"About six months ago," proceeded Nigel, "I picked up one morning what is known as a 'dock' brief. You know very well what I mean, Colonel, I've no doubt. For the benefit of Cecilia, however, I'll explain a bit more fully. Putting it—"

"Briefly," mocked Douglas in a grinning interruption.

"Shut up," returned Nigel patiently, "and let me explain. In a nutshell, it comes to this. A criminal in the dock, who hasn't briefed a barrister for his defence, is, in certain circumstances, allowed to choose one from those whom he can see sitting in the court. On the morning in question, there was an old ruffian in the dock, charged with burglary, and blow me if he didn't fix on me to take on the onus of his defence. Goodness knows *why* he picked on me—"

"Mentally deficient, in all probability," murmured my cousin. "I can think of no other reason."

"He was far from that," rejoined Nigel imperturbably, "as you will all be ready to admit when you hear a bit more. As it happened, however, I had very little chance against the prosecution, as the evidence against my chap was damning. There wasn't the vestige of a doubt, and to cap it all the old devil had a particularly healthy criminal record extending over a period of about fifty years."

"What was he then, by profession?" demanded Douglas, "an ex-alderman or a Member of Parliament?"

"Neither," countered Nigel. "He suffered from one great and chronic trouble. He had never been able to distinguish accurately between 'meum' and 'tuum'. In all probability he had never had the slightest desire to. He was a born thief, you see, in the true diabolic succession. Well, after I'd been at work a little while on the case, I realized that all I could go for, with any hope of success, was a reduction of sentence. So I pulled out the sympathetic stop when I addressed the jury, harrowed their feelings no end, painted a glowing picture of a repentant sinner and instead of the old devil getting a pretty long 'stretch', he got away with a mere six months' hard labour. I flatter myself that I made a damned good speech and there's no doubt—"

"You couldn't have been yourself, that morning, old man," put in Douglas decisively, "but don't let that worry you, the affair was only temporary."

"And there's no doubt," repeated the complacent Nigel, completely ignoring the interruption, "that the old thief in the dock realized what he owed to me and was really grateful for what I had done for him."

"Got him six months' hard, do you mean? The old bird must have been extraordinarily easily pleased," said the irrepressible Douglas.

"If you like to put it so," went on the stoical Nigel. "Anyhow, our friend rolled off to clink and served his sentence. He was released about a fortnight ago and within about forty-eight hours took the last count from an opponent that always wants a lot of beating. Pneumonia!—The 'Pneumococcus' bird always makes the bout short and sharp, and plays to a finish. Moreover he's never awed by such a thing as a reputation. My poor old client snuffed it, in a Stepney 'doss-house'. The day after he was gathered to his fathers I received this." He fished in his pocket and produced a rather dirty-looking piece of paper. Opening it, he spread it out on his knee. It was an ordinary sheet of common notepaper. I could see that quite well from where I was sitting at his side.

"It was delivered by post by somebody with particularly dirty fingers."

"I knew it had something to do with a Trades Union," contributed Douglas. "I was sure of that from the first."

"I'll read it to you. At this stage of the explanation, please don't interrupt, Douglas, for a moment or so. You will have ample opportunity to exercise your powers of satire a little later on. Anyhow, this is it. Listen carefully, please, all of you.

"November 2nd.

"Dear Mr. Strachan,

"Forgive the scrawl, but I am very ill. So ill that I'm pretty certain I'm dying. I have only one male relation in the world, the swine who married my only child, and I hope he burns in Hell when his time comes, like a celluloid cat that's been dipped in petrol. Judge, O ye Gods, how dearly I love him. There are only two people in this world who have ever lifted a finger to help me. You can lay the flattering unction to your soul that you're one of them. To you and that other I mentioned, I'm going to give an equal chance of a fortune. A fortune that not another living soul has any inkling of. There is just this to it. The one with the best brains will pull it off. Here goes."

At this juncture Nigel broke off, to interject something of his own. "What I'm going to read to you now is a piece of doggerel. Gibberish, if you like to describe it as such. Douglas might even go farther. I expect that he'll welcome the opportunity. Personally, I'm of the opinion that it's a sort of cryptogram. Still—I'll get on and read it and you can judge for yourselves." He resumed the reading of the letter and I will reproduce the cryptogram as I then saw it.

"No Dancers need apply"

First find the Bull, that flowers more bright
   than Daffodil or Crocus white.
Look neer for Sun, but seek the shade
   from Sky they came, on the Death Parade."

$$16\,P - \tfrac{1?}{1?8} + \tfrac{10}{23?} + \tfrac{1?}{1?2} + \tfrac{19}{7?} = 50{,}000\ L$$

"Good luck to you, Mr. Strachan, is the dying wish of old

SAM TROUT."

Nigel paused, folded up his sheet of paper and then looked up into the ring of our faces.

"Well," he asked quietly, "what do you make of that?"

Before I could give utterance to the main thought that was racing through my brain, Uncle Ian's voice broke the silence. "What name was that you said, Nigel?"

"Trout," replied Nigel Strachan. "'Sam Trout'. I might add, that amongst his own fraternity in the thieves' kitchen, the old boy was always known as 'Salmon' Trout. You can readily see how he came by the nickname. It was so obvious a sobriquet that no member of the underworld, for instance, could resist it."

"The devil he was," exploded my uncle. "Before you go any farther, Nigel, my lad, listen to what I've got to tell you. Thanks to the sharp ears of Cecilia here." Uncle Ian leant forward and told the story of the incident at Moroni's. He told it without a single interruption.

# CHAPTER III
# NIGEL'S STORY

"GOOD LORD," exclaimed Douglas when his father had finished. "This gets better and better, blowed if it doesn't. Long John Silver, Captain Kidd, Ben Gunn, Ancestor Jorico and the whole crowd of 'em aren't going to be in it with us. See to the stockade and post guards at the back entrances at once, or the man with the throaty voice will have gained admittance. Then serve out a double ration of rum! When you've done that I'll hide in the apple-barrel and cry for a piece of cheese. Anybody got a snuff-box?"

"Don't rot, Douglas—please." Nigel was deadly serious. "Unless I'm very much mistaken, this is going to be a ticklish business, with a great deal more in it than appears on the face of it. And what the Colonel has just told us, only makes me more certain."

My uncle nodded. "I'm inclined to agree with you, Nigel. One of the men whom we heard talking is, I should say, evidently the chap that I can describe as your co-legatee. He received his letter from the old boy about the same time that yours came, so that you can be said to be starting on level terms. But, coming to what I think is mainly puzzling most of us, what's it got to do with my bungalow?"

Douglas joined his father. "That's exactly what I'm bursting to know, Guv'nor! I knew, of course, in the beginning, that old Nigel was as keen as mustard on you buying this place, but the wily old bird has never let on the reason why. That's what I'm sitting up to hear—*now*. For there's certainly more in it than meets the eye."

Here I made my first contribution to the conversation. "I can guess what's happened," I cried excitedly. "Nigel's been clever and read the cryptogram. Confess now, Nigel, you have, haven't you?"

Nigel looked at me with something approaching admiration. "You're partly right, at least, Cecilia. You can take it that I've read the meaning from some of it. The rest beats me altogether. However, let me put this cryptogram jargon on the table so that you can all see it properly." He walked across the room and carried out his suggestion. We crowded round, each of us fairly buzzing with uncontrolled excitement. Nigel's moment of triumph was imminent, and we forgave him, I think very readily, the soupçon of self-importance with which he seemed temporarily to invest himself. He proceeded to demonstrate. "Leave out for the moment the five lines of doggerel and concentrate, for the time being, on what I will call, for the purposes of distinction, the arithmetical or algebraical equation portion. It isn't that really, I know, but it looked something like it at the first glance, and we'll call it that for convenience and mutual understanding. What strikes you about it, first of all? Anything?" He looked round eagerly, obviously inviting our individual opinions. Uncle Ian frowned heavily at the paper, but Douglas cut in rapidly.

"What very forcibly strikes me," he said, "is that it's absolutely idiotic."

"In what way, exactly?" Nigel was still eagerness personified.

"Well," rejoined Douglas—"nobody with the slightest pretensions to a knowledge of even elementary maths, would ever show fractions in the form that they are shown here. They're not even in their lowest terms, for instance. It's as plain as a pikestaff that they have a meaning beyond the figures themselves."

"I agree. The same thing, of course, struck me when I first looked at it. Go on."

My cousin showed signs of hesitation. "Half a jiffy, Nigel," he remonstrated—"give a bloke a reasonable chance. This sort of thing wants thinking about, you know. You can't hit on a solution in a brace of shakes." He paused and considered for a moment. "It's the '16P' that is stumping me, for the time being."

"Never mind that. Leave that alone for the present." Nigel's tone was encouraging. He continued. "I don't pretend to say that I've solved that yet. Generally speaking, I am taking that, at this stage of our investigation, to stand for '16 paces'. Although I'm not absolutely certain that it is a 'P'. It might even be a badly-made 'D'. But leave it. Go on from there."

Both Douglas and his father looked at the paper and remained silent. I must confess that my imagination served me in no better stead that theirs was doing. I racked my brains in a futile endeavour to drag some meaning from some part of the puzzle. Nigel perceived our obtuseness and grinned.

"Well, I'll tell you how it appeared to me, when I found myself really at grips with it. First of all, take the four quantities that are shown in what we will call fractional form, and let us see whether you can travel with me down the avenue of my first piece of reasoning."

Nigel's tone now held a wee touch of pomposity but I think that we were all still full of forgiveness towards him. After all, the dear boy was very human, and at this moment, in these circumstances, a saint would have been hard put to it to revolve directly and exactly in the orbit of his halo.

"What occurs to you with regard to the circumstances of those four fractions? Anything?"

Douglas entered the breach. "Well, they're not in anything like their lowest terms. They can be reduced—"

"You said that before," remonstrated Nigel, shaking his head. "I don't mean that."

"Well, then, the preponderance of ones, twos, threes and fours in the denominators. They probably represent vowels." Douglas went on airily with the usual cryptogram platitude. "'E' is the most commonly-found letter in the alphabet, and 'E' no doubt is signified by—"

"Sorry, Douglas," replied Nigel. "I don't want to crush the fine flowers of your intelligence at so early a stage, but, without any finesse, you're talking 'tripe'."

Before my cousin could find adequate words of expostulation, I rushed in to draw a bow, more or less at a venture. "I don't know whether you'll call this 'tripe', Nigel, but I think I've noticed something about those fractions. It's this. In each case, in *every* case that is, the numerators are very much smaller than the denominators. Of course, I know I that's quite a possible contingency in a fraction of this kind, but I think you might have expected, in *one* case, say, a numerator *nearer* to the size of its denominator. See what I mean? It may be all nonsense, of course," I concluded timidly, "but you asked for opinions and that's mine."

As I finished my sentence, I knew immediately that my contribution was of some value. Nigel's eyes were shining now with a glow of gratification.

"Hooray," he cried, exultantly. "Cecilia sees! Or perhaps it would be truer to say that her mental eyes are opening just a trifle. Let me proceed, however, from the point whither Cecilia piloted us. The fact that all the four fractions are *small* in themselves, struck me. Whereas the largest numerator is no higher than nineteen, we have a denominator as high as two hundred and thirty-four. I thought it over and cudgelled such brains as I have, and then I counted the words contained in what we called the 'doggerel' part of the cryptogram. There are thirty-three of them. It is conceivable, therefore, that the four numerators might bear an eminently sound relationship to those thirty-three words, seeing that each of them is *less* than thirty-three and therefore might be contained *within* those thirty-three. Do you follow me, people? It's excessively simple, you must admit, so far." The three of us nodded affirmatively. "Good. Granted that, then, the next step was fairly obvious and also simple. It was to find the four words of the doggerel that were in order respectively, the fourteenth, tenth, sixteenth and nineteenth, because if my theory were tenable, they could give us something tangible upon which to get to work. Let's do it now, as I did it some days ago. The fourteenth word is 'Daffodil'. The tenth word is 'Flowers'. The sixteenth word is 'Crocus'. The nineteenth word is 'Ne'er'." Nigel grinned. "Do the four words suggest anything to you?"

Uncle Ian answered immediately. "Yes! Gardens!" Nigel nodded.

"On the whole, I agree with you, Colonel Cameron. Although the last of the four words *hardly* fills the garden bill. Does it? However, we shall see. We will admit that three are definitely horticultural." He paused and then almost at once went on speaking more slowly. "Having exhausted our first theory with regard to our numerators and achieved some measure of what I will term 'consistency', let us turn our attention to the denominators. Once again we are confronted with an unusual recurrence of certain figures. A recurrence that is beyond 'average' conditions. That's what you meant, Douglas, isn't it?"

"Yes—twos, threes and fours. I was trying to show you that—"

"Yes, but hold on a moment, please. You were a long way off the right track when you started talking about the prevalence of certain vowels. That was where you fell foul of my criticism. I looked at it quite differently. Of the ten unit numbers, it is significant, I think, that nought, five, six, seven and nine do not occur at all. What we have is by no means an impossible combination of figures, of course, but I think I should be justified in describing it as just a little unusual and out of the common."

I could see Uncle Ian furrowing his brow as he attempted to follow Nigel through this (to him) jungle of figures. Maths had always been amongst his blackest of beasts and the fact that the cryptogram seemed to be developing on these lines was far from consoling to him. I could almost hear him praying to be delivered from the power of the dog. But Nigel was undeterred by the look that had taken possession of my uncle's face. Unabashed, he sailed merrily and professorially on.

"Bearing that fact in mind then, it cannot be denied that the additional fact that there isn't a single word in the doggerel which contains more than eight letters is most distinctly interesting and in my opinion very definitely illuminating. It was when I realized this that light began to come to me. You shall look upon that ray of light with me and bask in its roseate hues. To make a start, we will take the fourteenth word. We saw just now that it was 'DAFFODIL'. Now the denominator shown beneath the numerator 'fourteen' is, as you can see for yourselves, one hundred and twenty-eight. We will split that one hundred and twenty-eight up into its three obvious parts—those of its three figures. There are one, two and eight. And the first, second and eighth letters of the fourteenth word 'DAFFODIL' are 'Dal'." Nigel waved his hand oracularly. I gasped, because I think I began to see then even more of Nigel's lights than was apparent to Uncle Ian and my cousin Douglas. I could hear Nigel continuing his lecture. "Applying the same plan to the tenth word 'FLOWERS', with the key figures of two, three, and four, we arrive at 'LOW'. Going on and adopting the same plan with regard to the sixteenth and nineteenth words of the doggerel, which were, if you remember, 'CROCUS' and 'NE'ER' and using one, three, and two and one, two, and four, we achieve the results 'COR' and 'NER'." Nigel bowed as though before the applause of a tremendously enthusiastic audience. "The whole emerges from its shell, therefore, as 'Dallow Corner'. And Dallow Corner is the district in which this bungalow is situated and from which the bungalow takes its name. Thank you, ladies and gentlemen."

"Jolly good, Nigel," exclaimed Douglas. "I've often wondered what was the real reason of your encumbering the earth and to-night's performance has given me just an infinitesimal fraction of an inkling."

"Dry up, Douglas," commanded my uncle; then turning to Nigel Strachan, "I presume, Nigel, my boy, that your knowledge of this lay behind your anxiety that I should purchase this place?"

Nigel flushed. "It did, sir, and in a way perhaps I should ask your pardon. It was no business of mine to drag you into anything. But I was aware, from what Douglas had told me, that you were keen on coming to this part of Sussex, and when I heard that this place was in the market and from its very name, no doubt, situated as it were in the very heart of my 'cryptogram country', I naturally wanted, if at all possible, to hurry things up and get off on the quest with a flying start." His face was still flushed when he finished.

Uncle Ian smiled grimly. "I guessed as much. Well, go on, my boy, and translate the rest of your blood and thunder legacy. There's no doubt that it will be as well for you to put your best foot foremost, in view of the fact that you have a rival in the field. What's the rest of it mean? Tell us all about that."

Nigel looked up at us a little shamefacedly. "There, sir, I must cry *'Peccavi'*. Candidly, Colonel Cameron, I must confess that I haven't the slightest idea. I simply think this. Somewhere in this part of the country known as Dallow Corner there's a fortune to be picked up by the man that's either clever or lucky enough to read all the message that lies in old Sam Trout's cryptogram."

We stared at him as the meaning of his words came home to us.

## Chapter IV
# THINGS BEGIN TO MOVE

"That's all very well, but I'm afraid I'm not so sanguine as you are, Nigel." It was Douglas who spoke. "A lot of it seems to me to require much more explanation than shows on the surface. I think you're too ready to jump to conclusions."

"I'm listening, Douglas. Let's have what's in your mind. That suits me down to the ground. I want the whole thing ventilated as much as possible. I want to see it from every conceivable angle. That's the only way by which we shall solve it. Now, what's your first point?"

"This chap—Sam Trout—or 'Salmon' Trout as you called him. How is it possible for him to be dealing in fortunes? How does he fill the bill as a trafficker in doubloons? Have you thought of—"

"I have. All the same, I'll say this. I can quite understand you raising the question. Sam Trout, as I knew him on a slight acquaintance, was an ordinary thief, of the common-place 'burglar' type. I shouldn't think, from the look of him, from his general circumstances, or from what I've been able to glean about him in inquiries I've prosecuted since, that he ever pulled off a really big 'job' in his life. On these counts, I admit that it all seems preposterous. At the same time though, Douglas, there's just another possibility. That's how the affair appears to me."

"What's that?"

"Look at it like this. He may have come into contact during some part of his career with somebody bigger than himself and in some way have been put wise to a secret that wasn't his own in the original instance. For all we know, he may have been in 'clink' and run across somebody in there who passed the news on to him. It's been done before now, you know. See what I mean?"

"Hardly likely, I think," grunted my uncle with a shake of the head.

"Perhaps not," admitted Nigel, "but possible all the same."

"I don't think you're right," I intervened rather emphatically.

"About what?"

"About the secret having come to Sam Trout from somebody else."

Nigel regarded me somewhat curiously. "Give me your reasons for that, Cecilia."

"Well," I answered, warming to my subject, "I haven't very much to go on, but I'm basing my opinions on Sam Trout's letter to you. That's fair, isn't it?"

"Yes," said Nigel, "go on."

"Well, in that letter, Sam Trout is trying to reward you for something that you've done for him. It appears to be a piece of genuine gratitude on his part. Either you, or another person to whom he is grateful for some service rendered or kindness performed in the past, is meant to benefit. I think that shows that the secret belonged to Sam Trout and to nobody else. Otherwise, he might be offering something to you which was not his to give and which a third party might have collared long ago."

"I see your point, Cecilia. But this third party from whom Nigel suggests Sam Trout may have obtained the secret, has died, perhaps, and left Sam in the field alone. Don't overlook that possibility. That's a fair assumption, too, isn't it?"

I shrugged my shoulders. "I am a woman, and therefore, I suppose, illogical, Douglas. I don't think so. I think the secret or whatever it is, belonged to Sam Trout and Sam Trout alone, and nothing will convince me to the contrary. I'm positive of it."

"What sort of man was this fellow, Trout, from an academic point of view? Was he—er—cradled in the terminology of the schools, to any degree?" Uncle Ian asked the questions rather aggressively.

"Fairish, I should say," returned Nigel. "No more. I didn't see a great deal of him, naturally, but I should be inclined to class him as a cut above the usual burglar type from that particular standpoint. At any rate, you've got his letter to go on. It's decent, isn't it?"

"But that's my point, Nigel! Have we? For example, can we be sure that Trout himself wrote it? Would you expect a common burglar, of the type that you say he was, to have even the elementary knowledge that this letter indicates?"

"I don't see why he shouldn't have," returned Nigel doggedly. "There have been much more remarkable instances than this one. The late Mr. Charles Peace, for instance, had not only I believe a passion for the fiddle, but also the finest collection of bric-à-brac in all Peckham."

Douglas then proved his worth. "Well, there's one thing pretty certain. Arguing in this fashion won't get us anywhere. While we're yapping about probabilities and possibilities, Nigel's rival may be scooping the treasure, which doesn't suit my book at all. What about the other part of the cryptogram? How about having a shot at solving that? That'll cut more ice than anything."

"Douglas speaks sound sense," said my uncle—"let's see what we can make of it together. Although it has been said that an embarrassment of chefs does harm to the consommé, nevertheless in this instance four heads should outclass one. Especially when one of them is as pretty as Cecilia's."

"Read it out again, Nigel," suggested Douglas. Nigel complied with the request.

"Take it line by line," said Uncle Ian, "that's the best method; let's see where our joint conclusions lead us."

"To me," confessed Nigel, "the first line is a first-class rock-bottom snag. 'No Dancers need apply'. Why on earth should there be anything special about the gentle or jazzing terpsichorean, that its devotees should be excluded from the territory of Trout?"

"There is just this point to be considered. Are we right in taking the actual words as they stand?" asked Douglas. "Mightn't there be another meaning hidden in them on similar lines, shall we say, to the way the figures operated?"

"It's possible, certainly," admitted Nigel. "I had thought of that myself."

"I don't think so," affirmed Uncle Ian. "It's fairly obvious to me, that this treasure, whatever it may be or whatever form it takes, is buried somewhere in a garden situated in this district. Look at the context all round. Damn it all, it sticks out a mile. It's a handicap certainty. 'Bulb', 'flowers', 'daffodil', 'crocus', 'sun', 'shade', and 'sky'. Every one of these words may be said to have a horticultural significance of some kind. The key to the garden's situation is contained somewhere in these five lines. When we find it, if we ever do, sixteen paces from somewhere we shall have to dig."

"How far down, sir?" grinned Nigel. "Fifty thousand leagues under the soil?"

My uncle took the satire good-naturedly. "You can chaff, Nigel. But those that live longest will see the most. Anyhow, I'm tired, and I think we'll sleep on your cryptogram until to-morrow morning. Perhaps by then, something will have turned up." Nigel laughed and within an hour or so, we had temporarily forgotten the cryptogram and had gone to bed. We little knew what was lurking round the corner.

* * * * *

Next morning about half-past eleven I was in the front garden tidying one of the paths—they had been neglected for some little time—when I noticed a tall, handsome, military-looking man coming down the road in the direction of the bungalow. I was first attracted to him by the sound of his footsteps on the road. When he drew level with our gate he stopped somewhat abruptly and then walked towards me as I stood in the garden watching, I am afraid, rather discourteously.

"Pardon me," he said, raising his hat gallantly, "but can you tell me if I am anywhere near Dallow Corner?"

"This is Dallow Corner," I said, pointing to the name on the gate of our bungalow. His eyes brightened perceptibly as he read it and realized its significance. Then he twisted his mouth rather charmingly, I thought.

"I am a little puzzled," he continued. "Perhaps I have lost my bearings a little. I had imagined that Dallow Corner was a place on its own. I had no idea that—"

"It is," I interrupted him. "You have made no mistake with regard to that. Our bungalow happens to be named after it, that's all." I pointed vaguely away into the distance. "All this is Dallow Corner. As far as Quoynings."

His eyes followed my pointing finger with a kind of eager understanding.

"Thank you," he said, "I understand now. I'm glad that I met you. Also, I may see you again. There is just the chance that we may become neighbours. Is it very cold here in the winter? I have a reason for asking. I've been in India recently."

I shook my head. "I'm sorry—but really I can't tell you from experience. We only moved in ourselves two days ago. My uncle, Colonel Cameron—"

His face beamed. "Colonel Cameron? Not Colonel Ian Cameron of the Queen's Own Cameron Highlanders by any chance?"

"Yes," I nodded.

"How remarkable," he exclaimed. "Would it be troubling you too much to tell him that Major Gilbert Neale, late of the Glebeshires, is standing at his garden gate?"

"Better still, come in and tell him yourself," I invited him.

He smiled his attractive smile again and followed me up the garden path. It was then that I first noticed that he walked with a limp. But although he walked slowly, he was dignified and debonair. That was the manner of Major Gilbert Neale's coming to Dallow Corner.

## CHAPTER V
# THE GATHERING OF THE VULTURES

MY UNCLE was delighted to see him. I could tell that immediately. He had to rake his memory at first, when I introduced Major Neale to him, but eventually from data that the Major gave him, was enabled to piece little fragments of history together and "connect" the man that stood in front of him.

"I lost sight of you after Givenchy, Neale, like I lost sight of so many others. So you must forgive me if I was a trifle slow to remember you."

Major Neale gave his easy smile in return. "It was at Givenchy that I clicked for this." He pointed ruefully to the lower part of his leg. "Some enterprising Boche plugged me very neatly through the heel. Damaged the Achilles tendon. It will be a permanent memento for me." He laughed again, this time with a fine carelessness. "Mustn't grouse about it though, I suppose. I might have fared a lot worse. Thousands did."

My uncle nodded gravely. "Too true, Neale. Thousands of the best who could ill be spared. Such grand youngsters, too—'poured out the sweet red wine of Youth'. I lost my only brother at Ploeg Street. This young lady's father." Major Neale expressed his sympathy very courteously. "Lieutenant Graeme Cameron, V.C.," continued Uncle Ian proudly—"you must remember him." Major Neale twisted his mouth in an effort to remember. "Afraid I don't, Colonel Cameron. There were so many, you know, that one met here, there and everywhere and then forgot. They that succeeded them seemed to push the memories of their predecessors right away from one. At least, that's how I found it—recurring continually. Didn't you find something of the sort with yourself?"

Uncle Ian nodded agreement. "I know what you mean. Anyhow while you're here, what about a 'spot' of Scotch? I'll ring."

"Don't trouble Mrs. Veitch," I said, "I'll bring it in for you." I knew that Mrs. Veitch was busy and I also knew her fervent dislike of fugitive interruptions at this particular time of the morning. When I returned with the Scotch, the siphon and the glasses, the Major and my uncle were still indulging in reminiscence. I heard my uncle say, "And where did you land yourself after that, Neale?"

"Well, of course, my Army career was finished. It took me years to walk as well as I do now even. I had to scratch round for a job of work. After a spell in India, several billets were put in my way, but I didn't care particularly for any of them. In the end I determined to use the one bit of influence that I've got. My aunt, you know, is Lady Charlotte Hexham and she's able to pull the strings a bit. She got on to old Hexham who prodded the Prime Minister in the region of the intercostal. Eventually I received sufficient 'kick' from those high up in the seats of the mighty, to land me up as Governor of H.M. Prison at Wandle. I've held it ever since. Or at least until I retired a month ago. A pretty filthy job, too, taking it all round."

"What are you doing down in this part of the world, then?"

Neale laughed. "Very much the same as you, Colonel Cameron. Although I haven't travelled quite as far yet along the road. The fact is, I'm thinking of coming to settle here for good. You see, I love this corner of Sussex. Always have done. The air is incomparable, for one thing. For another, my father retired here and I've always cherished the idea of following his example. Now that the time's come, I'm eagerness itself." He bowed in my direction. "I find, directly I come to it, that it has gathered additional attractions."

Uncle Ian coughed discreetly. "I share your love of the district, Neale. And as you say, the air's like champagne. Where exactly are you thinking of coming? Have you a place in your mind, in your eye, or are you intending to have one built for you?"

"That's still in the air. I haven't decided yet, Colonel. If I see a place that captures my imagination and it's conveniently 'gettable', I'll have a shot for it. If I fail to run across anything suitable, I'll choose my spot and have my own place put on it. Have it built to my own design."

"Not a bad idea, Neale, from many points of view. Where are you staying now? In the village?"

"Yes. At the 'Red Stag'. I came down last night."

"Comfortable?"

"So-so. It's not the 'Ritz', of course, but I'm an old campaigner, so what's the odds? I can put up with most things, you know."

"Well, come and dine with us this evening. My son's here with a friend of his, and we have two more people coming down from Town. You will be welcome."

Major Neale accepted the invitation gratefully. The two people to whom Uncle Ian had referred in his last statement were Lois Fletcher and my aunt, his own sister, Mrs. Munro; she had been a widow almost as long as he had been a widower. She was an exceedingly hard-headed and highly capable person. Uncle and I went to the station to meet her. Lois was coming by road. The nearest station to Dallow Corner, by the way, is a matter of four and a half miles from the bungalow, over at Quoynings. I drove the Daimler that evening, as earlier in the day Hardy had asked for the evening off. His married sister was ill, somewhere near Tufnell Park, and wished to see him specially. Douglas and Nigel had walked over to Cranwick to play golf on the Cranwick course and at half-past four hadn't returned. Dinner was at seven, and naturally, Uncle and I were anxious to get back home before either Mr. Armstrong or Major Neale arrived. Aunt Elspeth's greeting, as she alighted from the train at Quoynings, was typical of her.

"Goodness gracious, Ian!" she exclaimed, "what in the name of all that's wonderful induced you to bury yourself down here in this God-forsaken hole? It's a positive abomination of desolation. Look at this station! Look at the way it's lighted! Or, rather, isn't lighted! It won't surprise me if I lose my way in the dark and walk off the platform on to the metals themselves. The idea of asking me to come down here to—I didn't see you, Cecilia. How are you, my dear?" She kissed me in her fussy, odd way and then turned to rend my uncle again.

"It's been pitch black for miles and miles. I've tried to look out of the carriage window, but it was useless. The darkness was Stygian. I could see nothing. Positively nothing."

Uncle Ian smiled at her vehemence, and commenced to remonstrate with her gently. "You wait till the morrow, Elspeth. You'll alter your opinion then. Providence and a better judgment 'will come with the light'. You'll be charmed. More than that, you'll be the first to admit what delightful country it is."

"I don't know so much. I've heard that sort of story before. And from you, more than once. Is there a church near? Or is it a—"

"A dear old place, Elspeth. Over at Dallowdene. You'll fall in love with it directly you set eyes on it."

"Oh, shall I?" she sniffed. "More than likely, I shall find that it's on all fours with your railway station, and that it's got nasty, smelly oil-lamps and a parson who preaches in black gloves. Dear old place, indeed!"

Uncle piloted her to the car, wherein she gradually simmered down into a state of comparative quietude. When we got back to the bungalow, Lois had turned up and Douglas and Nigel had returned from their golfing exploits.

Lois listened to Aunt Elspeth entirely unsympathetically. "Stop grumbling once and for all," she said authoritatively. Remember that you're down in Sussex by the sea, where if you are to believe them, hundreds of people are positively pining to be. That should be sufficient to satisfy you. Regard it as your daily dose. When you feel all snappy and snorky, repeat to yourself as many times as you can without taking a breath, 'I'm in Sussex by the sea, I'm in Sussex by the—'"

"Stuff and nonsense," interrupted Aunt Elspeth. "There's as much lying rubbish about Sussex as there is about Aberdeen. Did you ever hear such a libel on the Aberdonians as that story of the grit-proof confetti? I'd like to—"

The bell interrupted her and I could hear Mrs. Veitch admitting Mr. Armstrong and Major Neale. It struck me as a coincidence that they should have arrived together. I dashed into my bedroom to change into an evening frock and to put the finishing touches to my hair. Now the night was a very dark one, even for the middle of November. The moon was in its last quarter and there was a touch of frost. My bedroom was in the front of the bungalow and overlooked the road that ran between Stretton and Quoynings and through Dallow Corner. As I stood at the glass attending to my hair, I heard the ring of footsteps on the frost-bound road outside. Besides being dark, the night had turned cold very suddenly with that deadly chill that nearly always characterizes a sudden cold spell in November, when a frost takes charge. The road, hard and frosty, threw up the noise of the man's steps and the sounds came to me with that crystal-clearness that sometimes, in certain weathers, distinguishes the notes of a gramophone. Now it was rather unusual for anybody to be on the road at this time of night. Although we had been in the bungalow for so short a period, we had already remarked that the road where we were seemed completely deserted after about four o'clock in the afternoon. It was well off the route for regular cars. It led to no town that harboured industry; tramps of the old variety were few and far between. Because of these facts, I suppose, I went to the window of my bedroom and peered out into the blackness. Naturally I was not able to see anything beyond the blurred shape of the trees that fringed the other side of the road. Their branches were stretched out like the monstrous arms of stark and tattered giants clutching at air in the rather vain hope of gripping something more substantial. Then, just as I looked out, the footsteps slowed down and stopped. Almost, it seemed to me, as I looked out, right in front of our gate. I stood and listened for a second or two, although had I been taxed for a reason for so doing, I should have been unable to have given one. For a few minutes or so I heard nothing more. Impulsively, I switched off the electric light and then silently unfastened the catch of the casement window. This accomplished I leaned out, just a little. It was now bitterly cold and I found myself regretting my impulsive action almost immediately. "Idiot," I whispered to myself, "priceless idiot to—" And then I stopped dead in my whispering and my heart began to go nineteen to the dozen. For soft voices were coming from almost directly outside. There was just a low murmur, that to my ears, tainted with the fever of fearful imagination, seemed ominous. How I longed for the light—of either moon or stars—that I could see who it was that lurked so close to me. So near, we can say, and yet so far. But even this longing was summarily cut short.

I heard something that made the blood thump in my veins and set my heart racing perilously. I heard a low, horrible laugh. It was the laugh, that Uncle and I had heard behind the screen in the restaurant, on the evening that we had first come to Dallow Corner. I shut the window noiselessly and stood there, mastering an overwhelming desire to scream.

*　*　*　*　*

My hand shook a little, I think, as I opened the door of the dining-room. They were all in there and waiting for me. Lois uttered a scathing remark that covered time, taste, and toilet, and Douglas had just joined in the onslaught of banter, with Mr. Armstrong gallant in my defence, when there came a sudden and startling interruption. I can still remember, that, to me at that time, it sounded exactly like a summons. A tocsin. A summons that must be implicitly obeyed. A summons that was not only imperative, but inevitable. The bell rang! Once, twice, and then a third time. We all stopped talking and looked at each other.

# CHAPTER VI

# WE MEET "FLAME" LAMPARD

AT LAST the silence was broken. "Who the blazes is that?" Uncle Ian frowned bad-temperedly as he put the question.

I can't remember that anyone of us answered. I think that we were all listening to Mrs. Veitch. We heard her go to the front door and then we heard an exchange of sentences between her and whoever it was who had rung the bell. Eventually there came the sound of Mrs. Veitch's returning footsteps, and following upon that, a tap on the door of the dining-room. My uncle replied to it. "Who is it, Mrs. Veitch?" he called out heavily.

The housekeeper entered to answer him. "If you please, sir," she said, "there's a man at the door who says he must see you, sir. On official business, he says. I told him you were at dinner and had company and couldn't be disturbed, but he said he was sorry to disturb you—he must see you. He refuses to go away, sir."

Mrs. Veitch delivered her message with the air of one who has an unpleasant job which had best be got over with all possible celerity.

As I looked at him, I thought my uncle was on the point of explosion. "Send him about his business—whoever he is," he exclaimed vehemently. "Tell him that I'll see him in the morning and not a minute before. I don't care if he's the Chancellor of the Exchequer himself. Or even the Archangel Gabriel," he uttered in a kind of vindictive afterthought.

At this Douglas seemed to recover himself somewhat. "First that which is natural," he quoted, "afterwards that which is spiritual."

Mrs. Veitch turned on her heel to go. But a form suddenly appeared in the doorway behind her and a strangely-hoarse voice spoke over her shoulder towards us. "Neither the one nor the other, Colonel Cameron." The figure that I saw framed in the doorway gave me a shock. To say that it was huge does it much less than mere justice. The man to whom it belonged was more tremendously massive than any man I have ever seen. He must have stood at least six feet four in height and in addition to his unusual tallness, his girth was simply staggering when you first beheld it. I was reminded of a mighty tree. His face was abnormally pale. I have never looked upon another of such ivory pallor, and, to cap it all, his head was covered with a thick mass of flaming red hair. As the light of the room caught it and held it, there was the illusion that his head was actually ablaze. I heard it said afterwards by a detective from Scotland Yard that people never looked upon "Flame" Lampard for the first time without experiencing a physical shock. I can subscribe to that opinion without the slightest reservation, for, as my eyes first fell upon him, when he addressed my uncle, I felt a little shiver run through my frame. Lois said, later on in the evening, that she felt exactly the same, so there must be something of truth in the statement that I have just advanced. My uncle's coolness, knowing him as I did, surprised me—now that the actual moment of clash had arrived. He rose to his feet very quietly, but with dignity.

"What do you mean by this unwarrantable intrusion?" he asked. "Please explain your presence in this room."

The man laughed and I shivered again, both at the laugh and the reminiscence that it occasioned. Then he spoke—menacingly hoarse, as always.

"I wouldn't call you hospitable, Colonel. In fact, from your manner one might think that I harboured evil designs upon you. Believe me, I'm incapable of such a thing. It's contrary to my nature." He laughed again and almost contemptuously regarded the various occupants of our room. His eyes travelled from person to person, with a careless and cavalier flicker that gave one the impression that, had he willed, he could, with a gesture of a finger, have destroyed them all. Destroyed, too, with the sense of annihilation. He seemed to dwell on Major Neale's face a little longer than on any of the others, but this idea may have been merely a fancy of mine.

Douglas blazed across the table at him. "Look here, my man, state your business, or clear out."

"You weren't in the front row when courtesy was dispensed." His steel-blue eyes blazed at Douglas for an infinitesimal part of a second; then the flare and flicker in them died down as quickly as they had leapt up, and a cold, merciless malevolence took their place. "Have a care," he muttered. "You might try my patience overmuch. So much so, that I might do something for which I should sorrow afterwards. Which would pain me intensely." He turned again towards my uncle. "I will waste no more time, Colonel Cameron. My business is with you. In time to come, you may thank me for what you are pleased to term an unwarrantable intrusion. The truth of the matter is that I am the bearer of a warning, and when 'Flame' Lampard warns, it's as well to take heed. Take care that the air of this place doesn't prove unhealthy for you. And besides taking care, take a piece of advice as well. Advice for which I'll make no charge. Clear away from the vicinity of Dallow Corner while you can. Otherwise, Colonel Cameron, it may be too late. Good night."

Before Uncle Ian could find words with which to reply, he pivoted on his heel like lightning, pushed the trembling Mrs. Veitch from his path, and disappeared from the range of our sight. Silent for the moment, and swept temporarily off our respective balances by the audacity and effrontery of the intrusion, we heard the slam of the front door, and it echoed through the bungalow as though the person who had made his exit had left an empty abode behind him—an abode that harboured only ghosts and phantoms.

My uncle turned to Mr. Armstrong and Major Neale. "Gentlemen," he said, "my apologies for this most unfortunate happening. All I can plead in defence, is that the man is a perfect stranger to me, and that he entered the room under the element of surprise. He must have got hold of my name somewhere, but I can assure you that I haven't the remotest idea of what he was talking about." He motioned to Mrs. Veitch. "If the soup isn't too cold, Mrs. Veitch, kindly serve it. We will endeavour to forget the occurrence."

During dinner I think that it was Nigel who was affected most by the circumstances of the interruption. I could see that he wished we had been dining simply and ordinarily amongst ourselves— with no guests at all. He was excited and worried. He had read into the occurrence, I felt moderately certain, a new development that was connected with the Trout cryptogram. For a long period he said nothing at all. Mr. Armstrong, irreproachably tactful, behaved as though the incident had never taken place, but about the Major there was the unmistakable air of one who is deliberately averting his head from a too intimate contemplation of the vertebrae of the family skeleton. Douglas fidgeted and chafed under the restraint his father had so obviously placed upon him. Resentment at the whole business was his dominant thought. It was plain that he would have dearly liked to have had all the cards on the table and the entire matter thoroughly thrashed out while the heat was still in it. Lois seemed puzzled at the extraordinary turn that affairs had taken, and even Aunt Elspeth, for once at least, seemed subdued by an occurrence that was so far removed from the commonplace. Certainly she subsided into what I call "comfortable" conversation. Dinner over, we adjourned to the lounge, and after the conversation had touched upon a variety of subjects, all more or less sketchily, Nigel put a question to Mr. Armstrong that, I confess, startled me.

"What sort of a garden did the previous occupants of this place keep, Mr. Armstrong? It's been let slide a bit lately, I imagine, which makes it difficult to tell, apart from the question of the season. Was it well-kept when they were here?"

Mr. Armstrong nodded affirmatively. "It was very fine indeed, Mr. Strachan. Mr. Christie was exceedingly proud of it, and as for Mrs. Christie, his wife, well—I've rarely met a person as passionately fond of all flowers as she was."

"What was the speciality?"

"Speciality?" For the moment Mr. Armstrong seemed at a loss.

"Yes, most gardeners have a special flower, into the cultivation of which they put their best. At least, I think that's been my experience, and I've known a good many in my time. Wasn't it so here, with this chap Christie?"

Mr. Armstrong smiled. "I see what you mean, Mr. Strachan. But in Mr. Christie's case I don't think your point quite applied. The seasons, and I think all flowers, came alike to him, and in consequence, the garden here always looked a picture. I've seen it in spring, summer, and autumn, and I don't know when it held the greatest beauty."

Nigel was just about to reply, when I decided to step in and help him. My uncle and Major Neale had settled down to a discussion on military tactics under ultra-modern conditions, and Lois, with Aunt Elspeth, was chaffing Douglas about some incident of his early boyhood that my aunt had remembered—after the unfortunate manner of aunts—and had recounted with fearful and unholy relish.

"I love spring flowers," I said. "Daffodils, hyacinths, crocuses, freesia, narcissi—what did Mr. Christie, grow? All of them?"

"All, I think, Miss Cameron. I've never seen a finer show than his tulips in this garden last spring. They were really magnificent. He had such an army of colour. I remember that they commanded universal admiration."

I tried hard to avoid Nigel's gaze, for I could see from the corner of my eye that he was looking at me intently, in an attempt to catch my glance. Old Trout's lines floated through my brain. "That Flowers more Bright, Than Daffodil or Crocus white." Following upon them came Mr. Armstrong's last statement. Tulips were perhaps the most resplendent of the bulbs that clothed the earth with spring. I attempted to take a chance and to force the issue. "It's pretty evident, then, that we shall have to try to emulate our predecessor, Mr. Christie. We shall have to see whether we can't go one, or even two, better. You'll have to help me, Mr. Armstrong. I expect I shall be head gardener." I believe I cultivated a degree of archness as I made the proposal.

He smiled cordially in reply. "I shall be charmed, Miss Cameron. But tell me how."

"I'm bound to do most of the work in the garden. You see, Douglas won't be here overmuch, and Uncle Ian's dreadfully lazy. That's what makes him so fat. I thought you'd be able to show me the best position to grow the various kinds of flowers. See what I mean? A lot depends on things like that."

"Of course. I can even go part of the way with you now. Look here. Outside this window"—he pointed to the front window of the lounge—"Christie had his rose-garden. At the side there, when the time came for the roses to be the blooms of yesterday, he grew his autumn stuff, chrysanthemums, dahlias, and such-like. Over on the other side, where the dining-room stands he had his spring beds. The tulips were right in the centre of them. Looked superb when they were in full flower." He shook his head dubiously. "I don't want to discourage you, Miss Cameron, but you're flying at high game to try to outdo Christie."

I rallied him upon his misgivings. "Wait," I announced. "Wait, before you sit in judgment. Don't be so ungallant. What man has done, woman can do. You never know."

As I spoke and before he could reply, I noticed that Major Neale had left my uncle's side and had come over to stand behind my chair. It was clear, too, from his opening remark, that he had overheard some, if not all, of our conversation.

"So you're going in for gardening, eh, Miss Cameron? That's splendid news. We shall have to compare notes. I'm an enthusiast, also."

I shook my head. "You mustn't be too optimistic, Major Neale. Don't hope to learn anything from me. Mr. Armstrong has been making my mouth water with stories of what the garden here was like before we came. That's what fired my enthusiasm."

Nigel laughed meaningly. "Here's an offer, then. Count on me as your chief assistant, Cecilia. Every holiday I shall rush down here complete with spade, fork, and trowel. Fertilizers will ooze from my pockets, and instead of calling for a Bronx or a Cupid's Kiss, I shall yell for something dainty in 'weed-killers'."

Later on that evening, after our guests had gone, Nigel turned to me in high glee. "By Jove, Cecilia! You're worth your weight in rubies. You froze on to my idea in a flash. You helped no end. It took the edge off a bit, you jumping in as you did. Do you think we've progressed?"

"Angels, Nigel," I said, with mock severity, "rush in, where fools only commence to tread. You opened the carriage door. I scrounged the corner seat with my back to the engine. You wallowed heavily in horticultural generalities. I tiptoed elegantly through the tulips. By the way, Nigel, how does old Christie's tulip-bed strike you? Are you at all interested?"

He grinned with every sign of encouragement. "So much so, Cecilia, that I consider it calls for a fairly immediate investigation. What say you yourself?"

I kissed the tips of my fingers to him provocatively.

"To-morrow is also a day. In the morning, Sir Nigel."

But as it happened my prediction, to be strictly veracious, was not fulfilled. It was about half-past eleven that evening when I went into my room to bed. I had helped Mrs. Veitch with one or two little jobs in the kitchen and, feeling very tired and a wee bit excited, I decided to turn in. Uncle Ian and the two boys were sitting up for a last smoke and a final "spot" of Scotch, as was their usual custom. It was colder than ever, as may well be imagined. I was no sooner into bed than I dozed off into an uneasy sleep, to awake at the footsteps of the three men passing my bedroom door on their way to their own bedrooms. As they passed, I remember that I looked at the illuminated dial of my wrist-watch. The time was twenty past twelve. After that, I think that I must have dozed off again. Certainly I am unable to remember lying awake for any length of time. Suddenly I was awakened with a terrific crash. I sat up in bed blinking my eyes and collecting my senses, and it must have been a second or two before the full realization of what had really occurred came to me. The glass of the middle window of my bedroom had been shattered by something. There was a gaping hole in front of me through which the intensely cold night air was pouring. I shivered, both physically and mentally. Almost at once, Uncle Ian's voice sounded outside my bedroom door. If he had been asleep when the shot had been fired, he had been marvellously quick to have got there.

"Cecilia," he cried, "what is it? Are you all right, my dear? What on earth has happened?"

I unlocked my door with all the haste that I could muster. I thought it was the best answer in the circumstances. At any rate, it told him that I was safe. He came in. I pointed to the window with what, I am afraid, was a shaking finger. "Look, Uncle." He walked over to the shattered glass.

"That's a bullet, my girl," he exclaimed. "You've been shot at, Cecilia. There are no two opinions about that. You've had a narrow escape, my dear. Now what the—"

As he spoke, there came a second report from the back of the bungalow somewhere, and for the second time that night we heard the crash of shattered and splintered glass.

"I think, Uncle Ian," I said, with a tremor in my voice, "that it's pretty evident Flame Lampard's warning had some truth in it."

## CHAPTER VII
## THE CAMPAIGN DEVELOPS

I SLIPPED on a *négligée* hurriedly, and we made our way to the other rooms. Aunt Elspeth and Lois were already out of their room, and I shall never forget how absurdly idiotic Aunt Elspeth looked in the garments that did her service for the night. She reminded me of one of those flannel things that are put over egg-cups to keep eggs warm after they have been cooked. Without wasting words, Uncle Ian banged on the door of the boys' room.

"Are you all right, Douglas? And you, Nigel?"

I was relieved to hear my cousin answer cheerily as he pulled the bedroom door open: "We're O.K., guv'nor. But what's the little Bisley business? Some blighter has popped a bullet through our window here. Moreover, it seemed to be the second of its kind. Nigel swears he heard a shot before this one. Is that so, does anybody know? Was anybody else favoured?"

"I have been," I answered. "A shot came through my bedroom window a minute or two ago just the same as one seems to have sailed through yours."

"Nice place to invite anybody, Lois, I must say," exclaimed Aunt Elspeth. "I might have known what to expect, and that being so, sympathy would be wasted on me. It serves me right for coming. I have only myself to blame."

"I've read it," laughed Lois. "It's by Princess Bibesco. And if you ask me, I think the whole business is rather attractive. It's a dull old world nowadays, and say what you like, a thrill's a thrill all the world over, even if it does come in the early hours of a cold November morning."

Nigel spoke to my uncle. He looked very grave and very serious. "What are we going to do about it, sir? Do you think there's any likelihood of a second performance? Or shall we go out in the garden and reconnoitre?"

Uncle Ian shook his head. "They're gone by now, whoever they are. My counsel is that we lie low inside until the morning. In the morning we'll prowl round, watch points, and investigate generally. Go back to your beds, you girls, and get what sleep you can. Cecilia's got the worst of it. I'm afraid she's going to find her bedroom rather draughty. Still, perhaps Douglas will be able to fix something up for you, Cecilia. Good night, all."

Douglas plugged the hole up in my window-pane as best he could, and after a pretty lengthy spell of troubled wakefulness I fell off to sleep and slept soundly. In the morning I was up first. Except, of course, Mrs. Veitch, who was always a particularly early riser. Hardy, you remember, was away. As you may imagine, I made what was very nearly a bee-line for the garden. There might be, I argued to myself mentally, some traces left there of our nocturnal visitor or visitors. I determined to have a careful look. I was just on the point of bending down to examine a mark on one of the paths when I heard a low cough from what seemed just behind me. I looked up quickly at the sound—a little startled. A stout man, in a double-breasted blue reefer suit, was standing at the gate of the front garden, leaning over in my direction.

"Morning, miss," he called out, directly I spotted him. "Could I have a word with you?"

Without answering, I walked down the garden path towards him. As I approached him I saw that he had a hard, fleshy, callous face. His dark eyes, something like the currants that children put into dough for their mothers to place in the oven, were shifty and vacillating, and travelled restlessly from side to side. I determined to make myself as imperious and as authoritative as I could.

"What is it that you want?" I asked severely.

"A little job of work, missy," he replied ingratiatingly. "I'm down and out," he added, "one of the few genuine unemployed. 'Aven't had bite nor sup since yesterday morning, and can't see where the next is comin' from."

I eyed him up and down for a second or so. "You don't look it," I announced critically. "You look well-fed and well-clothed to me."

He shook his head critically and lugubriously. "That's another of my many misfortunes. It's hereditary with me, too. My looks never did pity me, missy, and the suit wasn't made for me. It came off a stiff 'un. I'll give you my solemn affidavit that what I told you was true. I'm hungry. Damned hungry! But I don't want charity, I don't. I'm one o' them what's willing to work." He half-opened the garden gate and appeared to be on the point of entering the garden. "'Ow about digging up your garden for you? I can see it wants it. Bad, too. I'd 'ave that all shipshape in a couple o' days. At a moderate charge, too. Say an 'Oxford' a day."

At the mention of the word "garden" I felt myself stiffen, and at the same time I wondered if the man knew of it. I shook my head in dismissal of his offer. "No, thank you." My voice sounded strange to my ears; it was almost as though I were listening to another person speaking from a distance. "We have already engaged a proper gardener to do the necessary work, as it happens."

His little eyes were fixed on me malevolently, and they narrowed as he realized that my refusal was firm and definite. "Oh—you have, have you? Very nice, too. 'Ow about supporting home industries? And suppose I happen to be a proper—"

I heard steps flying behind me down the garden path, and as I half-turned to identify them, the sound close at hand of my cousin's voice. "What is it, Cecilia?" he cried. "What's the fellow want?"

"He asked for work, Douglas. Wants to dig up the garden for us. When I told him we didn't require his services, he didn't seem to like it."

Douglas turned on the man almost savagely. "Clear off—do you hear? Can't you take 'no' for an answer? We've no work for you here."

The stout man curled his lip viciously and showed his teeth, and I understood more than ever that he was a decidedly nasty-looking customer. "S'trewth!" He spat as an embellishment to the oath. "And they call it a free country! Talk about heroes, it ain't fit for pierrots to live in! A man down and out, what's done his bit over the other side, bin wounded and all, can't ask for honest work in a decent, civil manner without 'avin' his blasted head bitten off. All right, my young toff, them as live longest 'ull see the most. 'Ave a good look round the landscape while you can. Mind you ain't seen nearly all you're goin' to see." He thrust his hands into his pockets, turned and shuffled off down the road.

When we told Nigel, five minutes later, he looked more perturbed than ever. "They're after something," he exclaimed, "I'm certain of it. My legacy—if I can describe it as such—looks like proving an awkward business. The sooner we can read the confounded cryptogram, the better for all of us. But from these latter developments, it looks as though we're 'warmer' here than we imagined."

I agreed with him. Then an idea struck me. "Let Lois and Aunt Elspeth have a squint at it, Nigel. Neither of them's slow in the uptake. The reverse, in fact. And an extra head or two might make all the difference. If their ideas coincide with ours, on the general scheme of the thing, we might do worse than have a shot at digging up that bed where old Christie's tulips were."

Nigel showed signs of doubt and partial disapproval, and he hesitated a second or so before he replied to my suggestion. "I don't want to start digging operations on mere 'spec', Cecilia. I'd like to feel more sure of my—er—ground." His face changed and he grinned. "Frightfully sorry—but you know what I mean. I think we ought to have more data before we make any definite move—more *certain* data. Still, on the other hand, I like your idea of letting your aunt and Miss Fletcher have a look at old Trout's rigmarole. We'll rope them in after breakfast. I'm not going up to Town till this afternoon, so we shall have plenty of time. In a way, I wish I wasn't going, but there's a book in the British Museum I want to see badly." He said no more and I made up my mind not to press him. To my disappointment, however, neither Lois nor Aunt Elspeth was able to get us very much farther. Inspiration was fugitive from each of them. In fact, Lois, I think, retarded us more than anything. The first letter of the equation part of the cryptogram, she refused to accept as a "P" as we had been inclined to do. More than that, she came down very emphatically with the opinion that the letter was definitely a "D"—which, as I say, threw us back on our investigations, rather than brought us forward, What on earth a "D" could represent, other than "down" or "dig", none of us could imagine. Anyhow, my little suggestion re—the auxiliaries proved fruitless, and when Nigel and Douglas left us after lunch, with the expressed intention to return in the evening of the following day, no further progress with the cryptogram had been made whatever.

Soon after the boys had gone, Hardy returned. My uncle was more than pleased, as he had not expected him until the end of the week, and almost immediately, he commissioned him to take us all for a run in the car. I think it must have been for the especial benefit of Aunt Elspeth. The panorama of events had disturbed her, and it appeared to give her new life directly the trip was mooted. We left Mrs. Veitch in charge of the bungalow and got back about half-past six. When we returned, we found the poor old woman in the kitchen, gagged and tied to a chair. In the garden there was a pile of newly turned earth, dug from a hole that fairly gaped at us when we came to it. As we undid the cords that held our old servant to the chair, and removed the padded handkerchief from her mouth, my uncle's face was black with anger, and to use a phrase of the boxing game that I have heard Douglas use very frequently, the time had come, I could tell, for "seconds out of the ring". For Uncle Ian swore softly to himself as he released Mrs. Veitch from her wholly unenviable position. And when Uncle Ian swore softly, it was a sure sign that he meant business.

## Chapter VIII
## THE FIRST DEATH

"Now, now, Mrs. Veitch," he said comfortingly. "You're all right, I think, and there appears to be no great harm done. Take your time, pull yourself together, and then tell me exactly what's been happening." As may be expected, however, the woman's nerve had gone to pieces completely. When he realized the fact, my uncle turned to me at once. "Bring me some brandy, Cecilia. Be as quick as you can, my dear."

Lois and I dashed off to the sideboard in the dining-room, and I quickly found the brandy and poured out what was wanted. Within a moment or so the stimulant slowly brought the colour back into Mrs. Veitch's cheeks, and after sitting quietly for a little while, she collected herself very creditably and started on her story.

"You hadn't been gone much more than half an hour, sir, when there came a sharp ring at the front bell. Of course, I answered it at once. I had half an idea that it was you come back for something. It was one of the gentlemen who were here to dinner last evening. The one called Major Neale. He asked for you, sir, and naturally I told him that you weren't in. He asked how long I thought you would be, and I told him that I couldn't say to the minute. I said that you'd gone for a run round in the car with the ladies, and wouldn't be back probably until it was dark. He thought for a minute or two and then said he wouldn't wait, if that was the case. He went away. About a quarter of an hour afterwards, I should think, there was another ring at the bell. As I went to answer it, I had the same sort of idea as before, only this time I thought it was the Major come back." She paused and sipped another mouthful of the brandy. Uncle and the others of us waited patiently for her to resume. I mention this, because in the ordinary way Uncle Ian is very far from patient. Mrs. Veitch seemed to sense that she was being made the recipient of something extra special in the way of consideration, for she looked up very gratefully and appreciatively, as she proceeded with her story. "Well, sir, when I got to the door the second time, there were two men standing there. One was the man who pushed in here last night, the man with that awful red hair, and the other was a man I'd never seen before. He was a big, burly, thick-set man with a swollen sort of nose. Bulbous, I think they call it. As I opened the door, and without so much as a 'by your leave', they pushed their way past me just as the red-haired man had done on the other occasion, shut the door and caught hold of my two arms. I was too surprised and too frightened to struggle much. I didn't seem able to resist at all. 'What shall I do with her, boss?' said the thick-set man, and the man with the red hair said: 'Stick something in her mouth to prevent her giving tongue and tie her to one of the chairs.' As he spoke he laughed a horrible laugh that made my blood run cold. They hustled me into the kitchen, stuck something in my mouth, and trussed me up to a chair—the same as you came in and found me."

"What did they do after that?" interjected my uncle sharply, his natural impatience mastering him at last.

Mrs. Veitch shook her head rather mournfully, I thought. "I'm sorry, sir, but I can't tell you very much about that. Except that nothing happened here in the kitchen. They gave the room a sort of quick glance round and then went straight out. After that, all I can tell you is that they tramped round all the other rooms. I know that, because I could hear them. Then, after a long time, I heard them go out. That is to say, I heard the front door shut."

Lois looked as though she had thought of something important, and I could almost see a question trembling on her tongue. She looked at my uncle almost pleadingly.

"May I ask Mrs. Veitch a question, Colonel Cameron?" she inquired.

My uncle quickly nodded his consent. "With the greatest pleasure, my dear. What is it?"

Lois turned to Mrs. Veitch. "How long had the men been gone when we came back? As nearly as you can tell, that is. You couldn't see the clock on this mantelpiece from where they put you, could you?"

Mrs. Veitch shook her head. "No, miss, I couldn't. My back was to it and I couldn't turn my head. That's why I can't be certain of any of the times. But let me think now. I should say that you were back here within about half an hour of the time I heard the men go away."

"Are you pretty certain of that? Because it's going to be important."

"Yes, miss. It wouldn't be more than half hour. I'd almost swear to that."

"Good. Now tell me this. When you heard them moving about in the other rooms, did you hear their voices? Did you hear them say anything? Did you hear them *talking to each other*, for instance?"

Mrs. Veitch nodded vigorously. "Yes, miss! I did."

"All the time?"

"Yes. All the time—on and off. They kept up what you could call a running conversation."

Lois intervened quickly. "They were *inside*, then, all the time that you were in here tied up?"

"Yes, miss."

"Then, Colonel Cameron," exclaimed Lois, turning to my uncle semi-triumphantly, "if that's the case—and Mrs. Veitch seems pretty certain of her facts—*who dug up the garden*? Tell me that!"

Uncle Ian looked at her steadily as her meaning came home to him. "You mean, Miss Fletcher—"

"If they left the house about half an hour before we came back, after being inside all the time—mark you—they wouldn't have had time to dig that yawning hole in the garden, would they? Therefore—"

I interrupted. "There were three of them! Two worked inside and one outside. Isn't that what you mean, Lois?"

"Exactly," said Lois.

"Looks very much like it, I grant you," agreed my uncle. "But who could the—?"

I went on hastily. "I know who the third man was. It was my gardener acquaintance of first thing this morning. He's had his wish, after all."

Uncle Ian nodded. "Looks very much like that, too, Cecilia." My uncle spoke very sternly. "I seem to have routed out a proper hornet's nest for my retirement, don't I? I certainly owe Nigel something for this. Confound his damned legacy, as he calls it!" He strode across the kitchen with the utmost vexation. "Legacy or no legacy—to-morrow morning, if I'm alive, I'm going to call in the police. Let's see what damage these blackguards have done."

We followed him round as he made the tour of the other rooms. There was enough disturbance. Pictures had been turned round, drawers opened, carpets and rugs moved, and there was every indication that a quick but pretty comprehensive search had been made for something in most of the likely places.

Lois again proved her worth in emergency. "There's one fact that issues plainly from all this," she observed, puckering her brows reflectively.

"What's that?" queried my uncle. "I'd welcome anything 'plain'."

"Why—that the people responsible for these outrages are very much in the same position as Nigel and we are. They know something, but not *all*, and they're chancing their arm. Which is comforting, after all—from Nigel's particular point of view."

"Perhaps, Lois," I returned, "and yet, perhaps not."

"How do you mean, Cecilia?" she demanded chatteringly.

"Supposing they 'chanced their arm', as you put it, and were successful. Supposing their arrow hit the mark? For instance, take the hole that they've dug in the garden, supposing they found in that what they were looking for? How then?"

"I'll concede that it's a bare possibility, Cecilia," she countered, "but no more than that. I'll tell you why. Let me reason things out for you. If they'd known that what they wanted was hidden in the garden out there, known it for a certainty, I mean, they would never have wasted their time tramping about the rooms, would they? That's common sense, isn't it? Do you agree with me?"

I nodded in acquiescence. "Yes, I think I see what you mean."

"Well, then," she continued, "if they didn't know exactly where to dig in the garden, it's easily a thousand to one that they didn't strike it first time in such a short period. They would have been appallingly lucky if they had done." She swung round impulsively on to my uncle. "That's sound, isn't it, Colonel Cameron?"

"Very," he answered. "I certainly agree with you, Miss Lois, and I congratulate you on your reasoning. Nigel's legacy, as we have come to call it, may be regarded, I think, as still intact. And if they think they're going to frighten us with these tactics, they don't know the Cameron men. In the meantime, let's have some dinner."

Mrs. Veitch did her best in the circumstances, and we had just finished the meal when Major Neale was announced. Uncle Ian, who, during the courses, had relapsed into a brown study, brightened up considerably at this addition to our forces, gave our visitor an account of all the happenings, and at length came out, with what, to me, was a most surprising suggestion.

"Neale," he said, "do me a favour, will you? Stay here with these girls while I take a stroll. I'd very much rather not leave them alone. I want to have a word with Armstrong. I wouldn't go, only I want to see him particularly. I'll be back by eleven. What time did you want to go?"

"I'll wait with the ladies till you return, Colonel Cameron— that will be all right."

"Thanks, Neale, I knew you would. I won't be later than eleven, I promise you. I'm not taking the car, so Hardy will be at hand if you want anything." He grinned. "To help, I mean, if there's a rough house. But there won't be. I'm absolutely convinced of that. You'll find that operations are suspended for the time being."

"Do you think you're wise to go out, Uncle?" I asked him.

"Wise?"

"To go alone."

He laughed, and the laugh held a tinge of excitement. "I'm not exactly alone, Cecilia." He patted his pocket. "Trust me for that. I've got something in here that will protect me quite well if need be. Loaded in all six chambers. Cheerio, Neale. Don't leave any of that Scotch."

It was just like him, the action, the mood, and the speech. He had always been absolutely fearless, supremely contemptuous of risk, and, I believe, revelled in the thought of the possibility of what he always termed "sporting" danger. All this passed through my mind as he left us. I heard him go into the lounge, and then, after an interval, I heard the front door close.

Major Neale proved a really charming and entertaining conversationalist, and although Lois was not too talkative, Aunt Elspeth was very quickly captivated by him. The time passed on veritable wings, and it was eleven o'clock before any of us realized the comparative lateness of the hour. The chiming of the clock on the mantelpiece was the first agency that reminded us.

"Your uncle's late, Miss Cameron," remarked Major Neale. "You remember what he said."

"He is," I replied apprehensively, "but don't you wait if you want to go, Major Neale. We're quite all right, you know. Hardy, our chauffeur, is in his room."

"I'll stay a bit longer, Miss Cameron," he replied. "I shouldn't think he'd be very long now."

A further half-hour passed and then became an hour. I looked anxiously at the clock. Eventually Major Neale rose. Aunt Elspeth, too, was beginning to show signs of apprehension. The Major made a suggestion. "How would it do if I go to meet him? There's only the one way back here from Armstrong's, isn't there? By the road?"

I nodded. "It's dreadfully dark and lonely."

He smiled at my description. "I know. I'll pop along. Don't worry. I'll bring him home, never fear. Something's kept him, no doubt."

I shall never forget his face when he came back to us about twenty minutes later. Mrs. Veitch let him in, of course, and he came into the lounge to us ever so quietly.

"You ladies must be brave," he announced. "The news isn't too good. Colonel Cameron's lying against the hedge about midway between here and Mr. Armstrong's. I think he must have been taken ill, or perhaps fainted. If you tell your chap Hardy to get the car out, he and I will drive up there and bring the Colonel back with us. Then we'll see if we can pull him round. Have some brandy ready for him on our return."

I gestured to Lois to get Hardy and then sank back helplessly into my chair. For I knew at that minute, beyond any possibility of doubt or contradiction, not only that Uncle Ian was dead, but also *that he had been murdered.*

## Chapter IX
## FOUL HORROR

When Hardy was ready, I made a decision. "I'm coming with you, Major Neale," I announced quietly but firmly. "I'm not afraid, not the least bit afraid, and I think I ought to come." My words must have sounded braver than they really were, for I found myself trembling and shivering all over as I spoke them.

He looked at me strangely and curiously, as though weighing me up and attempting to assess my courage and determination at their true values.

"I think you are foolish, Miss Cameron," he said quietly. "There is no need, really. But if you insist, of course, there is nothing more for me to say. Now, Hardy. Drive straight up the road towards Mr. Armstrong's, and stop just above the little stream on the right. Mind your arm in the door of the car, Miss Cameron."

A few horrible minutes passed, with my thoughts but a confused medley of sick pain, menacing doubt, and stultifying horror, when suddenly I heard Major Neale's voice speaking, as it were, from the other side of the world. It brought me nearer to my normal self and back to realities with a sudden and sharp mental jerk.

"Just here on the right, Hardy. Under the hedge there." He was speaking to the chauffeur, with his head out of the window of the car.

Hardy pulled the car up gently in the lee of the hedge, and there, on the other side of the road, lying just as Major Neale had described to me, I could see the body of my uncle. We went to him, the Major leading, with Hardy and me following closely in his wake. Major Neale bent down and felt my uncle's heart. Then I saw him try for a pulse with his two fingers. For a minute or so there was silence, each one of us, I think, being afraid to speak. Then Major Neale shook his head gravely, and eventually motioned to Hardy, keeping his head averted from me.

"Help me lift Colonel Cameron into the car, Hardy. We'll get him home. After that, you must find the nearest doctor."

The two men raised the body of my uncle, and I helped them lay him on the seat at the back of the car. On the short journey home neither of us spoke. When we reached the bungalow, I told Aunt Elspeth what had happened as briefly as I could, and Hardy was dispatched post haste for medical assistance. He was gone nearly three-quarters of an hour. The period of waiting did not seem to me so intolerable as one might imagine, for I was convinced that Uncle Ian was beyond any help that this world might bring to him. It was plain to anybody who looked at him that he had been dead for some little time. When Hardy returned, he brought with him a square-headed, taciturn sort of man, whom he introduced to us as Doctor Vallance. The doctor undid my uncle's tie and collar and then opened his shirt. For some time he never spoke at all. I found myself trembling again and shivering just as I had shivered before, as I awaited his first words. So much, it seemed to me, depended on the way in which this doctor was going to look at things. How I wished either Douglas or Nigel were there to remove some of the responsibility from my shoulders. It wanted a *man* to reach down in the depths and pluck with naked hands at the horror that I knew was lurking there. If a woman did it, or even attempted to do it, a charge of hysteria would be launched against her and much capital made out of her vague imaginings. I heard Doctor Vallance speaking.

"Was Colonel Cameron walking, do you know, when he had the seizure?"

"We presume so, doctor," replied Major Neale. "Perhaps it may help you if I recount the full circumstances."

Doctor Vallance listened, and when the Major had finished, nodded his head. "Exactly. Just as I feared. He knew that he was later than he had probably intended to be, and was hurrying home. This hastening threw a strain on his heart. There is cardiac weakness and a certain amount of fatty degeneration of the heart muscles." He paused abruptly to look at Aunt Elspeth and me. "My sympathy, ladies, in what must be a great shock to you. A shock that is all the greater on account of its suddenness. You have the satisfaction, however—perhaps comfort would be a better word for me to use—to know that Colonel Cameron's death was very, very quick and almost painless. The death, no doubt, that all his friends would have wished for him."

Neither of us made him any answer. I nodded mechanically, and Aunt Elspeth looked blankly across the room. My tongue seemed powerless of effort. I wanted to cry certain things aloud, to shout them from the house-tops, but found myself completely unable to do so. Doctor Vallance went on speaking when he saw how matters stood.

"Tell me," he said, "has Colonel Cameron had any medical advice recently? Has he attended his own doctor, say, during the last month or so?" He looked at us, shrewdly questioning under his bushy grey eyebrows. Aunt Elspeth replied for me.

"Yes, doctor. My brother, I know, has been to his own doctor two or three times this autumn. And what's more, knowing all that we know now, he never ought to have come down to this abominable place. I said so before and I say so again. If only I had insisted on him listening to me."

Doctor Vallance ignored the unnecessary embellishments of the reply. He concentrated on the first statement that my aunt had made. It provided him with all that he required. "Just so. In that case, then, if you communicate with his doctor, this doctor whom he has been attending, I will confer with him, and I don't think there will be any difficulty with regard to a certificate. None at all." He turned away from us to pick up his hat. "Good night, ladies. Good night, sir. I'm very sorry indeed. Believe me."

When he had gone back in the car, with Hardy driving, I turned to Major Neale. He was the essence of kindness and consideration.

"Get to bed, Miss Cameron, do. Take my advice, please. You can do nothing more. You've done all that there can be done. If it's any help to you, I'll stay till the morning. A shake-down in one of the easy chairs in the dining-room will be ample for me. As you know, I'm an old campaigner and can make myself comfortable in conditions that most men would find appalling. Take her to bed and look after her, Miss Fletcher."

I thanked him, and my aunt joined me in the thanks. I made one provision, however. "Before I go to bed, Major Neale," I said, "I'm going to look at my uncle's body again. I want to look at his clothes, his boots, his hat—everything about him."

He looked at me as though puzzled and wondering. "Do you think that would be wise on your part, Miss Cameron? Especially at this time of night. You are bound to distress yourself by so doing, and it will serve no useful purpose. What possible benefit can come from it? You heard what Doctor Vallance said just now—why not rest content with that until the morning at least?"

I shook my head decisively. All my nervousness and apprehension, all my literal fear and trembling had now passed from me. I seemed to be filled with an icy-cold, calculating, almost inhuman relentlessness that would impel me to prosecute my inquiry into the cause of my uncle's death to the bitter end. No matter what it cost or whomever it hurt, there would be no drawing back on my part.

I faced Major Neale squarely, so that he could read without any doubt at all the purpose in my eyes. "I heard what Doctor Vallance said, but all the same, I don't believe him. I am certain, as certain as I am that my name is Cecilia Mary Cameron, that my uncle did *not* die from natural causes. He was murdered, Major Neale."

He shrugged his shoulders pityingly, and the action almost maddened me. "You are endeavouring to associate the visit of the other night with the death of your uncle, Miss Cameron? Perhaps it is a natural act on your part. At any rate, I can quite understand you so doing. I am sure, however, that you will find it to be a mere coincidence."

"Come with me," I said simply, beckoning to him.

He followed me again into the lounge where the body of Uncle Ian lay, for I had already noticed something when Doctor Vallance had made his examination. I made up my mind not to tell Major Neale yet, what it was that I had observed. I intended to look in other directions before I gave anything away to anybody.

"You remember," I said to him, "that when Uncle Ian went out this evening, he carried a revolver in his overcoat pocket. You remember what he said about it, don't you? Would you mind seeing if it is still there?"

He went to my uncle's overcoat that lay over the back of the chair, as we had placed it when we had brought him home, and felt in the side pockets. "It's here all right, Miss Cameron." He looked at it closely. "And what's more, it hasn't been used. The six chambers are still full."

I said nothing, and realizing this, he proceeded to follow up the temporary advantage that he considered the fact had given him. He tapped my uncle's revolver with his forefinger. "You must admit, if you are logical, that this in itself, Miss Cameron, possesses a very valuable significance in support of Doctor Vallance's diagnosis. If your uncle had been murdered, as you are trying to suggest to me, or even merely attacked, would he not have used in his defence the weapon that lay so close to his hand? The weapon that he took with him when he went out with the intention—"

"If he had had *time*, Major Neale—*yes*. But what if he had no time? What if they were on him in a flash?" For the moment my questions silenced him, and I determined at this opportune moment to change my plan and confront him with what I had seen when Doctor Vallance had first examined my uncle's heart. "I will tell you something, Major Neale," I said, "something is missing from the top left-hand pocket of my uncle's waistcoat."

He wrinkled his brows in perplexity as he looked at me. "Missing?" he queried.

"Yes," I answered, "something that he always carried with him, something he never went out without."

"What is it?"

"His fountain-pen," I replied prosaically. Again he shook his head dubiously.

"There's nothing in that, Miss Cameron. Most likely fell from his pocket when he collapsed. I've no doubt that we shall find the pen in the morning somewhere near where we found your uncle."

"Perhaps," I responded, not entirely convinced. "It's a point, anyway." I went across to the body as it lay there and looked over all the clothing with the utmost care. There was nothing, however, to excite the most trifling suspicion on my part, and my heart sank a little when I appreciated the difficulties that were in my path and the apparent hopelessness of establishing my position.

Major Neale watched me with the same look of sympathetic pity that I had witnessed on his face a short time before. "There's nothing there, Miss Cameron—really," he declared. "I looked myself."

Without thinking, and certainly without knowing exactly why I did it, I went to my uncle's overcoat and held it up in front of me with the inside turned towards me. As I did so I was conscious of a feeling of unutterable faintness and nausea. For the moment, I was unable to account for it, but suddenly the reason was revealed to me. From the inside breast pocket of the coat there came an odour that I can only describe as the most revoltingly loathsome stench that I have ever experienced. The only smell to which I could possibly liken it with any degree of accuracy was the smell of foul and rotting fish.

"Come over here, Major Neale," I said very quietly. He came—wondering. "Smell there." I indicated the pocket. He frowned. "Well," I asked a moment or two later, "are you going to tell me that you suspect nothing now?"

"I can make nothing of it, Miss Cameron," he said at length. "Nothing at all. Frankly, it's out of my depth—absolutely beyond me. I'm beginning to think that there's something in what you say, after all."

"Go and have your shake-down, Major Neale," I said, with sudden determination, "and I'll go to bed. I've done what I wanted to do. In the morning we'll talk things over. Perhaps Mr. Armstrong will be able to help us. Uncle Ian must have been all right when he left there. That will give us a starting-point at least."

He nodded his agreement and left me. When he had closed the door, and after I heard the sound of his retreating footsteps, I went over to the body again. For an idea had occurred to me. Was it possible that he had endeavoured to use his pen?

I went to the pocket of Uncle Ian's jacket. What I found there brought me unhesitatingly to a decision. Without waiting even for Douglas to agree when he returned, and without consultation with Aunt Elspeth, I determined to send for Anthony Bathurst first thing in the morning.

# Chapter X
# ENTER ANTHONY BATHURST

Hardy went down to the post office in the morning and sent off four wires, to Douglas, Nigel, Doctor Emery of Wimpole Street, Uncle Ian's own doctor, and Anthony Bathurst. To my cousin and to Nigel I simply said, "Come at once," and addressed them at the private hotel at Harrow where they were both staying. To Doctor Emery I stated the facts very briefly. To Mr. Bathurst I made myself a little more explicit. My telegram was as follows:

> Dallow Corner,
> Near Quoynings,
> Sussex.

Please come at once for most urgent consultation. There is deadly peril here.

> Cecilia Cameron.

It may seem strange to many readers of this story, but I never had any doubt about Anthony Bathurst coming, right from the moment when the thought of turning to him for help first flashed through my worried mind. Helen Considine, Sir Charles Considine's daughter who married Dick Arkwright, was an old schoolfellow of mine, although five years my senior, and an even greater friend of Lois Fletcher's. I reasoned to myself in this fashion. If I wait for Douglas and Aunt Elspeth to agree to my idea, I shall have to waste *some* time. If he argue about it and pooh-pooh my views, I shall waste *more* time! To waste time, in an affair like this, is absolutely fatal, and I knew not what the nature of the peril was that hung over us in the bungalow at Dallow Corner. All I knew was that it was there, and that therefore no time should be wasted. After Hardy had gone to send off the wires, I think I went through my worst moments. I was never so near to fainting in all my life. The strain of everything I had gone through seemed to come to a head precipitately. I called out to Aunt Elspeth, but she was with Mrs. Veitch in the kitchen and never heard me. However, Lois came in to me in the dining-room and looked after me like an angel, and shortly afterwards Hardy returned with Mr. Armstrong. The latter came over to me and took my hands. "My dear young lady," he said, "I don't know what I can say to you. To find words on occasions like this is one of the most difficult of all tasks. I saw your chauffeur in the village—and he told me." He said no more than I have written down, and the written words look bare and crude, but the sympathy his voice held meant much to me at the time, and I thanked him very, very gratefully. His words, too, did more than comfort me. They caused me to pull myself together, to brace myself up, and I shall always be thankful for Mr. Armstrong's visit to me that morning. If it did nothing else, it stimulated me to the task I had set myself.

"Was Uncle all right when he left your house last night, Mr. Armstrong?" I asked.

"He seemed to me to be in perfect health, Miss Cameron. I've never seen him look fitter. I'm only sorry I didn't carry out my intention of accompanying him part of the way home here. Do you know, I offered to. I actually made the suggestion to him. I felt that I should love a walk and I wanted, too, to convince him in an argument that was under way between us. But he wouldn't hear of it. Said he couldn't think of dragging me from my fireside at that time of night." He broke off and shook his head sorrowfully. "Perhaps if I had gone, I might have been able to have helped him."

"Don't reproach yourself, Mr. Armstrong. What was to be, had to be, I suppose," I said. "Doctor Vallance says that he probably suffered very little."

"Who found him?" he asked. I told him. "He was dead, then, when Neale first saw him?" I nodded. "Is there anything I can do for you, Miss Cameron? If there is, please command me. We haven't known each other very long, it's true—but forget all that, if I can serve you. Think of me as the oldest of old friends."

"You are very kind, Mr. Armstrong," I said, "and I appreciate your offer tremendously. But Lois here is a host in herself, and I have wired to my cousin and to Mr. Strachan. They should be here in an hour or so. I shall be pretty well protected, shan't I? If I want you for anything, I'll let you know." I paused, to proceed almost at once. "If I wanted you this afternoon, would you come over?"

"I'll come at any time, Miss Cameron. You have only to say the word and I'll come straight over."

"Thank you, then. I'll send Hardy over if I do."

He hesitated. "May I see Colonel Cameron before I go? I should like to—if I may?" I nodded in understanding.

"Come with me," I said. He followed me to the door of the lounge where my uncle's body lay, and stood on the threshold.

"This will do, Miss Cameron," he said quietly.

"I won't come in the room." He stood there for a moment or so and then very reverently raised his hand as though in farewell. "Don't forget, Miss Cameron," he said, "*any* time." He turned, shook hands with Lois and me, and took his departure.

It was, if I remember correctly, about ten minutes to one when I heard the noise of a car approaching the bungalow. Thinking that it must herald the approach of either Douglas or Nigel, or both of them perhaps, I walked out to meet it. The man in the big heavy coat who swung himself from the driver's seat would have commanded instant attention anywhere. He was tall, lithe, and muscular, and moved with that easy swinging grace that always characterizes the born athlete. In addition, his keen grey eyes and sensitive, mobile mouth stamped his face with a scholarly intellectuality that seemed to be the perfect complement to his physique. He was not as Charles Wogan, "a scholar that had been twisted awry into a soldier", but the most perfect combination, in appearance, of scholar and athlete that I have ever been privileged to see. With one hand on the door of his primrose-wheeled Crossley, with his other he raised his hat.

"My name is Bathurst," he said quietly. "Have I the honour to address Miss Cecilia Cameron?"

I gave him my hand impulsively. "I can never thank you enough, Mr. Bathurst," I said, "for coming to me so quickly. Will you please come in?"

He smiled with a smile that lit his face up and followed me into the dining-room, which I was pleased to find unoccupied.

"First," I said to him, "have you lunched?"

He smiled again, and as he faced me the grey eyes took on an added charm. "Trust me, Miss Cameron. I've a perfectly vicious appetite. Don't worry about that sort of thing now. First—what is your trouble that you bring me hot-foot to help you?"

I gestured to him thankfully. "Sit down. I'll tell you."

He took the big easy chair by the fire. "Tell me in your own way, Miss Cameron. As far as you find possible, in proper chronological sequence. I will endeavour to refrain from interruptions. If I fail occasionally in that direction, forgive me."

I told him the whole story, to the best of my ability, from my hearing the voice behind the screen, to the events of the previous night. As I finished, feeling that I had made a poor job of the telling, he congratulated me, and to my sharp annoyance, I felt my cheeks flushing at his praise.

"Splendid, Miss Cameron! Your attention to detail is a most unusual quality, especially, if I may say so, in a lady. The treasuring and husbanding of the apparently tiny matters are worth their weight in gold to the investigator when he comes investigating. Most people, you see, content themselves with vague impressions which usually lead nowhere." He stopped and eyed me shrewdly. "Now, Miss Cameron," he said gently, but with infinite persuasion, "leaving the question of the cryptogram for the time being, show me the piece of evidence that so far you have been keeping for me." He held out his hand in invitation.

"How do you know?" I gasped.

He shrugged his broad shoulders. "You would hardly have sent for me so urgently on the data that you have supplied so far. Especially when we consider the verdict given by Doctor Vallance. I am therefore compelled to think that you know more than you have so far been pleased to tell me." He pointed to the front of my tweed frock. "You have it somewhere there, I think, Miss Cameron. Three times your hands have strayed towards it." The smile he gave me encouraged me. I gave him my uncle's diary.

"I told you his fountain-pen was missing, Mr. Bathurst. In conjunction with that fact, look at the diary. Turn to the end of the present month—November."

He did as I directed. "Part of a page torn out? H'm!" he observed. "Significant, you think, eh? Part of what is a blank page, too. Have you found the missing page, Miss Cameron?"

I shook my head.

"Have you looked for it?"

Again I shook my head. "Where could I? Where was there to—"

"My dear Miss Cameron! There is one place surely that commends itself to us above all others? Where your uncle's body was found. There was nothing in his hand, of course, when you picked him up?"

"Nothing," I replied.

He frowned as though in consideration of some point, the explanation of which was eluding him. "Major Neale, according to your story, I think, had found your uncle first, and then came back here to tell you. I am right in that, am I not?"

"Yes, Mr. Bathurst."

"H'm! It's a chance, and perhaps a slender chance, but we'll take it, Miss Cameron. We will take it. It's just on the cards that for once the fates may take a hand on our side! They sometimes do, you know. Please come with me at once. We'll run up in the car to the place where Colonel Cameron was found. Even before I look at his body. You must direct me. Come along at once."

We ran through the bungalow to the utter astonishment of Lois and Aunt Elspeth, who had emerged from the kitchen and watched us almost open-mouthed. As the Crossley ran swiftly along the road, the very same road that I had travelled with Major Neale only the night before, Anthony Bathurst remained silent in the driving-seat. It was I who eventually broke the silence. Leaning forward, and touching him upon the arm, I watched for the hedge, and at last said, "Here." He brought the car to a standstill just as Hardy had done the night before, and as he did so, the whole thing seemed like a nightmare to me from its beginning to the stage that we had now reached. We got out and stood by the hedge.

"Pardon me asking you, but it's important. Are you sure that this is the *exact* spot, Miss Cameron?" asked my companion.

"As close as I can bring you," I answered.

"Thanks. Now take a hand and try to help me. If, as you suggest yourself, your uncle attempted to send a message to you as he lay here dying, by tearing a piece from his diary, it's just possible that the flimsy piece of paper upon which he wrote may have blown away from him somewhere and be lodged comparatively near. Caught in somewhere or held by something, for example. Very possibly, it seems to me, in the hedge itself. Now, let me see, which way was the wind last night?"

"It was almost due north," I replied promptly,

"it has been for several days now."

"I agree with you, Miss Cameron. So that our best plan, then, is to work in that direction." He pointed up the road. "You take that side of the hedge, Miss Cameron, and I'll confine my attention to this side. Cover the ground as carefully as you can, won't you?" He walked to the side of the road and looked over the hedge towards the little stream that ran below. Suddenly I saw him crouch forward, and from the eagerness of his attitude, I felt certain that he had seen something that he considered of importance. I walked over to him, endeavouring to master my excitement.

"What is it, Mr. Bathurst?"

He pointed to a little patch of ground that was completely devoid of grass. "What do you make of that, Miss Cameron?"

I looked hard at where he pointed, but failed to understand. "Where?" I queried, blankly.

"There—look! On that little portion of ground there, from where the grass has been worn away. Can't you see?"

I looked again, in vain. "I'm sorry if I seem dense," I ventured, "but I can't see anything there at all. Perhaps I don't—"

"You aren't dense, Miss Cameron," he answered with one of his rare smiles, "my eyes are better than yours, that's all. Or let us say that they've been trained to be keener." He paused and then continued. "That sounds very selfish and ungallant, doesn't it? What I mean, really, is that my eyes are seeing a bit farther than yours are. Follow me."

He pushed his way through the hedge and then turned round and helped me to follow. "Now you can see what I mean, surely." This time he was right, and I nodded. There was a pink smear that was fairly heavy where it began, almost red in fact, and which trailed away as you followed it, getting less and less until it disappeared. Anthony Bathurst dropped to the grass and extended his lithe length by the side of the pinkish stain. Inclining his head to one side, he strove to obtain true alignment. From his pocket he whipped out a magnifying glass. He examined the mark with his lens with the most assiduous care. Then he crawled back along the grass to the hedge, and more than once I heard him utter a little cry of satisfaction. For some time he lay close to the hedge, turning over old leaves and broken twigs. At last he rose, and came to me again.

"You are prepared for the worst, Miss Cameron, I know, otherwise you would not have called me in to help. Those pink stains that can be seen there are blood. Blood, I am very much afraid, too, that came from your uncle."

## Chapter XI
## THE MISSING MESSAGE

I know that I went ghastly pale at his words, but I don't think that I gave any other sign that I was disturbed. Fierce resentment still possessed me and I felt glad that we had passed another milestone, as it were, on the road to tangibility and to discovery. After a moment's cogitation, I nodded.

"Now for the missing piece from the diary, Miss Cameron. We will carry out our original plan, I think. I'll stick to this side of the road, as I said I would before. Look carefully in the hedge itself, will you? That seems to me the likeliest place, by far. Anything like paper could get caught up there."

I obeyed his instructions to the very letter, bending down as closely as I could, so that I could see the lower parts of the hedge as it ran along the length of the road. Across the way I could see that Anthony Bathurst was doing exactly as I was. But he was much quicker than I and, as a consequence, covered much more ground, and within but a few moments had gained several yards on me as we made our respective ways along the sides of the road. I was just feeling that, on this occasion, Fortune had averted her smiles, when I heard a whoop of triumph from my companion-investigator. I looked up. Mr. Bathurst beckoned to me commandingly.

"Here, Miss Cameron, quick! What about that for a stupendous piece of luck? Look down there, curled against the hedge itself."

My eyes followed his pointing finger, and there, as he had said, I saw the piece of the leaf that Uncle Ian had torn from his diary. Anthony Bathurst bent down and carefully retrieved it.

"No sign of the fountain-pen, you see, Miss Cameron, but there may be a very good explanation of that. It may have rolled down somewhere or even been kicked away. We shall find out, doubtless, before very long. Now let's see what this tiny piece of paper has to tell us."

I ranged myself at his side, bubbling with curiosity to read what I could of Uncle Ian's last message to the world. It was easy to see that the piece of paper exactly fitted the diary as I had shown it to Anthony Bathurst half an hour previously. I reproduce it here as we looked at it then.

"You were right, Miss Cameron," said my companion gravely. "Colonel Cameron was murdered without a doubt. Your instinct was absolutely and completely sound. This is, as you surmised, his dying message. It was doubtless meant primarily for your eyes."

"How was he murdered, then, Mr. Bathurst?" I gasped. "And what does this mean—this last part that he was able to scrawl?"

He considered it carefully. "The first part of the message is, of course, quite lucid. I think that the explanation is that your

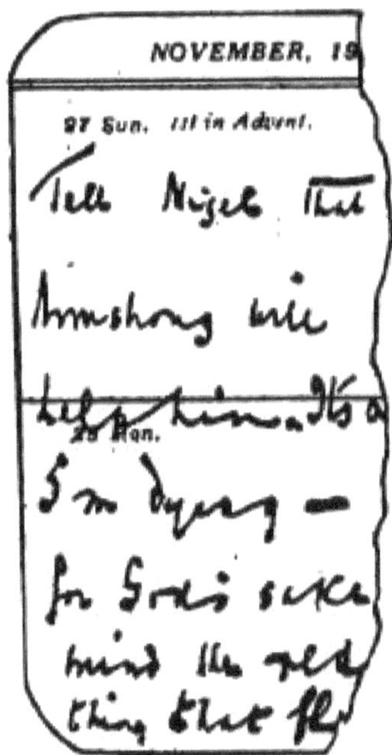


uncle realized that his enemies had got him, but that at the same time he didn't know *how* they had done so. And if *he* didn't know, who was there, and the man actually attacked, how shall we ever know, we, who come after him?" He furrowed his brows as he stood there in deep thought. "For God's sake, mind the red thing that—what?" he quoted questioningly.

"The two letters of the last word that he commenced to write are 'f' and 'l'," I answered. "I know Uncle Ian's handwriting too well not to know that."

"Then what is the word, Miss Cameron? That is what we must establish. To know that will assist us immensely. What are the words that we can conceivably fit to it?"

I shook my head wonderingly.

"There are, we can say, Miss Cameron, 'flames', 'flies', 'flings', 'flares', 'flicks', 'flogs', 'flags'." He stopped. "There must be many others, though. Can you suggest any?"

"Flourishes," I suggested half-heartedly.

"I think not, Miss Cameron. Look here at this paper. Consider the space into which Colonel Cameron attempted to write the word that we find unfinished. Judging from that alone, I should say that his intention was to employ a word of not more than five or six letters at the most. Now which of the words that I have already suggested fits the context best, do you think?"

"Flies," I answered—"the red thing that flies." I shivered. "It sounds ghastly and horrible," I added, "but don't you think it may be that my uncle was dying when he wrote the words and that his imagination was overwrought? It may even be that he was only semi-conscious."

Mr. Bathurst regarded me gravely, and then very slowly shook his head in denial of my suggestion.

"I think not, Miss Cameron. Consider what we know already—all that you yourself have told me. There isn't the slightest doubt that we are in very deep waters. I doubt if we shall be in a position to measure them accurately for a considerable time. When we do—" He stood there, his hands plunged deep in his pockets, thinking hard. Suddenly he turned to me. "We will go back I think, Miss Cameron. It is essential that I should see the body and act at once." He drove the car back at a great speed and after I had told Aunt Elspeth and Lois who he was, and how he had come to be there, I took him into the room where the body of my uncle lay. That quality of excessively rapid action that I had already observed about Bathurst was again strikingly in evidence. He wasted no time at all. Walking quickly across to the body, he bent over it and examined the features carefully. Then he pushed up the two sleeves of my uncle's coat and looked closely at his two forearms, paying particular attention to the wrists. This done, he opened the shirt and exposed the neck and chest. I saw him shake his head doubtfully as though sorely exercised in mind as to some point or another that was apparently—temporarily at least—eluding him. Suddenly he pivoted round to me with a quick question. "The overcoat you mentioned that your uncle was wearing, Miss Cameron, the coat with the pocket that attracted your attention. May I see it, please?"

I walked over to it, took it off the chair where it was hanging and handed it to him silently.

"The inside breast pocket, I think you said?"

I nodded to him. He sniffed at the depths of the pocket indicated. "The odour of which you spoke has almost disappeared by now. However, I can just detect it. I doubt, though, whether I should have done, had I not been previously informed." He looked very carefully over the other parts of the coat and then handed it back to me. "Thank you, Miss Cameron."

I replaced the coat on the chair and he returned to my uncle's body on the settee. "Draw the curtains away from the windows as far back as you can, do you mind? I want all the light that I can possibly obtain. The tiniest speck may—"

I obeyed him and he pushed the settee nearer to the window with the daylight bearing full on Uncle Ian's face. Bathurst then knelt by the settee and moved the dead man's head first one way and then the other to catch the full measure of light. I was startled by an exclamation that fell from his lips.

"Come here, Miss Cameron, please." I went slowly to the settee. "Bend down here and look carefully at this." He pointed to the flesh just under the ridge of the right lower jaw. It was very slightly puffed and I could see tiny marks, very tiny marks, as though the skin had just been broken or cut into.

"I can see what you mean, Mr. Bathurst," I said. "What is it?"

"Can you see these extremely tiny incisions?" he asked me.

I nodded. "Yes."

"Tell me. How many are there to the best of your vision?"

I looked at them with the most careful scrutiny of which I was capable. "I think *three*."

"So do I, Miss Cameron, so do I. Tiny bites, perhaps, that might very well elude the eye of a doctor who wasn't looking for them. The ordinary medical practitioner in this country, having had no experience of such a thing, would never dream of, or suspect even, their existence. They're as much like the marks left by the pocks remaining after an attack of Chicken Pox, as anything I've ever seen."

"But what could have caused them, Mr. Bathurst?" I cried anxiously. "What is it that could have—"

He cut me short. "If I knew the answer to your question, Miss Cameron, I should be a long way towards a solution of my case. As it is at the moment, I'm as sorely puzzled as you yourself are. Let me see Colonel Cameron's revolver, will you?" I handed it to him and he looked it over. Then he handed it back to me without comment. "Dr. Vallance you say, the doctor who first examined the body, announced his intention of conferring with your uncle's medical adviser. Have you yet communicated with the latter?"

"Yes. I meant to tell you that. I thought I had told you of everything, but somehow that slipped my mind. I'm sorry. It's a Dr. Emery of Wimpole Street. I wired to him at the same time that I wired to you. Your answer to the wire, you see, was more prompt than his was." I gave him a half-smile. For a moment or so he made no reply.

"Still, we may reasonably expect him here to-day or to-morrow, even allowing for the fact that he may be excessively busy. He can hardly ignore the pressing nature of your summons, can he. When he comes, I should like to have a word with him. What's the nearest 'phone, Miss Cameron?"

"In Quoynings, I should say, without definite knowledge. We have not lived here very long, you know."

"And how far's that?"

"About four miles—going by road," I answered.

"Straight?"

"Couldn't be straighter. Keep to the road, follow it round and you'll run into it."

"Good! I'm going to send several messages. Some for myself and some on your behalf. Expect me back here, however, under the hour. I should think your cousin would be back by then, and possibly his friend, the Mr. Strachan about whom you've told me. Before I go, describe this man Lampard to me again, will you? In the fullest possible physical detail."

I complied with the request. Anthony Bathurst listened eagerly and nodded his head once or twice as though in approval. When I had finished my description, he turned and ran down the garden path, and within a moment I heard his big car purring along the road to Quoynings. Somehow the movement and the noise of the car gave me comfort and solace. A kind of "grateful coolness in the heat." For I felt within my heart that my uncle's murderers had a man to grapple with them at last, and more than that even—a man that I had definitely chosen for the part. If anybody could track them down and bring them to justice, this man would. It occurred to me, as I walked back into the dining-room, that he was already hot-foot upon their trail. You can judge the confidence that he had already installed into me.

## Chapter XII
## BATHURST CASTS THE LINES

THE PRIMROSE-WHEELED "Crossley" ran into the main street at Quoynings well under a quarter of an hour after leaving me, and Bathurst found a telephone booth on the corner of the market-place. His first call was put through to the Lewes police.

"I want to speak to Inspector Baddeley, please, if he's available. Tell him it's urgent and immediate." Within a moment, Bathurst heard the familiar voice of the Inspector at the other end of the line.

"Good Lord, is that you, Mr. Bathurst? Well, this fairly beats the band. At any rate, I'm pleased to hear from you. What is it this time?"

Bathurst gave him a brief outline of the business at Dallow Corner. "I want you, if you can, to come over at once, Baddeley. You know I wouldn't trouble you unnecessarily. Bring Dr. Elliott with you, if it's convenient. O.K.?"

"Right you are, sir. I'll be over in an hour."

Sir Austin Kemble, in his arm-chair at New Scotland Yard, frowned uncompromisingly at his telephone as it rang on his desk, and removed the receiver with an action that bordered closely upon an ill-grace. An observer would have seen his frown change into a smile of intense pleasure . . . such was the personal charm of Anthony Lotherington Bathurst—when he chose to exert it. The Commissioner listened interestedly. "Sounds an extraordinary affair, Bathurst! But one, I should say, after your own heart. What? . . . What did you say, Bathurst? Lampard? 'Flame' Lampard? . . . Can't say that I have!—Still—that's quite inconclusive, you know. He might be quite well-known and yet not touch me personally. I'll put MacMorran on to it for you with pleasure. He'll know all that there is to be known. What was that other name that you mentioned? I didn't quite catch . . . Trout? Yes . . . that's more familiar. I know a bit in that direction. I can get his 'dossier' almost at once . . . very well. No. I can't very well . . . I'm full up with this Prime Minister business at the present moment . . . he's got the 'wind up' properly this time, I can tell you. Of course, of course, my dear boy. You know that you've merely to ask me. *Carte blanche*, of course, and I'll send MacMorran's reports on to you as soon as they're available. I knew Colonel Cameron, by the way, if it's of any interest to you. I met him at Camberley some years ago. Convey my sincere sympathy and—er—condolences—to his niece, will you? Very likely I'll be able to manage a day next week if you're still there by then. Where are you . . . wait . . . I'll make a note of it. . . . The 'Red Stag', Dallow Corner, Sussex, right then. . . . Good-bye, Bathurst—good huntin'. . . ."

Dr. Emery, the eminent heart specialist of Wimpole Street, was more than a little on the frigid side. It was easy for Bathurst to tell that the doctor resented what he considered was Bathurst's deliberate intrusion into a private matter. He listened courteously, but with a definite suggestion of off-handedness and detachment. In the initial stages of the conversation, he was entirely non-committal and gave Anthony no help whatever. "I have Miss Cameron's wire," he admitted. "As a matter of fact I received it early this morning. But I have two important consultations on hand that are demanding the whole of my immediate attention. After all, my dear sir, I cannot shut my eyes to the fact that Colonel Cameron is dead. I have other patients, you see, who are alive, and they come first. You must see that." Bathurst poured honeyed words into the receiver. It is on the cards that Sir Austin Kemble might have blushed had he been privileged to hear them. Dr. Emery became more human and more interested. "Let us leave it at this, then, Mr. Bathurst," he conceded eventually. "I will endeavour to run down to Dallow Corner early to-morrow morning. Tell Miss Cameron to expect me. That is as far as I can commit myself at the moment. Good-bye." As he caught the note of frigidity that had come again into the doctor's voice, Bathurst grinned to himself contentedly and replaced the receiver.

When he returned to me at the bungalow after a cruise round in the "Crossley" he found that Inspector Baddeley had already arrived.

I will admit that I took a liking to the Inspector at once. I gave him a pithy resume of the case, supplementing what Bathurst had told him, and when he came in, Anthony Bathurst found that we had already established a very pleasant condition of "good terms" with one another.

"Looked at the body yet, Baddeley?" he asked curtly.

"No, Mr. Bathurst, not yet. Dr. Elliott will be here very shortly. I left word asking him to follow me over. I said how obliged you'd feel if he did. He wasn't handy when your first telephone message came through. All the same though, I don't suppose there's much that you've missed." He turned to me by way of explanation. "You know, miss, he's a rare fellow for seeing all that there is to see—and even a bit more sometimes."

As I nodded my belief in the truth of his statement, Aunt Elspeth and Lois came in and I informed them what was happening. My aunt seemed too taken aback at the turn events had taken, to reply coherently, but Lois expressed her approbation of my decision and uttered a warm "good work, Cecilia!" The Divisional Surgeon from Lewes, the Doctor Elliott to whom reference has already been made, put in an appearance about half-an-hour afterwards. I accompanied him and the two other men to the room where my uncle's body still lay. I noticed that Bathurst offered no remark whatever to Dr. Elliott whilst the latter conducted his examination. Eventually the Divisional Surgeon turned to Bathurst and the Inspector, and shook his head with a sort of puzzled dubiety.

"Well, I'm sorry, Bathurst, and all that, but I can't see anything to worry about here. There is undoubtedly heart trouble and I shall expect to find no little inflammation and a certain amount of fatty degeneration. I should be inclined to suggest that Colonel Cameron died of endocarditis. It certainly looks to me like it."

Bathurst nodded as though signifying his complete approval. "I am not surprised at your saying that. Dr. Elliott. As a matter of fact, Dr. Vallance gave an opinion that was very much the same. Do you mind, however, if I call your attention to something?"

Dr. Elliott frowned. "Go ahead then. Where and what is it?"

Bathurst walked to the body. "Please look here, Dr. Elliott. Tell me what you make of that, will you? Those marks there." He pointed to the places under my uncle's right jaw. The Divisional Surgeon bent over the body and as he looked, the opinion came to me that the marks had died down considerably since Bathurst and I had looked at them an hour or so previously. Certainly there was very much less puffiness to be observed about them, and almost all the little patch of inflammation had subsided, and I didn't wonder at all that Dr. Elliott had missed seeing them. Under the ridge of the jaw as they were, the negligence, if it can be so called, was eminently excusable.

"Well, Dr. Elliott," reiterated Bathurst, with persistence, "what do you make of them? Extraordinary to say the least—don't you agree with me?"

The Doctor grunted an unintelligible reply. "H'm, I certainly see what you mean." He bent more closely. After a moment or so he ventured to express an opinion. "Do you know what I think, Bathurst? These marks look as much like injection marks to me as anything else. But I don't know that I could put a name to—"

It was now Bathurst's turn to frown. "The marks of a hypodermic, do you mean, Doctor?"

"No—not that, certainly." Dr. Elliott was emphatic. "Not a needle, but something else of that nature. Something that has been used to pierce the skin. I admit again that I can't put a name to it. Perhaps you can yourself, Bathurst."

"I can't, Dr. Elliott. Because I don't agree with you. Which is a good reason, you must admit."

Dr. Elliott came to the point. "What, then, is your conclusion—about which you seem so confident."

Bathurst laughed carelessly. "I won't press it, Doctor. For the moment that is, at any rate. But assuming that your own theory of the injections holds good, are you prepared to concede that it almost certainly upsets your previous diagnosis? For instance, Colonel Cameron on your own showing, may very well have been poisoned. Well, Doctor?"

There was no hesitation about Dr. Elliott's answer. "Your reasoning is sound. It would make a difference, certainly."

"And it would cause you to think twice before you issued a certificate?"

"Yes. It certainly would."

Bathurst addressed the Inspector. "That's all I want, Baddeley. And if Dr. Emery finds the same difficulty when he comes to examine the body, your course is clearly indicated." He swung round on Dr. Elliott. "All the same, Doctor, what you have said tends to disturb my own theory." As he spoke there came a ring at the front-door bell. I heard Mrs. Veitch answer it and a moment later the sound of Nigel Strachan's voice in the hall. Then I heard her talking to him. I excused myself to the others and went to greet him. He was wearing his big overcoat and looked very tired. Apart from that, he appeared to be very fit. Checking at its birth, the flood of sympathy with which he attempted to engulf me, I thanked him and told him that I knew all that he desired to say to me and that there was sterner work afoot. Then I told him of the manner of Uncle Ian's death.

"I have already moved, Nigel," I explained, "the police are here now. The police and Mr. Anthony Bathurst."

He looked incredulous, but as the idea matured and took possession of his brain he nodded his approbation of what I had done. "I think you've done splendidly, Cecilia," he asserted, "and I, for one, thank God that you've done what you have done. To act quickly in these matters is more than half the battle. I've a reason for saying that, beyond anything that you yourself know." He paused awkwardly, as though uncertain as to how he should best proceed. I sensed the doubt and put my emotion into questioning words.

"What do you mean, Nigel?" I cried. "What has happened since I last saw you that I don't know? Tell me—please."

He hesitated. "There may be nothing in it, Cecilia. One can't always be sure. All the same, if you can't help me, I'm convinced that the matter's serious. But perhaps you may be able to. When did you last see Douglas?"

I looked at him wonderingly. "Why, when he left here with you, of course. Yesterday afternoon."

He returned my look searchingly. "You're sure that he hasn't returned here? That he didn't come back some time last night?"

"Of course I am. Don't be ridiculous, Nigel. If he had come back here, I should know, shouldn't I? I haven't set eyes on Douglas since he went away with you."

Nigel shrugged his shoulders with a gesture of hopelessness. "In that case, then, Cecilia, Douglas has disappeared. Nobody has seen him since somewhere about seven o'clock yesterday evening."

# CHAPTER XIII
## THE ENEMY CLOSES IN

KEYED UP as I was by recent events, his words terrified me, and I shivered as I stood there listening to him. It came home to me at that moment that our opponents, whoever they were, were definitely too many and too strong for us, that we were waging a frightfully unequal warfare. That they were slowly but inexorably closing in on us, and that nothing I could possibly do would fend them off. As the thought took shape and heavy being, the position grew in hopelessness, and I fear that my voice, when I addressed my next remark to Nigel, betrayed the full extent of my apprehension. For at that moment I was the companion of Despair.

"It's the cryptogram, Nigel, it must be," I whispered to him— "they're ruthless, merciless. What have they done to Douglas. Is he dead—too, do you think?"

He protested his disagreement, but he failed to convince me. "No—no, of course not. How could they? They wouldn't dare."

"They dared to kill Uncle Ian," I cried resentfully, "say what you like about it. Oh, Nigel, why did you ever—"

"I know what you're thinking, Cecilia. Don't reproach me more than you can help, for even as it is, I shall never forgive myself. I curse the day I ever gave the thing a thought."

It was at that moment that I remembered that I hadn't asked him for any of the details concerning Douglas's disappearance. "Tell me about Douglas," I said to him, "tell me the facts. When did you—?" I stopped short as I remembered. "What a priceless idiot I am," I cried.

He regarded me with amazement. "What do you—"

I cut him, summarily. "Anthony Bathurst," I exclaimed, "here, in the next room, as I just told you. And I've been wasting time, gibbering to you, with possible salvation close at hand. Come with me, and you shall tell him and me what has happened. It may help him, too, besides helping us. Who knows but it may throw light on a spot that needs it most?"

Without waiting for him to answer me, I dragged him to the door of the drawing-room and called to Anthony Bathurst.

"In one moment, Miss Cameron," he answered me.

I waited patiently for his appearance. When he came, Baddeley and the Divisional-Surgeon from Lewes accompanied him. Dr. Elliott bade us farewell and I asked Aunt Elspeth to show him out. When we had settled ourselves again, I called upon Nigel Strachan to tell his story and as it was as new to me as it was to Bathurst and Baddeley, I listened to every particle of it with the utmost attention.

"Tell us all you know, Mr. Strachan," advised Bathurst encouragingly, after I had introduced Nigel to the others, "and Inspector Baddeley and I will see if we can piece anything out of it. Take your time and tell it in your own way."

"I haven't a great deal to tell," commenced Nigel, "so it won't take very long if we start from the time that Douglas and I left here yesterday afternoon. As you know, I wanted to have a squint at a certain book in the British Museum, and Douglas—"

"One moment, Mr. Strachan. I find this interesting at the very outset. You will pardon me, I am sure, and forgive me, too, if my question appears impertinent. What was the book?"

The direct nature of Bathurst's question took my breath away. Nigel, however, manifested neither surprise nor displeasure.

"*Le Courvoisier on 'The Science of Cryptograms and Ciphers'*," he answered imperturbably. "It's the recognized authority on those matters."

"Thank you, Mr. Strachan. Proceed, please."

"And Douglas had a job of work to do in chambers. In the train, however, on the journey up, he seemed to come over 'nervy' and 'jumpy'. Talked about coming straight back here, on the plea that he ought never to have left his father with all this extraordinary business hanging about. I talked him round eventually and arranged to see him again that evening at the private hotel near Harrow where we invariably stay when we're detained in Town. I went down there, in accordance with the arrangement, but Douglas never turned up. I knocked about in the billiard-room till about half-past ten playing 'snooker' and at length turned into bed, assuming that Douglas had changed his mind about joining me, had given way to the influence of his early intentions, and had come back here to Dallow Corner. When I got Cecilia's—Miss Cameron's—wire this morning I began to wonder if my surmise in this direction were correct. Why had it been she who had wired to me and not old Douglas? The more I pondered over the affair, the greater my doubts and suspicions became. At length I decided to put an end to them by going straight round to Douglas's chambers in Lincoln's Inn. Inquiries of a stout lady I found there, wielding a business-like broom, elicited the fact that Mr. Cameron had been there late yesterday afternoon, but had gone out about a quarter-past seven. Since then he hadn't been seen there. More than that, she couldn't say. All I can say, therefore, gentlemen, is this: if he didn't come to Dallow Corner, and if he didn't come to Harrow to join me as we had definitely arranged, where did he go? And also, where is he now? Taking it in conjunction with what Miss Cameron has told me with regard to her uncle's death last night, it seems to me to assume very sinister aspects. The two affairs seem to be connected somehow—don't they?"

Bathurst pulled at his upper lip whilst Baddeley caressed the ridge of his jaw. There was silence for an appreciable period. Then Bathurst looked across at Nigel Strachan and came to the point. "What is your own solution, Mr. Strachan? I should be pleased to hear it."

"Solution?"

"Don't you follow me? What I mean is this. How would you explain Mr. Cameron's disappearance? That is to say, the *cause* of it. Don't be afraid to give your imagination a run. Would you hint, for instance, at foul play?"

Nigel hesitated before he framed his answer. "Considering all the circumstances as we know them—*yes*."

"In that case, then," intervened Baddeley, "the people responsible for these outrages must have pretty ample resources. If they worked a job down here and a job in London on the same night there must be several of 'em in it together. Looks like a gang at work. That's obvious, isn't it?"

"Do I understand, Mr. Strachan," questioned Bathurst, "that the only information that you could obtain in regard to Mr. Cameron's movements yesterday came from a woman that cleans his chambers?"

Nigel nodded. "Yes. That is so. I could find nobody else who could tell me anything."

"Did you make very careful inquiries?"

"Do you mean, did I thoroughly investigate the affair?"

Bathurst smiled a half-smile. "Put it that way if you like, Mr. Strachan. I think you understand what I mean."

Nigel, a trifle resentful, embarked upon an explanation. "When I went to Douglas's chambers, please remember that I knew nothing beyond the fact that he hadn't turned up at the Harrow hotel the night before. I didn't go as you might have gone, on the trail of something. I went as a friend, making an ordinary inquiry in an ordinary way. You would have gone as an investigator. I clutched at any information that came my way and when I ran across the charwoman whom I mentioned to you, and she told me what she knew, I accepted it as good evidence and came away. Quite a natural thing for me to do in the circumstances, I think. I didn't see what could be gained by stopping."

"I should have thought that you would have tried to get into touch with his clerk—if he has one—or with one of his colleagues. Surely there must be someone there with more intimate knowledge of him than this woman has? She only cleans there, you know."

Nigel looked aggrieved at Bathurst's criticism, but I felt and saw the justice of the remarks. "Anyhow," Bathurst went on, "the fact remains that you didn't, and there's an end of it. It's no good us going over that ground again. Tell me! Has Mr. Cameron a clerk?"

Nigel shook his head. "Not altogether. But I will explain. As a matter of fact, he shares a clerk with another barrister. He has hardly enough work to occupy a man all his time, so he divides him with a certain Mr. Kenwyn Grey. Quite frankly it never occurred to me to rout this chap out and see if he knew anything. Sorry I made a fool of myself." Bathurst ignored the satirical apologia.

"What's the name of this clerk? Do you happen to know it?"

"Oh—yes, Judson."

Bathurst turned to Baddeley. "Assuming Mr. Cameron doesn't turn up during the next twenty-four hours—and I may state that I don't think there's the slightest chance of his so doing—I think it would be as well, Baddeley, if you put a few inquiries round at his chambers. Don't wait, either, for the twenty-four hours to elapse. Get on the job at once. I'll arrange matters with Sir Austin Kemble. For the moment, at any rate, he'll leave the job to me. I've already spoken to him about it."

"Very well, Mr. Bathurst." Baddeley accepted the suggestion immediately. I began to notice that it was a habit of his when Bathurst directed the plan of operations. "I'll get along up there at once."

When he had gone, Bathurst turned again to Nigel. "I am in Miss Cameron's confidence, Mr. Strachan, so you needn't harbour any apprehensions as to my good faith in the matter. The whole affair appears to me to be most complicated. The strands are many and also, alas, they are twisted. It will be our duty to try to straighten them out. I am afraid though that it will prove to be a dark and sinister business. I am dealing with forces the like of which have not been arrayed against me before. Repeat to me, if you please, the exact terms of the Trout Cryptogram." He had scarcely finished speaking, when I am certain a look of annoyance flitted across Nigel's face.

It occurred to me that he was about to resent Bathurst's interference. Surely, he didn't expect that I should call in a man of Anthony Bathurst's calibre and reputation to investigate the murder of my uncle, and at the same time withhold from him information of the most paramount importance? However, he eventually submitted to Bathurst's request with somewhat of an ill-grace. He began by asking a question.

"By 'terms', do you mean its whole history or only the actual words used in the cryptogram itself?"

"Tell me all about it in your own words, Mr. Strachan. *All* about it! Everything of which you can think. Miss Cameron has already given me an excellent idea of the affair, but you, with your first-hand knowledge, must necessarily be in a position to assist me more than she has been able to. Now you talk and I'll listen." He assumed an attitude that I discovered afterwards to be a favourite one of his whilst in the capacity of an audience. Stretching out his long legs to their limit, as he sat in his chair, he thrust his hands deeply into the pockets of his trousers and closed his eyes. Nigel commenced his narrative, and I listened to it intently. Although I had been privileged to hear it before, I nevertheless listened to it on this occasion, as though I were in Anthony Bathurst's place and were attempting to unravel something from the story that would set my feet on the road that led to elucidation. Nigel traced his first meeting with Trout and how he had been requested to defend him. After a very short interval, Bathurst made his first interruption.

"One moment, Mr. Strachan. Can you give me the date when you undertook the defence of this man Trout? The exact date, if possible. It may or may not be important—one never knows." Nigel furrowed his brows as he attempted to remember.

"It was either the thirteenth or the fourteenth of May," he answered. "I am certain that it was one of the two. I could find out for certain by referring to my professional diary."

"Good enough! That will do for the moment. Proceed, Mr. Strachan."

Nigel obeyed and finished his story without further interruption. "This is the letter that he sent me, Mr. Bathurst," he said in conclusion, "just before he died."

Taking Trout's now famous sheet from his pocket he handed it to Bathurst. I saw the latter con it critically. He pored over it carefully for the matter of perhaps a minute.

"I will provide you with a copy, Mr. Bathurst," promised Nigel, "as soon as I have time to get one done. I expect that you would like to have a shot at—"

Bathurst shook his head in refusal. "Thank you for the offer, Mr. Strachan, but I won't trouble you. I have committed the cryptogram to memory."

Nigel stared in some amazement, but there was no note of vain-glory in the speaker's voice. Bathurst had made the statement in that quiet, level, well-ordered voice that always characterized him, and it seemed to me just as though he had made a plain statement of fact that brooked no possible denial.

"I am lucky enough to have the gift of being a quick study," he added in explanation. He rose and faced Nigel. "I understand that you have already let some measure of light into the cryptogram, Mr. Strachan? Yes?" Nigel nodded and opened his lips to speak. Bathurst stopped him with an uplifted hand. "No—no—don't tell me of your success. Let me approach the problem with an entirely open mind. I am a great believer in that, although it is obvious, I think, that this bungalow must be strongly indicated in some way."

Again Nigel stared in frank and open wonderment. To him, Bathurst's statement, based upon such a meagre acquaintanceship with a complexity that had exercised his own powers of intellect and ingenuity so considerably, bordered upon black magic. His face changed from wonderment to scepticism. What had Bathurst been already able to see that enabled him to assert his opinion with such confidence? How had he had time to work it out? Whilst he was considering this standpoint, he heard Bathurst's voice in continuation of his previous statement. "Everything points to it, you know."

"I want to ask you something, Mr. Bathurst," I said to him in return. "I'm not a coward, I hope, but at the same time I must plead guilty to a whole heap of natural fears. It is one of those natural fears that has prompted me to ask you the question at which I hinted some little time ago."

He nodded sympathetically as though he understood perfectly what was passing through my mind.

"Ask on, Miss Cameron, and I'll see whether I can answer it for you satisfactorily. Sometimes, do you know, I almost enjoy answering questions." He looked at me steadily and I returned his gaze, with, I hope, an equal measure of composure.

"Mr. Bathurst," I said, "what I want to know, is this. Are we in any danger here? Do you think that there will be an attack, for instance, on the bungalow to-night? We are four women with only two men here, Nigel and Hardy, my uncle's chauffeur. We don't exactly offer what can be described truthfully as formidable opposition, do we?" My tone was rueful.

He paced the room once or twice before he answered me; then, wheeling round suddenly, he voiced his opinion. "Frankly, Miss Cameron, since you have asked me the question, I think that there is the strong possibility of danger threatening both this bungalow and you, directly darkness comes on us. Not only to-night, but on other nights to come." He paused and went to the window to look out across the road. "I am expecting certain data concerning your man Trout, Mr. Strachan, and your friend, 'Flame' Lampard, Miss Cameron, to reach me from New Scotland Yard within a very short time from now. Until I receive that information, I am uncertain as to my campaign, for I may as well tell you that much of my future movement will depend upon what I hear. In any case, however, I intend to spend the greater part of the evening here with you. Also, I may enlist the services of your neighbour, Mr. Armstrong, and that rather intriguing colleague of your uncle's army career, Major Gilbert Neale. You will then have two extra men here, besides me, Ample, don't you think, Miss Cameron?"

He had scarcely finished his sentence of reassurance to me when I heard the voice of Lois outside the door. "There's a telegraph boy here, Cecilia," she cried. "With a telegram for Nigel. Shall I bring it in to him?"

"Of course," I called back in reply.

Nigel, however, anticipated her entrance by crossing to the door and taking the telegram from her himself. "Thank you, Miss Fletcher." He came back towards the middle of the room opening the buff envelope. As he read the contents, his face appreciably fell.

"I am sorry, Cecilia," he announced with some disturbance, "most frightfully sorry, but you won't be able to count on me for to-night. This message calls me back to Town on business of the most urgent importance. It's absolutely vile luck, but it's to do with the Yorke-Singleton forgery case and I simply dare not ignore it. Will you excuse me? I think that there's a train up in about half-an-hour's time. That should land me up in Town in good time for this consultation." He tapped the telegram with his forefinger. Anthony Bathurst looked at him gravely.

* * * * *

As I saw the tail of the car that carried Nigel to the station disappearing down the road a wave of doubt and misgiving surged up in my mind and threatened to engulf me. Everything seemed to be going against me. The tide seemed to be permanently set. I turned to Anthony Bathurst, who was standing at my side. "Something has just occurred to me," I said meditatively. "It has come to me during the last few minutes. I feel within my bones that that telegram is a trap to entice Nigel away from here to-night, so that I shall be left almost alone. I can't explain why I think so, but I do, and try as I will I can't get away from it."

Anthony Bathurst regarded me with a look of extreme interest and a half-smile played round the corners of his mouth. "Do you know, Miss Cameron," he said quietly and almost sadly, "you compel my sincere admiration. For I formed the same conclusion myself directly the wire was delivered to him."

I swung round on him challengingly and I'm afraid indignation showed both in my eyes and voice. "Then why did you let him go? Why didn't you stop him? He may walk into the same deadly peril that killed my uncle, that may, for all we know, have killed or be threatening Douglas, that may—"

"He may walk into it, Miss Cameron, as you suggest," returned Mr. Bathurst. "I wouldn't deny the possibility of that for a moment. If he does, however, my old friend Inspector Baddeley will walk with him. That I think will ensure him a comparative measure of safety and us a definite amount of knowledge. I will arrange it forthwith. I know where to get Baddeley." He held out his hand. *"Au 'voir."*

A thought struck me and I sought succour from him. "Till this evening?" I said questioningly.

"Before that, Miss Cameron," he replied earnestly. "I hope to be with you again as soon as it grows dark."

I think my eyes shone my gratitude to him.

## Chapter XIV
# THE REPORT FROM SCOTLAND YARD

ANTHONY BATHURST's choice of the "Red Stag" as his place of stay was dictated by two reasons. Besides the comparatively satisfying nature of its ménage, there was also the (to him) distinctly alluring fact that Major Neale was also in temporary residence there. He was unable to disregard the fact that Neale had been relatively close to Colonel Cameron on the night of the latter's murder, had been a colleague of the murdered man during his earlier days, and had been the first person to come upon his dead body. Moreover, I had disclosed more than one important detail to him—details that only he and Bathurst knew. Anthony Bathurst has confided to me since that at this stage of the case he was more irresolute and undecided as to his best plan of attack, than he had been on any one of the many cases that had previously engaged his attention. He asserts that this state of mind that held possession of him was very largely due to the existence of the cryptogram. A complication of a kind that he had never before encountered. In other words his main problem resolved itself into this. Would he fare better by attacking the secret of the Trout message than by concentrating on the circumstances of the murder itself? It must be remembered that Bathurst is a truly remarkable man. I had exceptionally good opportunities to study his methods whilst he handled my uncle's case. His brain always seemed to belong to a mental huntsman who was invariably questing after the elements of truth. He would always argue that the essential characteristic of all mental activity must be movement. The mental process can never be static; there is always, as it were, in the mind, a deep central area of active conception. Despite his intense individuality, however, there was not a fragmentary particle of egotism about him whatever. He had none of that intellectual arrogance that resides in disdainful isolation and supreme contempt for the opinions, beliefs, and aims of others. Whilst responding with a kind of warm courtesy to the impetus of praise, he craved, I discovered, neither power nor position, recognition nor reward.

As he entered the coffee-room of the "Red Stag", the landlord of that hostelry, Stephen Hoad, came forward to meet him.

"I have reserved a room for you, sir, as you requested. Will you dine now, sir, or will you wait for a while?"

"That's very good of you, Hoad. I'll dine at once. I can see that you and I will very soon understand each other. What are you giving me?"

Hoad was a grave-faced and slow-thinking host who reacted to the conditions of cordial intimacy very slowly.

"Nothing at all elaborate, sir, I'm afraid. We can't go in very much for that sort of thing. Mrs. Hoad has cooked you some mutton cutlets with tomatoes. I think you'll find them satisfactory, sir." He turned to depart and Bathurst was mentally conscious of a movement of hesitation on Hoad's part, as the man reached the door and fumbled with the handle.

"Did you want to ask me anything, Hoad?"

The landlord came slowly back from the door to the middle of the room. "Yes, sir. As it happens, I did. Would you have any objection, sir, if another gentleman shared your dining-table? Or would you prefer to take your meal separately?"

Bathurst's thoughts were rapid and conclusive. He sought knowledge. Conversation must always lead to a certain amount of mental exposure. The thoughts and opinions of others are dragged from their hiding-places and rub their eyes before the light. He would take the chance. After all, it was right in his favour. He had nothing to lose thereby and something possibly to gain.

"Not at all, Hoad," he answered. "Who's my companion to be."

Hoad became reassuring. "Quite a gentleman, sir. You need not be afraid on that account. I know what's what and I wouldn't mix gentry with scum."

Anthony Bathurst grinned at the landlord's distinctions.

"Don't be too hard on me, Hoad. In these democratic days, you know, there is always—"

But the landlord went on, impervious to his visitor's pleasantry. "For instance, to explain what I mean. I've had three men staying here who cleared out yesterday. But I wouldn't have put one of 'em in with either you, say, or Major Neale. I know my business better than to do a thing like that. They were rough stuff without a doubt, and I ought to know, for I've met a few in my time."

Anthony Bathurst pricked up his ears. "What were they like, Hoad? You interest me."

"One was a tremendous, great fellow with flaming red hair; the two others were just ordinary, as you might say. One was clean-shaven and stout, and the other was a pretty sturdy chap with what is usually called a 'grog-blossom' nose."

The information suited Bathurst as far as it went.

It ran true to form, in relation to what he had already heard from me. He nodded to Hoad his acceptance of it. "Oh, by the way, sir," added the latter as though remembrance had just come to him, "there's a package come for you, sir, while you've been away. A young gent on a motor-cycle brought it, said it was to be delivered to you personally. I'll get it for you, sir."

Returning, he put the package into Anthony's hands. A quick glance at it told Bathurst that the sender was Sir Austin Kemble. He opened it immediately and sat down at the table to peruse it. As he had expected, directly Hoad had mentioned it, it contained the information for which he had asked in relation to the two men, Trout and 'Flame' Lampard. He took the two reports in that order. There was little about Trout, however, that he did not know. The report stated that after a varied career of crime, chiefly of the burglarious type, for which he had in turn and time served many sentences of varying periods Trout had died of pneumonia at a very recent date at a common lodging house situated in Jubilee Street, Stepney, kept by a Mr. and Mrs. Luke Morton. Trout appeared to have come under the observation of the police authorities first, when he was about twenty-seven years of age and of the man's earlier days there wasn't a great deal that was known. He was believed to have come of a fair family and to have received a reasonable amount of education, but little could be gleaned with regard to this that was even moderately conclusive or definite. The report terminated with a list (with dates) of the man's successive misdemeanours, arrests and sentences. He had served "stretches" at Maidstone, Reading, Wandle, Wormwood Scrubs, and Portland, all within a span of eleven years. His last arrest had been in the spring of the present year of grace; the sentence for this breaking of the law had been pronounced on the fourteenth of May, and Trout had been released on the twenty-seventh of October.

Bathurst read the report a second time, very carefully made a note of the various dates, and then turned with perhaps even more eagerness to the "dossier" of the interesting gentleman whom he knew as "Flame" Lampard. What he read therein, occasioned him some surprise, as it did me an hour or so later, when he passed the information along to me. In the second instance Scotland Yard had comparatively little against the man. He lived, it was stated, in a turning off Club Row. His alleged business was that of an importer of foreign animals, Lampard having been employed by Jamrach's many years previously. But although nothing serious was known against him, there was, at the same time, hanging round and over him, much that was unusual and even suspicious. Anthony Bathurst read on with eager interest. For despite the statement that he had just encountered, that Scotland Yard had little against the subject of the "dossier", there was positive belief in the minds of several of the higher personages operating at the

Yard, that "Flame" Lampard had been on the fringe, at least, of five of the biggest cases that had occupied their attention during the past few years and which had remained unsolved. The outrage on Clapham Common when the Polish Jew Mottiniski had been found with his brains battered out, the theft of the Duchess of Pangbourne's historic diamonds from the "Luxuriant Hotel", the notorious assault on Guilfoyle the banker, on the outskirts of the New Forest, the amazingly audacious murder of Dr. Page-Burnup in his surgery at Chislehurst within a period that could not possibly have exceeded two and a half minutes, and the sensational vitriol-throwing case when Patrina the *prima donna* of Vienna lost her beauty and her rubies, all impinged upon this man "Flame" Lampard from several directions. Directions, however, that were too indefinite and nebulous for the police authorities to collect evidence that would justify them in making an arrest. From the information in front of him, Anthony Bathurst learnt that, in the affair of Guilfoyle the banker, had the detective in charge of the case left Brockenhurst a matter of three minutes earlier, Lampard would have been very hard put to it to explain adequately the reason for his presence in the hotel at Lyndhurst where Guilfoyle had stayed on the previous evening. But the detective had dallied, and there was time for Lampard's defence and alibi to be made cast iron. Reference was made in the dossier to the man's magnificent physical proportions, his absolute fearlessness and utter contempt for personal danger, and his most remarkable gift for handling and controlling the largest and most savage animals. There had been an occasion at his establishment near Club Row, soon after his departure from Jamrach's, when a python had escaped from its glass case, and had seized one of Lampard's attendants by the arm. Lampard, sensing the exigencies of the matter with lightning-like apprehension, had used his enormous strength upon the reptile's neck, and had succeeded in holding the deadly monster at bay until a battalion of help arrived and the python was overpowered and safely housed again. Of recent times, Lampard had been comparatively quiet, and this very quiescence, it appeared, was causing the police some anxiety. It was considered by them to be ominous in itself. Sir Austin

Kemble himself, in a special footnote to Bathurst, expressed the opinion that it would only be a question of time before the man would be laid by the heels on a capital charge. "When this does come, my dear Bathurst," he wrote, "you can take it from me that it will be something pretty colossal. But they all make a mistake, if we only wait long enough, and this man won't be any different from the rest."

Bathurst folded the reports up and put them in his breast pocket. There was much there that not only excited his curiosity, but that also fanned the flames of his imagination. All that he had heard and seen in relation to my uncle's murder, and the circumstances surrounding the case concerning the Trout cryptogram, told him unmistakably that Lampard was a man and an opponent to be feared. He determined, if possible, to obtain further particulars of the two men who had been Lampard's companions. The two men who had stayed at the "Red Stag" with him. At the same time he realized that this might not prove to be too easy. All that he had to go upon, were the descriptions of them given to him by Hoad, the landlord of the "Red Stag", and before that by me. During this exercise of meditation, the door of the coffee-room opened to admit Hoad carrying the constituents of dinner, and in his wake there came Major Neale. The latter nodded a friendly greeting. Bathurst returned the nod, and following upon one of those quick decisions that he is wont to make, announced to Major Neale both his identity and his intentions.

"Please pardon me," he opened, "you are Major Neale, I believe. My name is Anthony Bathurst. I am here at the instance of Miss Cameron. You can guess why, and there is no need then for me to say any more."

Before Neale could reply a fork clattered from Hoad's hand and fell noisily on to the table. The landlord was evidently perturbed by something—either that he had seen or that he had heard Bathurst say. Bathurst glanced at him questioningly.

"You will excuse me, sir," declared Hoad all of a flutter, "but is it true that there has been a death up at Dallow Corner? I've had the news brought to me by more than one person, and I've been wondering if there's any foundation for it. Farmer Ratcliffe's carter who was by here just now, on his way to Quoynings, says that it's the military gentleman that's just taken the place."

"Unfortunately, it's only too true, Hoad. Colonel Cameron was found dead last night on the road between his bungalow at Dallow Corner and the house inhabited by Mr. Armstrong. He'd been on a visit to Mr. Armstrong's and was on his way back home."

Hoad caught his breath as his face whitened at the news. He moistened his lips. Bathurst waited for him to amplify his previous statement. There was no doubt in his mind that the man was badly shaken, and all Bathurst's instincts bade him exercise the greatest care in dealing with the situation which he was positive would require very delicate handling.

"Where did you say the body was found, sir?" Hoad stammered.

"On the road, about midway between Dallow Corner and Mr. Armstrong's house. Why? Why do you ask?"

"I—I—wasn't sure if I heard you correctly, sir," replied Hoad. He appeared to make an effort to pull himself together. "If either of you two gentlemen require anything else, just ring the bell, please, and the missus will bring it in to you." He turned, strode rapidly across the room and closed the door sharply behind him.

Bathurst looked across to Major Neale and raised his eyebrows. "Strange how one runs across little tufts of information sticking out in the most unexpected places, isn't it, Major? I little thought when Hoad brought in these really excellent cutlets that he possessed anything of value to pass on concerning the case itself."

Neale nodded, but the nod was unconvincing and accompanied by a frown. "Information?" he queried. "Is that the word, do you think? I can't see that he *gave* you anything that may be said to fall in the category of information. In fact, I could almost put it the other way. It seemed to me that he asked for information, rather than supplied it. You told him certain things, he told you nothing. Tell me if I'm wrong, won't you?"

Bathurst ignored the invitation. "Very true, Major Neale," he assented cheerfully. "It is impossible for me to deny the truth of what you say. Hoad told me nothing. All the same, he will. When I want him to. That man knows something, Major Neale, and I am going to know it, too. It may be something that he has imagined, it may be that he harbours a ridiculous opinion or an absurd belief, either of which may prove ultimately to be absolutely valueless, but there is always the possibility that it may not. We shall see, even if we have to wait and see."

Neale frowned again, and for a moment made no further contribution. Anthony Bathurst continued the explanation on which he had embarked before Hoad's intervention. "I let you into my secret, Major Neale, and I rely on you to treat it as confidentially as is reasonably possible. You can naturally understand—er—Miss Cameron's distress and her genuine desire for help."

Neale rose and walked to the window to pull the curtains, and for the first time Bathurst noticed the man's limp. "It's getting dusk," said the Major in explanation of his action. "I hate feeding in a half-light. Never could stand it from a child. I'll light the gas, if you don't mind."

When he resumed his seat at the table, Bathurst looked across at him intently. "I am very much afraid, Major Neale, that Miss Cameron and perhaps even those with her, are under the shadow of a great peril. A peril, too, that is as unusual as it is real. Your intimation to me just now that the daylight is failing reminds me of a promise that I recently made to her. As soon as we have finished this meal, I'm going to ask you to accompany me to the bungalow at Dallow Corner. Miss Cameron has only two friends in this district upon whose aid she can call—you and Mr. Armstrong. I purpose calling for him on our return journey. We shall need all our resources."

Neale looked up sharply. "I shall be only too pleased to help Miss Cameron, as always. I should like her to rest assured of that. All the same, what you tell me surprises me to some extent. I thought that I understood her to say yesterday that her cousin, Mr. Douglas Cameron, and his friend, Mr. Strachan, would both be back with her at Dallow Corner this evening. What has happened to them to change their plans?"

"Mr. Cameron has not returned from Town, and at the same time, unfortunately enough, Mr. Strachan had been recalled to Town upon important business. Those two facts are mainly responsible for my appeal to you and to Mr. Armstrong. There is no doubt, I take it, that we shall find him perfectly willing to take a hand in the game?"

Major Neale nodded his assent and at once rose from the table. "In these circumstances, I shall be at your service, Bathurst," he said very courteously, "within a matter of a few minutes. I have one or two things to do, that's all. Where shall I find you?"

"My car's down in the inn yard," replied Bathurst. "If you come down there when you're ready, you'll find me waiting for you."

Major Neale took his departure from the coffee-room, and Bathurst turned to the fire that burned cheerfully on the hearth of the old-fashioned fireplace. As he stretched his hands towards the comfort of the flames, there came a tap upon the coffee-room door, and at his immediate cry of invitation, there entered again Hoad the landlord. Anthony Bathurst felt a glow of expectation as the man advanced towards him. He wasn't at all surprised that Hoad should have returned to the room. As he had previously surmised, the man had something to impart, and he felt certain that the moment had come for this exchange of confidence. Probably Hoad had waited for Neale to leave the apartment.

"Sit down, Hoad," he said, with every sign of encouragement. "What is it, about which you wished to see me?"

The landlord took the chair by the fire that Bathurst had indicated, but sat rather gingerly on the edge. Moreover, he fidgeted with his hands. "It was about the death of Colonel Cameron, sir. You see, I'm not quite sure how to proceed, but do you happen to know, sir, what the poor gentleman's supposed to have died of?"

Bathurst determined not to help him out. He finessed. "I'm afraid I don't quite follow you, Hoad. Do you mean, has the doctor given an opinion—"

Hoad interrupted him. "I mean this, sir. Is it known for certain if the Colonel died from natural causes, or was he—" Hoad hesitated.

"Murdered—are you trying to say, Hoad?"

The landlord looked apprehensively round the room, and his glance strayed to the door. As his gaze shifted slowly back to Bathurst's face, he sighed audibly with what was evidently relief that his companion had so quickly understood him.

"You've said the word, sir," he said very quietly. "It's a nasty word, but it's what I was trying to say."

"Why on earth do you ask these things of me?" countered Bathurst.

Hoad again hesitated for a moment or so before he replied. "That's a difficult question to answer, sir, and I may be quite out of my reckoning. But I've got a strong sort of feeling that you're down here because of Colonel Cameron's death. I can't explain why I think so beyond the fact that the missus first put the idea in my head, and she's got a knack of seeing through most things. I know this. She can always see through me." He leant forward in his eagerness and touched Bathurst on the knee. "Am I right, sir?"

As the result of a quick decision, Bathurst crossed the Rubicon. "You may take it, Hoad, that I do represent Miss Cameron, and that we are far from satisfied as to the manner in which her uncle met his death. I will leave it at that for the present."

A tiny gasp came from the landlord, but Bathurst ignored it and went straight on. "It is now my turn to ask you a question. It is clear to me that you were not inquiring about the death of Colonel Cameron merely out of curiosity. You must, I think, have a much more vital reason for asking than a mere whim. What is the reason?"

Hoad leant forward again. "I have a reason, sir, and yet I'm so doubtful about everything. I don't know what to tell you. I don't know how to put it. I'm worried." He paused, as though searching for the right words with which to clothe the ideas that were running through his mind. Bathurst looked at his watch and then walked to the window. Hoad began. "After we closed last evening, sir, I went on an errand to—" He stopped abruptly, for the door of the coffee-room was flung open very suddenly to admit Major Neale. He stood on the threshold temporarily irresolute. Bathurst turned quickly.

"I'm sorry to have kept you waiting, Major Neale," he apologized, "I have been detained."

Without waiting for Neale to reply, he advanced towards Hoad, and extended his hand.

"Good-bye, then, Hoad," he declared, "I'm sorry, but I really must go. We will discuss that other little matter you mentioned, first thing in the morning. But I stick to my guns. Saddle of mutton must have red-currant jelly." He smiled one of his irresistible smiles. "After all, the other can wait. I don't suppose it will prove to be tremendously important."

## CHAPTER XV

# BATHURST PREPARES TO RECEIVE VISITORS

LINGERING for but a moment, Major Neale entered the primrose-wheeled Crossley that stood there. Bathurst closed the door after him and spoke through the open window of the car.

"I believe I'm right, Major, in assuming that if I take the turning to the right at the bottom of the hill, and work round, I shall come to Dallow Corner eventually, and at the same time pass Armstrong's on the way?"

"That is so," returned Neale. "Going that way, you will. I will point the house out to you directly we come to it."

For some time Bathurst drove in silence, and seemed to awake from the lethargy of thought when Major Neale intimated to him that they had reached Armstrong's house. Anthony swung quickly from the driver's seat and called to Neale as he pushed open the wooden gate that led to the house: "Stay there, please, if you don't mind. I won't keep you waiting long. I hope to be back with Armstrong in a moment." He reached the porch and rang the bell. One quick glance at the man who opened it told him, with the knowledge that he had from my own description, that the man he sought—Armstrong himself—stood in front of him. Introducing himself, he quickly explained his business, and the exact conditions and purpose of his errand.

Armstrong understood immediately. It was a habit of his, as I had already found.

"Allow me, sir, one moment to get my hat and coat, and I shall be ready to accompany you. As a matter of fact, I half-anticipated a messenger of some kind from Miss Cameron, because I gave her an undertaking that I should respond to her summons, whenever the occasion arose. From what Colonel Cameron confided to me last night, and from what I have seen during their very short stay at Dallow Corner, I feared that that occasion might materialize very, very quickly. In a way, I am gratified to think that my judgment was so accurate. You have a car, of course, Mr. Bathurst?"

"I have," replied Bathurst. "How did you know? You can't see it from here, can you?" He spoke truthfully, because the car was hidden by the belt of trees that swayed on the left of the house to and fro in the wind.

"I heard it. I heard you approaching from some little distance. My ears are good and the countryside is so silent. Direct me to it, will you?"

Bathurst piloted him down the path and through the gate. "I have an acquaintance of yours in the car, Mr. Armstrong, so that you will not find the short journey a solitary one. There is also another point. When the immediate business of to-night is over, I should like to interrogate you with regard to Colonel Cameron's visit to you last night. I imagine that you may be able to help me considerably. With the exception of the actual murderer, you must have been the last person to see the Colonel alone. For the moment, however, the most pressing need is the safety of Miss Cameron and those with her, and it is in that direction that all our present energies must tend." The car quickly ate up the short distance. "Here we are, I think." He opened the door.

"I agree with you entirely, Mr. Bathurst, over what you said to me," declared Armstrong as he alighted, "and I shall be happy to place my services at your disposal."

* * * * *

I welcomed my three visitors into the dining-room as heartily as I have ever welcomed anybody in my life. My gratitude for their presence was intense. Aunt Elspeth and Lois had refused to quit, despite my entreaties that they should leave me, with the help of my lieutenants, to see things through. But we were only three women.

"If I didn't owe it to you yourself, Cecilia," Aunt Elspeth had declared, "I owe it to the memory of my brother. 'An eye for an eye and a tooth for a tooth' is as sound a piece of doctrine as I know, and I'm hoping that before this case is finished I shall be able to collect a few physiological fragments myself. At any rate, I mean to have a real good try."

Anthony Bathurst opened with something like an apology. "When I remember my promise, I'm sorry to have left you alone for so long," he explained, "and I viewed the sudden and speedy descent of darkness with some apprehension, I assure you. But the one or two things, that I had to do, took me rather longer than I anticipated." He smiled. "After all, we're in time, and as yet there's no more harm been done. Shall I outline what I think will happen to-night and the plans that I have in mind to defeat the objects of the people that we will call for the time being our antagonists?"

I gestured my acquiescence, and then bethought myself of the two men whom he had brought with him. "Have you already explained them to Major Neale and Mr. Armstrong?" I inquired.

He shook his head. "Not altogether, Miss Cameron. But I understand that each of these gentlemen is as familiar with what has so far taken place as I am. From the little conversation also that I have been able to exchange with them, I feel sure that they realize with me that the people who have favoured you with a certain series of attentions are almost bound to continue their—er—patronage. I cannot believe for one moment that we can reckon on anything like another night's delay. In the circumstances, therefore, my intention is that we attempt to entrench ourselves, as it were, and consolidate our position."

Armstrong nodded. Neale, however, was silent. Armstrong immediately went further and translated his agreement into speech. "I know exactly how Bathurst here feels, for he has put into words what has been passing through my own mind for some little time now. Because of that, I propose that we ask him to explain what he wants us to do. What do you say, Neale? Do you agree with me?" As Armstrong put the question, Major Neale glanced towards me, and it seemed to me from the flash that I got of it that his glance held something in the nature of a question. I evaded it, however, and seeing that, he turned to Armstrong.

"Let's hear, then, by all means, what Mr. Bathurst's suggestions are."

"One minute! I'm in a little difficulty perhaps. Before we do that, I should like to ask Mr. Bathurst a question." The speaker was Armstrong, and the delicate lines of his face showed the emotion that he felt. Anthony Bathurst turned to him at once.

"Yes?"

"It is this. Is it absolutely imperative that we should submit to this attack? That we should *allow* these men to proceed, as you might say, with their villainy. Can't we move, ourselves, and take the offensive out of their hands? We know two things at least. We know that they threatened Colonel Cameron. I was here when it happened. So were you, Neale, and we know that they carried out their threat. Why not grasp the nettle danger and end the matter, once and for all?"

Anthony nodded in seeming acceptance of Armstrong's suggestion. "How?" he asked. "I am all for handling the matter firmly, even to fingering the sting, as I thought I had already made clear. What action would you take that would necessarily put an end to their mischief? Speaking quite frankly, I should be overjoyed to hear it."

Armstrong replied with firm decision and without a hint of hesitation. "Make no bones about it at all. Come right out into the open and put the entire affair in the hands of the police. After all, when everything has been said and done, that's where it will have to go eventually. Why postpone the evil day? As soon as a really reliable medical opinion has been—"

Anthony intervened quietly. "Let me set your mind at rest, Mr. Armstrong. The police are already at work. But they cannot bring about miracles. Look at it for yourself. What have they or we, come to that, against anybody in particular? You know that certain men broke in upon Colonel Cameron's privacy the other evening. You heard what 'Flame' Lampard said. We know that certain men assaulted Mrs. Veitch, the housekeeper here, and made certain domestic investigations both inside and outside this bungalow. But you'll pardon me if I say that that's all we *do* know. The Colonel is dead, it is true, and the Colonel was murdered. But again—what semblance of a proof have we? Tut-tut, Mr. Armstrong, I respect your motives and I look to you for real help, but to make a precipitate move now would scare our birds, and frighten them away, I fear, for good. Or bad! What do you think, Major Neale?" He swung round suddenly on the man addressed, as he put the question.

"I'm disposed to agree with you, Bathurst, on the whole. Although it's a habit of mine, I'll confess, to think that on ninety-nine occasions out of a hundred, attack is the finest method of defence. Perhaps this may be the hundredth occasion."

To hear the three men in discussion interested me profoundly, and I held back my own opinions purposely. Mr. Armstrong's next remark was in the nature of a surprise to me. "Look here, Bathurst," he cried, and his eyes held the fixity of purpose and determination, "be absolutely frank with us if you want us to march under your banner! Are you certain in your own mind that this is a clean-cut case? Where is Mr. Strachan? Where is Miss Cameron's cousin, Mr. Douglas? Are you positive that this man 'Flame' Lampard and his henchmen *are* the men who—"

"Hark!" cried Bathurst in ringing tones of interrogation. "What on earth was that?"

I had heard nothing, and the others expressed themselves in similar terms. I caught the tiniest suggestion of a flicker from Bathurst's eye in the direction of Armstrong, and then Anthony Bathurst himself took up the burden of the conversation.

"Time is getting on," he announced decisively, "and we must waste no more of it in futile discussion. Now, my plans are as follows. I am as certain as I ever shall be of anything, that Lampard and his gang will come here to-night. The question then arises as to what are our best means of foiling them. My proposals are, in a nutshell, these—Hardy shall run my car into your garage. By the way, is there room, Miss Cameron?"

"Yes. I'll tell him at once, shall I? Or, better still, I'll get Lois to tell him."

"Good." He came across to me and spoke in an undertone. I popped out into the other room to her and was back again with the men in a twinkling.

"O.K.," I said. "What's the next step? I'm eager to know."

"I do not think," he continued, "that Lampard has any reason to suspect that you have auxiliaries of strength with you. I kept my eyes open as we came down this evening, and I saw nothing to make me think otherwise. If that be so and I'm right in my idea, Lampard will reckon upon having to deal with three women (or four if we include Mrs. Veitch) and one man—your chauffeur, Hardy. He has taken steps, we will suppose, to eliminate your cousin and Strachan from the contest and will not consider the proximity of any one of us who is with you now. Which gives us advantage number one. Besides the undeniable strength of being forewarned, we are actually (if we are forced to employ Hardy) four men against his three. You are armed, Major Neale. So am I. How about you, Mr. Armstrong?"

Mr. Armstrong shook his head whimsically. He felt as I did, I think, that there was an incongruity about the suggestion. "I am a man of peace, Mr. Bathurst," he replied. "Count me out when you're travelling down the avenues of action. Give me a part that demands strategy and the power of seeing two or three moves ahead. There is always room for that, you know."

"Peace!" echoed Bathurst. "What hast thou to do with peace, eh?" he joked. "If you only knew it, you're a man after my own heart. Anyhow, when Lampard comes, it will be with the intention of searching the whole house. And he doesn't intend, let me tell you, to do it again after this. This is to be the very last time, for this time he hopes to get away with what he has come for."

"What is that?" I gasped. Bathurst shook his head at my question. "I'm sorry, but I don't know yet, Miss Cameron. I haven't had enough time to attack conscientiously the full secret of that cryptogram that you sprang on me. I cherish hopes that I shan't have the trouble. Who knows but what 'Flame' Lampard may, out of his supreme generosity, in some way lead me to it? Which will suit me and all of us down to the ground." He rubbed his hands at the anticipation.

Armstrong's eyes shone and Neale fidgeted uneasily. Bathurst proceeded.

"He will almost certainly force an entrance and hold these ladies up—probably at the point of the revolver. *But he won't know that we are here.* Unfortunately for him! Do you know, I almost think that we shall be strong enough to hold Hardy in reserve somewhere. Now, the first point is suitable hiding-places. Where can we find them?" He looked round, and my eyes followed his. The room in which we were, and to which I have always referred in this history as the dining-room, was the *pièce de résistance* of the bungalow. It was large with several windows. At one end we had the open fireplace, our big comfortable arm-chairs and divans which we were using at the moment, and at the other the long dining-table of reddish-tinted mahogany with its attendant dresser and chairs. Directly we had taken possession, however, my uncle had designed a simple and practical break-up of the room by the aid of a pair of screens. They had the effect of making the room smaller when we so desired it. Their mobility was an asset and greatly in their favour. We had no need of such a thing as a lath and plaster partition; we were able to have the screens here to-day and there to-morrow, as it were, without either trouble or expense. The two that we had brought with us to the bungalow were of Chinese type, of lacquer and embroidery. The effect they produced by reason of their unusual tallness was particularly fine. They seemed to lower the ceiling and at the same time to "furnish" the walls very wonderfully. As they stood, as Anthony Bathurst looked at them, they shut off an exquisitely cosy corner of the room to form my uncle's library.

"Those two screens," Bathurst declared, "are large enough to mask two of us three men. We will clear a direct way to them so that we can take up our positions almost instantaneously when the psychological moment arrives. We will use Hardy outside to prevent reinforcements reaching Lampard. We mustn't leave ourselves open to an attack of that kind."

"Just a moment, Bathurst, before you go any further," interposed Major Neale. "Aren't you overlooking something?"

"What's that?"

"We have but two revolvers amongst us, yours and mine. Armstrong hasn't one. What effective force will Hardy be able to employ externally, if he is unarmed, too? Also, what are we to do with Armstrong here? Shall we put him in—"

"May I make a suggestion?" put forward the man just named. "Must we use these ladies as a decoy? For that's what Bathurst's plan seems to me to come to. Need they be submitted to the indignity—to the unpleasantness? Can't we persuade them to go to another room, for instance, and deal with this gang of ruffians ourselves?"

Bathurst answered his two questions together. "Your point, Mr. Armstrong, is a good one. And, believe me, one that I've considered. Why I want Lampard and his men to 'hold up' the ladies is because I want a gun or guns from them. So that one of their guns, if necessary, may be available for finding its way into the honest hand of Hardy. Let's hope, however, that we shall manage without. Do you get me, Neale?"

The Major nodded his understanding. "What about Armstrong, though?" he added.

Anthony Bathurst rubbed his chin. "If I were only certain as to how much Lampard knows—if I were only sure as to how much Nigel Strachan knew when—" He stopped suddenly and I saw a strange light come into his eyes. "They must pass the lounge on their way here, Miss Cameron, mustn't they? If they come in from the front? Yes? And is Colonel Cameron's body still in there?"

I bowed my head in assent. Bathurst thought hard for a moment. "One of you two gentlemen go in there before our visitors arrive and listen hard as they pass by the door for the exact words of their conversation. He might be lucky enough to pick up something important. Once inside the room, however, and having taken up his position, he must remain in darkness and stay there until he gets the word of 'all right' from one of us. Otherwise, they would at once be placed on their guard. Who will go? You, Armstrong? Or you, Major Neale?" The latter hesitated, quite naturally, I thought, under the somewhat gruesome conditions. Mr. Armstrong, however, came forward with a fine and rare dignity.

"I will do what you want, Bathurst. As I said, I am no man of war; neither do I fear the companionship of the dead. But I appreciate your point. They may give something away. When shall I—"

The hoot of a motor-horn sounded outside, and Armstrong's sentence ceased abruptly.

"They are here," I cried, "there is no time to lose."

Anthony Bathurst smiled at my excitement. "On the contrary, Miss Cameron, they are *nearly* here. That was the signal I arranged with Hardy which would give us a few moments' grace to perfect our preparation. He himself will now assume his position as I outlined to you. Don't you remember?" He turned and nodded to Armstrong, who exited and made his way into the adjoining room.

"Bring the other ladies in here, Miss Cameron. From what I've seen of them they both seem self-possessed and pretty cool-headed, but tell them to keep their nerve, hold their tongues, and generally follow your example all through. Then they'll be as safe as houses, or shall we say bungalows? Now, Major! You and I will take up our insidious position."

At his use of the adjective I remembered my Latin, and a curious little thought struck me that such a reminiscence could have come to me at such a moment. Aunt Elspeth and Lois came in at my bidding, and I whispered to them the instructions that Anthony Bathurst had just given to me. Listening hard, I heard the wheels of a car draw up outside. Shortly afterwards there came to me the sound of the crunch of footsteps on the gravel. The bell rang as sharply as it had rung on the evening of our dinner-party. After a short interval, I heard Mrs. Veitch commence her journey to the front door. Before she could get there, a horrible thought came into my mind to assail me, and in the stinging sense of my fear I rashly imperilled our position.

"Mr. Bathurst," I called to him softly, and he slipped out from behind the screen. "Are we safe?" I asked him.

"What do you mean?" he whispered.

My face and voice trembled. "Remember the red thing that flies."

"Have no fear of that this evening, Miss Cameron. It will not fly within this room. He will not have it with him." He slipped back to his place, revolver in hand, and as he did so, I heard the voice of "Flame" Lampard booming down the hall. I heard it, and I shivered.

## CHAPTER XVI
## "FLAME" LAMPARD AT BAY

THERE WAS a sound of heavily-resolute footsteps along the passage that led from the front door. I tried to distinguish the sounds of different feet in order that I might be able to tell the numerical strength of our visitors, but in this effort I failed. The time was too short, the noise too confused, and the atmosphere too tense, and before I could really collect my thoughts to perform a process of intelligent thinking, I heard the handle of the door grasped, and then saw the door itself flung open. The huge man, at the sound of whose voice I had winced and shivered but a moment previously, strode in; his tremendous bulk seemed to blot out almost the remainder of the apartment. He carried a revolver in his right hand, and was followed into the room by two other men who were similarly armed. One was the man who had harangued me for work at the bottom of the garden, and the other was disfigured by a bulbous nose. Up to the moment certainly, Bathurst's prognostications had been absolutely correct, for the attack had gone exactly as he had predicted. Lampard removed his soft hat with a sweeping bow, and I saw Aunt Elspeth's eyes travel instantaneously to his flaming crown, as though she were fascinated by the man's wealth of hair.

He did me the honour of addressing himself to me. "It is my privilege, I believe, to be speaking to Miss Cameron, niece of Colonel Cameron of these parts. In the—er—regrettable absence of so many of the male members of that illustrious family, I must be forgiven if I regard her as the head of the house. The Cameroness of Cameron." His voice rumbled and shook into laughter in appreciation of his own pleasantry. "These other ladies are, I presume, merely friends of yours, and not authentic members of the ancient line. I may be wrong, of course, but I will assume that the march of the Cameron men has passed them by and left them unmoved." He laughed again, and his huge shoulders rocked to and fro in the effort. The eyes of Lois flashed in resentment at the sally, and Lampard's eyes mocked her in malicious response. But he wasted no more time in flippancy, and tossed his revolver on the table where the others had been thrown. "For the lethal weapons that obtruded somewhat upon our entrance, my sincere apologies. Put it down to my early training as a Boy Scout. One never knows what one may encounter, and therefore one must take adequate precautions. Also, I should prefer our proceedings to be as quiet as possible." He stopped abruptly, and I saw his nostrils twitching as he lifted his head a trifle higher. Suspicion was written in his eyes. Like a flash, inspiration and understanding came to me. He could smell the left-behind aroma of a cigarette that Major Neale had been smoking when he had first entered the room. Taking my case from the table at my hand, I selected a cigarette with a deliberate fastidiousness. For a moment my heart chilled and almost stood still. Would my ruse succeed? Would my opponent compare my cigarette with the stub of the one Neale had left behind? Lampard smiled—and I breathed again.

"I had almost forgotten, Miss Cameron," he announced pompously, "that nowadays—'girls will be boys'. For the moment I was a little disturbed. But only a *very* little, let me assure you." His face hardened. "Morton," he cried sharply, "station yourself in the doorway and let nobody pass. Nobody, do you hear? What did you do with the old woman?"

"She's locked in a cupboard out in the other room, 'Flame'—it's quite comfortable, and she'll do nobody no harm until she's let out. You can bank on that."

"Good. Allen! Keep an eye on these two ladies while I have an interesting *tête-à-tête* with Miss Cameron—or should I say, Cecilia? You can put your guns down, boys."

His face was now aflame with a mixture of anger and passion. Greed, rage, and savage cruelty were all to be seen on it as he spoke the words. If his face had been hard before, it was ruthless and fierce now.

"Now, Miss Cameron," he said, "hand over the goods and spill to me everything you know. Leave out nothing! Do you hear? Nothing!" He brought his huge fist down on to the frail table in front of him and shattered it in pieces. He pushed his face into mine. "Nothing! Or it will be the worse for you. In fact, it will go very badly with you indeed."

For the moment I was nonplussed. I did not feel sure, from a quick survey of the situation, what would be my most diplomatic reply. But I took comfort and solace from two directions. It was evident from Lampard's request that he was still *seeking* his objective—whatever it might be—and secondly, I knew that Anthony Bathurst was behind the screen at the back of me, could hear all that Lampard said, and could perhaps wring truth and sanity from words and phrases that might mean nothing or next to nothing to me when I heard them. I resolved, therefore, to let Lampard talk as much as possible in the hope that he might let his tongue slip and give something away. After all—silence is of the gods. Only monkeys chatter.

"I'm sorry," I said, with a quiet confidence that I was far from feeling, "but I haven't the least idea about what you're talking. If I had, I might try to help you. So don't make it too bad for me, will you?"

"Cut your lies out," he snapped roughly, "you've got the cryptogram the same as I have. Or somebody here has. Else why did you come? I've dug your bloody garden up and I've tested your rooms. You can say that I've toiled all night and caught nothing. So I've come to the conclusion that someone here has more brains than I have and that I'm a trifle late on the scene. All of which I propose to rectify, without the slightest waste of time."

"I'm sorry," I said again, "but you rush your fences." As I spoke I saw my next step clearly defined in front of me. It was a bold stroke, perhaps, but I determined to take it—regardless of the possible cost, and despite the chance, also, of it being a mistake on my part and contrary to the line of Bathurst's policy. "I've had other things to do," I continued, "than read your so-called cryptograms, even if I had the ability to do so. Amongst other things—my uncle has been murdered. I congratulate you. Your threats were curiously prophetic—Mr.—er—pardon me—but I'm not too sure of your name." He drew his head back with a sharp gesture as though my words had stung him into irritation. But the movement was but momentary, for he turned and flung a malevolent glance at his confrère of the bulbous nose.

"So—Master Allen—when the cat's away, the mice play, eh? Play with deadly things they know little about. Ah, well—that will remain as between you and me. But for only a little while, believe me. I don't take kindly to interference. It makes me see red."

The man Allen commenced an indignant expostulation, but Lampard roared an execration at him, and he stopped short. "Keep that for another time, you lump of scum. You're making the old lady tremble. Now, Miss Cameron, let us return to where we were." His face became more gentle. "To the cryptogram. Don't deny that you and your friends have in some way managed to read its meaning, and then hand over the spoils. When you do that, I'll clear out, and not before."

"You ask the impossible," I returned. "I know nothing. I've solved nothing. I have nothing. So that I can't hand anything over, can I? I shouldn't hesitate an instant, I assure you, if it meant ridding myself of your presence."

All the ugliness of expression of which he was capable crept back into his evil face. "Very well, then, young woman. Your blood be on your own head. I shall take possession of this bungalow from now on. For the sake of politeness, we will say that I and my two friends will be your guests. *And I shan't go until I have in my possession what I came for!* If it means taking out every brick, pulling up every floor, breaking the bloody place up in pieces, *I'll do it.* And if I'm still unsuccessful, I'll break you in pieces afterwards. You can't get help, for I shall see that no help comes to you. Your uncle's dead, and your cousin and Mr. Blooming Nosey Nigel Strachan in loving hands and well cared for. And, by the way, in case you're thinking of doing so, I shouldn't put too much faith in him if I were you. I'm not so sure but what he's tried to double-cross me, the swine, and it's not going to come off."

I shook my head, with an idea, I think, of shaking his confidence, and then Lois butted in for the first time. "You forget something, Mr. 'Flame' Lampard. Something that will upset *all* your calculations."

"Oh, my lady, and what's that?"

"Hardy, our chauffeur! He knows you're here. He saw you come in. When he finds that you don't come out—that you're apparently *staying* here, he'll go and get—"

Lampard smiled at her with a kind of mocking pity. "There's no harm in thinking," he replied, "and no harm in an ostrich who sticks his head in the sand. If he likes to do so, well and good. But my arrangements never leave loopholes for failure." He swung round on to me. "Why do people interrupt our little confidential conversations, Miss Cameron? It's most inconsiderate of them. They can't realize all we mean to each other—or they wouldn't do it. Anyhow, you understand the position, don't you? I'll tear up the bungalow and then, failing that, I'll tear up you. Although I'm gentleman enough to say that I hope the latter contingency won't be necessary."

A voice sounded just behind me, and I exulted to hear it. "Believe me, my dear Lampard, it won't be! There won't be the slightest necessity, I assure you. You won't mind putting up your hands, will you? And you two gentlemen as well. Right up, please. All the way. That's right. Thank you very much. I hate putting you to the inconvenience, but you leave me no choice. Don't move, Mr. Lampard, please!"

## Chapter XVII

# THE ATTACK ON MR. ARMSTRONG

Anthony Bathurst and Major Neale had stepped from their hiding-places behind the screens, and their levelled revolvers held command of the entire situation. Bathurst faced Lampard, and the Major confronted the latter's two companions. Aunt Elspeth heaved a fat sigh of ecstatic relief, and the imp of triumph danced in the eyes of Lois. Lampard's face was a study as his hands went slowly up above his head, and his two associates in trouble looked completely broken. His eyes travelled from the face of Bathurst to that of Major Neale, and as he surveyed the latter he appeared to be submerged by a wave of stupefied amazement. Neale, however, eyed him steadily and said nothing. He had evidently received instructions as to the part he was required to play. It was his duty to maintain silence and to let his companion do all the talking that was necessary. Bathurst proceeded to explain himself.

"Let me offer you my congratulations, Mr. Lampard, upon your second statement of this evening. It may be justifiably described as beautifully prophetic. Miss Cameron has already complimented you upon the first, and I feel that I must join her with regard to the second. I heard you suggest just now that better brains than yours had made their appearance in the little matter that is engaging our joint attention. Really, Lampard, I should hate to contradict you."

Lampard's lip curled. "You're top dog, whoever you are, at the moment. But every dog has his day, and there is such a thing as the tables being turned. My chance may come next time. What's your game, anyway? Also, what are you going to do with us? You can't—"

"Some of your questions are more easily answered than others. Count us as friends, not only of Miss Cameron here, but of the late Colonel Cameron as well. Whose cowardly murder, Mr. Lampard, we shall avenge. Have no doubt whatever on that score. That information may assist you in regard to your future intentions. As a matter of fact, there is more than one course of action open to me."

"Really," returned Lampard. "Dear, dear, how excessively interesting! Would you be good enough to tell me what they are?"

"I can tell you one," replied Bathurst, "one that occurs very readily to my mind. I could turn you over to the police. It would be the easiest thing in the world for me to obtain a warrant charging you with the murder of Colonel Cameron."

"You suffer from too vivid an imagination," sneered Lampard, "like most of the 'busy' class. I don't care two straws for fifty warrants. I never went near Colonel Cameron last night and I can prove it! I was miles away, in fact, and I have seven witnesses at least who can prove an alibi."

"And six at least, of the seven, decidedly 'suspect', I anticipate, if the truth be known. However, there is no need to look so far ahead. We will leave that little matter till the day when you stand in the dock, which can only be a question of time at the most. You asked me what I was going to do. You are asking a little too much there. I regret that I cannot supply you with that information. To do so, would be absurdly quixotic on my part. On the other hand, however, not wishing to be completely discourteous, I will tell you what *you* are going to do. Morton! Allen! Look at me." His voice rang through the room with a tone of command that brooked neither denial nor refusal. "You, Lampard, you, Allen, and you, Morton, will leave Dallow Corner this evening and you will not return. Do you understand? You will neither threaten nor molest Miss Cameron or any member of her family in any way from now onward. You will take no action, whatever against her or against any of her friends, from to-night until—"

He paused, and Lampard took advantage of the cessation to intervene with a caustic question. "Until when?" he demanded.

Bathurst affected consideration. "We will not attempt to be too meticulously precise as to the date. Let us say until the day of your arrest, Lampard, and in the meantime Mr. Morton can return to his doss-house in Stepney."

Lampard sneered. "You show me the strength of your case, Mr. Busy, with all your talk of warrants and arrests. For that's all it is—talk. You've got too much of what the cat cleans herself with. Suppose I take no notice of your orders—eh? What then? You can't shoot us in cold blood very well, can you, much as you'd like to?" His grimace was ugly.

"I could and I would without the least compunction, but I won't! I should have to make a lot of explanations, and quite candidly, Lampard, I question very much if you're worth them.

You can put your hands down. Collect their guns, Miss Cameron, will you, and give them to Major Neale."

As Anthony Bathurst spoke, my eyes caught sight of Lampard's left wrist, and what I saw there caused my heart to stand still again. "Mr. Bathurst," I cried, "I've something to tell you."

"Just one moment, Miss Cameron," rejoined Anthony Bathurst. "When Major Neale has seen to our visitors' guns that I want you to collect, I will hear what you have to say. Like our good companion, Mr. Lampard, I allow my arrangements to leave no loopholes for failure. That was the expression, wasn't it? Would you mind, Miss Cameron?"

I walked over to the table on which the three men had thrown their revolvers, picked them up, and handed them to Major Neale. One by one, using his left hand, he put the three revolvers in his pocket. Not one of our three antagonists moved a muscle.

"Now, Miss Cameron," proceeded Bathurst, "I shall be happy to hear what you have to tell me."

I dashed in at once. "Mr. Lampard was very eager and anxious just now to insist that we held nothing in the nature of evidence against him. I am able to contradict that statement." I pointed rather theatrically, I fear, at "Flame" Lampard's left wrist. "Perhaps he would be good enough to explain how it is that he comes to be wearing my cousin's wrist-watch? I know the slight dent in the rim on the left-hand side too well not to mistake it. Incidentally, also, the watch was a present from me, and I am absolutely positive of the truth of what I am saying."

"Excellent, Miss Cameron. A distinct hit to our side. I, too, find myself awaiting Mr. Lampard's explanation with intense interest. I confess that I should like very much to hear how he will justify such a—what shall we call it—coincidence?"

Lampard's eyes flashed into anger and resentment, but he yielded not an inch of his ground.

"'Pon my soul, you amuse me," he declared with a sneer. "Your performance grows more humorous every minute. Considering the many thousands of wrist-watches that one sees during the course of one's occupation, I think that you would find it extremely difficult to impress a jury with the accuracy of your statement.

Especially as I have a perfect explanation as to how this particular watch came into my possession. If you want to know, the Mayor of Bethnal Green gave it to me for a birthday present."

This audacious denial, a perfect piece of effrontery as I knew it to be, stung me into definite accusation. "You lie," I cried. "The watch belongs to my cousin, and you know perfectly well where my cousin is, that is to say, if you haven't already murdered him. For all I know, you may have enticed his friend, Nigel Strachan, away, too. You seem to be determined to leave no stone unturned to further your diabolical plot."

"Go across to him, Miss Cameron, and recover your cousin's watch. Don't get too much in front of him as you do it, but stand well to my right. You, Mr. Lampard, will remain perfectly still, please."

I did as Bathurst said, unfastened the strap and took the watch, and, as I did so, Lampard's eyes blazed at me with the absolute limit of vindictiveness.

"Returning to where we were," continued Anthony Bathurst, "you will eliminate yourselves from the immediate landscape on the terms that I outlined to you just now. Major Neale and I will act as your guides and counsellors until you have reached again the comfort of your car. If you find yourself in doubt as to the time, Lampard, let me recommend the suggestion that has become almost proverbial. Don't let yourself be put off by any trifling personal bias in that direction. Now, march." He gave the order with curt decision and nodded to Neale, who prodded Morton in the stomach with his revolver as a hint to him to form the van of the somewhat inglorious procession. Allen joined Morton, and followed by Neale, they made their way out of the room.

Lampard's face was white with rage as he watched his confederates disappear, but he had the native sense to realize that he had no option in the matter, and a moment or two later, when the others had got well away, he fell in the rear of the line, still menaced by Bathurst's revolver.

As we saw them go, I sighed with relief, and a few minutes later I heard the sound of the wheels of their car receding into the distance. Bathurst and Major Neale, accompanied by Hardy, were quickly back. As they came to the front door I suddenly bethought myself of Mrs. Veitch and her predicament. It was the work of a moment to release her, and as I cut the cords and heard the three men coming down the hall, I was astonished to hear at the same time a cry of distress—of agony almost—come from the direction of the lounge. I flew across to it, but Bathurst and Neale reached there before me. Despite the handicap of his limp, Major Neale was a pace or two in advance of Bathurst and was already inside the room. I was astonished to see that the electric light was full on when I came to the threshold.

"It's Armstrong," I heard Neale cry in alarm. "But how the devil could they have got at him in here? I made sure that he was alone."

Mr. Armstrong lay prone on the floor with his arms outstretched and his right leg doubled beneath his body. The settee, upon which the body of my uncle still lay, had been for some reason pushed from the middle of the room right over to the side.

It seemed to me, as I took in my first true visualization of the scene and its setting, that the settee had been pushed aside roughly, and not placed in its new position with any definite purpose, because it was askew, as it were—not positioned at all carefully. In the original position that the settee had occupied, right in the middle of the room, stood the largest and strongest of the occasional tables, and it was at the side of this particular table that the body of Armstrong lay. It may seem strange, perhaps, to the reader that I should have assimilated what may appear to be comparatively unimportant and perhaps irrelevant details, at the time when a fellow human being lay in front of me, either dead or in urgent need of help. But you must remember that it was my own room so to speak, and the unfamiliarity of its aspect not only surprised but startled me. Let me put it in a different way. It was as though my uncle had come back to me, for example, with his moustache shaved off. Bathurst and Major Neale rushed to the prone body, and thinking perhaps that no harm could come of it and possibly immediate benefit, I at once dispatched Hardy for the brandy. Major Neale turned Mr. Armstrong over on to his back and put his ear to Armstrong's heart. It was a moment or two before he spoke. "Thank God, he's not dead, Bathurst," he declared. "He gave me a rare turn. He's had a bad shock, though, of some kind, and he's unconscious, but I think he'll come round before very long."

"Good!—Ah—here's brandy. Splendid, Miss Cameron. Thank you, Hardy. Give him this, Neale, will you?"

Major Neale rubbed a little of the spirit on the unconscious man's lips, and after that, was successful in forcing a small quantity down his throat. I turned away to watch Anthony Bathurst. Nothing seemed to be escaping him. His eyes were everywhere, and I found mine following his. He turned suddenly, to catch me watching him, and pointed to one of the casement windows. It was open. Then he indicated, with the very slightest gesture of his head, the table that, as I said, had been moved to the middle of the room to take the place of the settee. I looked closely at it, to see what it was that had attracted his attention. On the surface of the table was a fragment of partly-dried mud. It passed my comprehension as to how it could have possibly got there, and whilst I was mentally debating the point, there came a groan from the lips of the man on the floor. Bathurst at once dropped on one knee at his side. He spoke rapidly, but his voice was soft and persuasive.

"What happened, Armstrong? Can you tell me?" he asked. "Summon all your strength and tell us if you can. It's so vitally important to us."

Armstrong looked blankly round the room as though semi-stupefied. Then he seemed to pull himself together a trifle and to recollect, not only where he was, but also the mission that had brought him there. "Thank God, Bathurst, for your help. Otherwise—I was standing by the door there," he said weakly, "listening to you putting it over those scoundrels, when I suddenly found myself grow frightfully cold. I can't explain it, but the chill in the room was horrible—almost nauseating. It was as though the room had suddenly been turned into a refrigerating chamber. I turned round in a kind of attempt to discover the reason or origin of my feeling, when there came a ghastly whirring kind of noise, like something zipping through the air." His voice broke and began to trail away into a mere whisper. "There was a *thing in the room,*

Bathurst," he whispered, "*that flew*. It flew at me. And I—" His head drooped again into the crook of Bathurst's arm, and he relapsed once more into unconsciousness.

## Chapter XVIII
# THE BODY IN THE INN-YARD

THIS ENTIRELY unexpected but positive confirmation of my uncle's dying scribble set me violently trembling again, and the thought that I had anticipated the presence of the horror when Anthony Bathurst had scouted its possibility, brought me no satisfaction, but, on the other hand rather, made me vaguely uneasy. Bathurst himself began to pace the room, and that he was mentally agitated I had no doubt whatever.

"Carry him into the other room, Major Neale," he ordered, turning in his stride, "it will at least be warmer in there than here. To say nothing of being much pleasanter. Can you manage?"

"Easily," returned Neale, "he's not a heavy weight by any means." He lifted Armstrong as though he were a child and carried him out through the door.

"Quick, Miss Cameron," whispered Bathurst, pulling me back as I prepared to follow, "tell me! There isn't a moment to waste. Were you surprised to find that window open when you came in here?"

"Yes," I replied quickly. "It was shut when I last saw it. I'm certain."

"Good!" He nodded as he joined me on our way to the other room. "I must ask Armstrong," I heard him say, almost under his breath, "and he must help me about these other matters, too. But I mustn't spend any more time than I can help on them."

Under the efficient ministrations of Lois, Major Neale, and Aunt Elspeth, Mr. Armstrong seemed to be well on the road to recovery. As he had foreshadowed when he entered, Bathurst wasted no time; he went straight across to him. "You had reached the point when you told us that something flew into the room,

Mr. Armstrong! Are you well enough to tell us what happened after that?"

Armstrong nodded.

"I couldn't be sure." He shook his head as though trying to piece together certain facts or incidents that were worrying him. "You see—it all happened so quickly. I had no time whatever to think. I heard the noise that I described to you. I turned round fully—I had half-turned before, you see—and the next thing I remember is coming to, with you and Neale kneeling at my side. I'm sorry to be able to help you so little, my dear boy." He smiled wistfully in consideration of what he evidently considered to be a culpable deficiency on his part.

"You can't remember, then, anything in the nature of an attack?"

Armstrong shook his head again. "No. Nothing like that at all. There was that repulsive chill, the noise—and the next thing was that I fell. I am grateful to you gentlemen, and to you, Miss Cameron, also, for what you did for me. On the whole, I'm rather ashamed of myself. I came to help you, you know, not for you to help me."

Bathurst cut in with a further question.

"Can you remember if any of the windows of the room were open when I sent you in there? That is to say, on Lampard's arrival?"

Armstrong thought hard. "I don't think so," he returned at length. "I didn't notice any. I think the sudden chill that I felt must have come from the opening of a window. That is how I should explain it myself."

"You were in the dark, of course, as we arranged?"

"All the time. I kept the door on the jar and stood close to it, listening."

"Behind it?"

"Yes—what you would call behind it."

"Yet the light was on as we came to the room," declared Neale.

"But you had passed the room just previously," I cried wonderingly. "When you saw Lampard and his friends off the premises.

What about it *then*? Was the light on *then*? Surely you would have seen—you would have noticed?"

Major Neale stared at me as though trying to assess my statement at its true value. He seemed like a man who had forgotten something.

"I can't remember. I was too intent on the job I had in front of me," he said slowly.

"But I can," intervened Armstrong. "When you were marching Lampard and Co. off, I was in the dark. Nothing had happened then. I was all right. I heard you and listened to you. The room was pitch dark."

"I can confirm that," added Anthony Bathurst. "Mr. Armstrong is right. There was no light from the room as I walked past it with Lampard." He paused and considered for a moment. "Mr. Armstrong," he proceeded, "I think that you have had the closest of close calls. I congratulate you upon your escape. There is something here that I cannot fathom. It's all *wrong*—all twisted and tortuous, and that's why it caught me unprepared. But I'll—" He broke off into more ordinary channels. "When you're feeling fitter, I'll run you back in my car. Will you come along, too, Neale? These ladies will be quite safe for to-night."

Neale was very sincere and straightforward in his reply. "I'll come if you particularly want me, Bathurst. I think you know that, but if you *could* manage to do without me, I'd be tremendously obliged. The fact is, I've a most important letter to write, and if I write it to-night I'll get the first post out in the morning." He rose, made his farewells, and limped from the room.

An hour later, Mr. Armstrong announced himself as fit to return home. We put him in the car and Bathurst drove off.

"I'll call on my way back, Miss Cameron," he cried. "I'll come round this way again specially, just to reassure you. Expect me as soon as Mr. Armstrong here feels well enough to release me. And one last word—be easy in your mind. There will be no further danger threaten you to-night."

I waved my hand to him thankfully, and the Crossley disappeared into the distance. On the journey back to Mr. Armstrong's, Bathurst more than once seemed none too sure of the complete recovery of his passenger. There could be no doubt that the man had received a very nasty shock. For Armstrong sat very silent and huddled up in a corner of the car. On two occasions, Anthony Bathurst, desirous of whipping him into something like mental activity, flung him a sharp inquiry, but each time Mr. Armstrong gave him a reassurance that the trouble had passed and that he was once more feeling himself, only to relapse again into a semi-stupor. By the time they reached his house, he had picked up somewhat, and Bathurst, after stopping the car, helped him to alight. He assisted Armstrong into the house, and upon a further reassurance from him that he was absolutely recovered, declined a pressing invitation to stay for a while. "It's awfully kind of you, but I won't trouble you now, Mr. Armstrong," declared Bathurst. "It would be inconsiderate of me to do so. But to-morrow, as I indicated to you earlier, I should like to have a few words with you, if I may, with regard to Colonel Cameron's visit to you on the night that he died."

"Drop in any time you like, Bathurst. If I can help you in any way, I shall be only too glad to avail myself of the opportunity. But you know that, my boy."

Ten minutes later I heard the Crossley draw up outside the bungalow again, and of course I flew to the door.

Anthony Bathurst smiled as he entered. "My reason for coming back, Miss Cameron, is not perhaps as altruistic as it may appear to be on the surface. Whilst realizing that it might hearten you to know that Armstrong is safe and sound indoors again, and that, as I told you before, you need fear no further trouble for the time being, it is in my mind to have a further glance at the room in which Armstrong was attacked. So now you know the real reason why I'm here."

I followed him into the front room. He turned to me. "There are three interesting points here for us to consider. You agree?"

"I think so. Yes. The window, the mark on the table, and—" I hesitated.

Anthony Bathurst helped me out. "The deliberate moving of the furniture within the room. That's what you were going to say, isn't it, Miss Cameron?"

"Yes. I should have said something like that. At all events, I know what you mean. Because it was the first thing that I really spotted."

He eyed me shrewdly. "Why are windows opened, Miss Cameron? Answer me that. For more than one reason, conceivably, eh?"

I nodded helpfully, and gave him answers. "To let somebody or something in—or out. For air—ventilation. Anything else?"

"It might be so. I have opened a window myself before now in order to see better."

"In the dark?" I queried.

"It's hard to say, but we must not omit such a contingency from our calculations, you know. We dare not! It's a dark and baffling case, Miss Cameron, deeper perhaps than any that I have previously encountered. Consider point number two. What caused the mark on the table? What do you think yourself?"

"Something was placed on the table or somebody stood there. I can't think of any other possibility." As I finished my answer I could see that he was thinking hard.

"No," he returned at length. "Neither can I. I incline to the latter idea myself, because such evidence as we have points that way. Why on earth should anybody want to *stand* on that table? Unless—This little fragment of mud will have to be carefully preserved." He walked over to the table and carefully scraped off the tiny piece of mud into an envelope. "In a sense, you know, we're making definite progress."

I shook my head in wonderment, for everything seemed to me as dark as ever. I turned towards him. "How do you mean?" I questioned.

"Oh—it's trivial, I admit. But, you see, even the most trivial things have their place and meaning, and at last I'm in possession of two facts that *fit*, as it were. Facts that don't scream out in glaring contradiction of themselves. I'll explain to you what I mean. You and I were puzzling just now as to why the disposition of the furniture in the room had been altered. We were groping mentally here and there, undecided and uncertain, seeking possibly something unusual, extraordinary, or even grotesque, to furnish us with the explanation. Then, quite suddenly, we are confronted with an explanation that after all is excessively simple. And why not? Similar experiences have come my way during previous investigations. Apparently incredible happenings, the meaning of which, for a time, have seemed impenetrable, have had bases that were founded in naturalness and simplicity. In this instance I suggest that the furniture was moved because that particular table was a necessity in the middle of the room—and for no other reason. A necessity of convenience. Somebody had to stand on it because the table suited his purpose better than anything else would have done. What could be more natural?"

I nodded. "It's feasible," I conceded. "All the same, however, there's one thing that we mustn't forget. Whatever happened in here, happened remarkably quickly. From the time that Major Neale left the lounge with those two men, Morton and Allen, to the moment when Mr. Armstrong cried out, couldn't have been much more than a couple of minutes. I would put it at three minutes at the most."

He nodded. "That, perhaps, is the strangest part of the whole business, Miss Cameron." He turned towards the door. "Well, I think I'll be getting back. I've some urgent business with Hoad, my landlord at the 'Red Stag'. Expect me fairly early in the morning. I've made arrangements with Inspector Baddeley in respect of Colonel Cameron's body. There will have to be an inquest, you know. The result of which, I, for one, await with very keen curiosity."

The big car quickly gathered pace and came to the inn where Bathurst was staying. Turning to the right, he ran gingerly over the cobblestones that formed the inn-yard to garage the Crossley for the night. About to pull up at a convenient distance, he uttered a startled exclamation. Stretched at full length across the big rough stones in front of him lay the body of a man. With a quick fear clutching at his throat, Bathurst leapt from the car and ran to the man's side. The man lay on his face, with his head pillowed on his right arm, which was flung clumsily and awkwardly away from him. Bathurst knew instinctively that the man at whom he looked was dead, for the body had that strange, sagged inertia about it, that tells so eloquently of the passing of the life within it. Bathurst turned the man over on his back, so that he might see his face. What he saw, confirmed his worst fears and for a moment or so he stood silent and motionless in the inn-yard. For the face at which he looked was the face of Hoad, one-time landlord of the "Red Stag."

## CHAPTER XIX
## NIGEL STRACHAN RETURNS

WITH A CHILL at his heart, Bathurst unbuttoned the dead man's overcoat, and then loosened his tie and collar. Taking his electric torch from his pocket, he allowed the light from it to play on the dead man's face and neck. His eyes soon picked out what they were seeking. Giving another sharp exclamation, he stared at the puffy pink mark that showed just under the ridge of the left-hand jaw. The triple bite again! Anthony Bathurst rose hastily to his feet and looked hurriedly round the yard. "Curse the darkness," he muttered to himself, "if only I had the light of day to help me. Then I might be able to—" Standing by the body of Hoad, he let his torch play round in all directions. He saw that the inn-yard sloped away from him, if anything, and in the straight direction from which he had entered. Then, very slowly, step by step, he made his way towards the entrance of the yard. He walked, too, with a definite plan. "If there's any here it will lie this way," he whispered to himself. "It must be. And if—" The whisper had scarcely been completed when his light threw up a little pool of water that had collected in the crevice between two of the largest of the cobblestones. This water was what he had been seeking. Bathurst knelt carefully by the tiny pool and made his preparations. After a moment or two he flashed the torch on the cobblestones that surrounded it; as he did so, he knew that his reasoning once again was sound, and his patience, therefore, rewarded. For, on the actual stone that fringed the little puddle on the side where lay the dead body of Hoad, there was a thin trickle of blood. Close to it, as Bathurst was, there was no mistaking it. It was just as though somebody had dipped a finger in blood and then drawn the finger lightly along the stone in a scrawl. Bathurst frowned as he looked at the pool of water. Could it be just possible that—? Feeling in his pocket he found the flask that he almost invariably carried and slowly removed the silver cup from the bottom. With the cup he baled the water drop by drop from the crevice between the stones. There was hardly enough to fill the cup and almost immediately the muddy dirt at the bottom of the puddle was revealed to him. "Not enough water there, of course," he muttered. "I'm an idiot. I ought to have foreseen that. A mile away, perhaps, by this time. For all we know, with the other one. Still it was worth trying." He rose to his feet again and walked straight to the door at the rear of the inn that was used as entrance and exit when the inn was closed. He tried the handle, and as he expected, found the door yielded to his push. Going quickly up the staircase, he knocked on the door of Major Neale's bedroom.

"Are you asleep, Neale?" There was no immediate answer. He called more loudly. "Neale! Neale! Wake up, man! I want you."

"Who is it?" came a sleepy voice. "Is that you, Bathurst? What's happened now?"

"Put your dressing-gown on, man, quick, and a greatcoat over it, and then come out here to me. There's trouble outside."

He had no sooner made the request than the door opened and Major Neale had joined him.

"What is it, Bathurst? Who—"

"Hoad," replied Bathurst laconically, "the landlord here. They've got him as they got Colonel Cameron, and as they nearly got Armstrong. His body's in the yard below; I ran across him as I came back in the car from Miss Cameron's. Had I been earlier I might have even run into them at their devilish work."

Neale looked at him completely incredulously. "Hoad?" he gasped. "Hoad? Why Hoad? What had they got on him of all people? Are you sure you aren't making a mistake, Bathurst, and that Hoad's met with an accident or something?"

"I am," responded Bathurst grimly. "Hoad's death is no accident, I can assure you. It's a natural sequel to something that has happened before. There's no getting away from that, Neale. He *knew* something and has paid the penalty for his knowledge.

He's as dead as a door-nail, poor devil. Come down and help me carry him. Then we shall have to break the news to his wife. Which is a job I shan't relish, I can tell you."

As he completed his speech, a bedroom door on the opposite side of the landing opened and a burly figure stood framed in the doorway. His head was bald and his face and neck were full and fleshy. His pyjama suit of mauve-and-white stripes only served to intensify his bulk.

"You will pardon me, gentlemen," he opened, "but I heard one of you calling out, and it occurred to me that there might possibly be a case of sudden illness in the house and that I might be of assistance. I happen to be a doctor, you see. My name is Emery. Can I help you in any way?"

The name stirred a chord of reminiscence in Anthony Bathurst's brain and he answered the stout man immediately.

"Good morning, Doctor, for it is morning now, to be precise. I am glad you have been able to get down here so quickly. We're old correspondents, you know. My name is Anthony Bathurst." He smiled.

Emery smiled in return. "I thought that it might be, when I heard your voice. I guessed that you might be staying here as it seems to be the only decent place in the neighbourhood. I decided this evening that I had arrived too late to see Miss Cameron before to-morrow. The train service from Town is positively appalling. What's the new trouble—eh?"

Bathurst explained rapidly and concisely.

"I'll have a look at him at once. Half a second, while I put something else on. It's confoundedly cold inside here, let alone out there. I should say that the bedroom that I've been put in, must be the coldest room in Europe. H'm," he said five minutes later. "Carry him inside. He's dead right enough. Though I'm hanged if I know 'how' or 'what'. Put him on the hearth-rug in the inn parlour. That will be as convenient a place as any. That's the room where I interviewed his good lady when I first blew in. This poor fellow had gone out somewhere, she told me. So, as it happens, I'd never set eyes on him in life."

Bathurst and Major Neale laid their burden where they had been instructed to place it; the former watched Dr. Emery with an expression that bordered on intense inquisitiveness. After an examination of some minutes, the latter looked up with a puzzled frown on his face.

"'Pon my soul, gentlemen, I'm almost inclined to suspect poison. I am—really. One of the more obscure poisons at that."

Bathurst craned his head to look at the body. The tiny mark under the jaw was declining rapidly. By now, much of the inflammation had passed and there remained but a very small abrasion that, as before, suggested the pock of past chicken-pox as much as anything else. As he looked down at it, Bathurst realized that it would take a very sharp-eyed doctor, indeed, unless under particular advice, to detect such a trifling puncture. He decided to force the issue.

"You may be interested to hear, Dr. Emery," he remarked, "that your old patient, Colonel Cameron, met his death in precisely the same way as this man. Although I am not in agreement with him, Dr. Elliott, the Divisional-Surgeon from Lewes, has been toying with the idea of an injection of some kind. Administered, say, by a hypodermic. Can you see anything here on Hoad's body which would support that idea. Would you mind looking? I should value your opinion tremendously."

Dr. Emery bent more closely to his task; Bathurst saw him stare at the mark under the jaw. "There's a mark under the jaw here that I hadn't noticed. Though I don't know that I can—"

"What is it, Doctor?" Bathurst put the question purposely.

Dr. Emery finessed. "I was thinking that, perhaps, after all, my colleague Elliott may have had reason on his side. Though if a needle's been used it's not of an ordinary type. I can assert that without fear of contradiction."

A slight noise behind them caused Major Neale to turn. A woman had entered the room. It was the widow of the dead man. To Bathurst's relief, the bare realization of her loss had already come to her.

"I have heard something of what you gentlemen have been saying," she said with simple directness. "Is Hoad dead?"

Dr. Emery nodded sympathetically.

"How?" she asked with laconic earnestness.

"We don't know for certain, Mrs. Hoad. But we fear that he may have been poisoned."

"Not—you don't mean that he's done away with himself?" she questioned fearfully.

"We have no reason to think that."

"Then you mean that he's been murdered?" Her stolidity was born of mental habit which is as fruitful of qualities as mental endowment.

Anthony Bathurst turned to her with celerity. "Are you altogether surprised, Mrs. Hoad, to consider that as a possibility?" His grey eyes caught and held hers before she essayed an answer.

"Not so surprised, sir, as I should have been, had it happened a week ago."

"Tell me why you say that."

"You'll get nothing from questioning me, sir, if that's what's running through your mind. I can't help you. For the simple reason that I know nothing. But Hoad's been funny for two or three days now. Funny! Queer! Not himself! Ever since he first heard of the death of the gentleman down at Dallow Corner."

"Worried?"

"P'raps." She shook her head with a kind of mournful resignation. "I don't know, really I don't."

"Did you know that he had gone out to-night?"

"Yes, sir. He told me that he was going. That he absolutely must. For about an hour, he said. No more."

"Did he tell you where or why?"

"No, sir, and I never asked him. I knew my place better than that, sir. Hoad wasn't the man to be curious about, when he was in that mood. He resented it, resented it hot and strong, as I've known to my cost more than once."

"When did he go out, Mrs. Hoad? Exact time, if you can remember it."

"Very soon after he had been speaking to you, sir. He came down to me after you'd finished your dinner—you and Major Neale here—and after a little while he went upstairs again. I thought, perhaps, he'd gone to see you again about something. Did he, sir. Did he go up to you a second time?"

"He didn't speak to me again, Mrs. Hoad, if that's what you mean. Did he speak to you, Major?" Bathurst spoke carelessly.

Neale shook his head in instant denial. "The last time I saw him was when I came in and found him talking to you. Just before we drove away in your car. You remember that yourself. I never set eyes on him after that."

Bathurst paced the room. He felt that somehow the kernel of the whole affair lay very close to him . . . now . . . here . . . in this room . . . if he could only summon the full power of his intelligence and reasoning power to his aid. He found, with himself, that more often than not, vigorous mental application over a very small period of time, brought forth a prompter power of accurate analysis than any other. Where was the truth of this intricate riddle? He must find it . . . and soon. Suddenly he swung round to the woman who mourned a husband.

"Mrs. Hoad—tell me! And, please, think carefully before you answer. It's most important. You had three men staying in the inn a few days since—your husband told me about them, so there's no secret about it. Was your husband worried and preoccupied, as you say he has been, *while they were here.*"

Mrs. Hoad looked at him—wonderingly. Then suddenly she seemed to sense what his meaning was. "It's rather difficult to say, sir. But I don't think that he was. I think that he changed after the three men had gone away from here."

"*After* Colonel Cameron's death and not *before*—eh?"

"To the best of my knowledge, sir, yes. Have the police been informed of this, sir? Hoad's death, I mean."

Bathurst shook his head at her. "Not yet, Mrs. Hoad. There has been no time. We brought your husband straight into here. Dr. Emery happened to be here, you see, and he saw him almost at once. There was no time wasted in that way. Your husband was past help when he was found. But you are quite right, of course, Mrs. Hoad. The police will have to be informed. I'll see to it at once. I know where there's a 'phone. I'll run down there in the car now."

On the way back to the "Red Stag" Anthony Bathurst continued to cudgel his brains. Could Lampard and his followers have killed Hoad before they came to Dallow Corner? It seemed to be a possibility. If so, what had transpired between Hoad's conversation with him and the time of the second murder? What devilish agent or contrivance had the murderer at his command, that he could kill so suddenly and so effectively and yet leave but little trace of his handiwork? If Hoad died because he knew too much, why then was Armstrong attacked as well? Why had the window been opened and the furniture moved and why had somebody stood on the table? Had the murderer then been forced to—His thoughts strayed again to the dying message of Colonel Cameron. It *must* be, he said to himself, "the red thing that *flew*". The words must have been intended to mean that. What sinister and grotesque instrument of death and murder could possibly be described in that way? Could my uncle's message be regarded as reliable and to be strictly trusted in the details of its description? It must be remembered that he was actually dying when he had scrawled it on the page of his diary. It was possible, therefore, that his imagination, distorted in extremis, *might* have played him false and led him to what were inaccurate conclusions. Anthony Bathurst's meditations had just reached this stage when his car swung round a bend of the road at Dallow Corner and came in sight of our bungalow. As he approached it more closely, he was rather surprised to see the figure of a man standing at the front gate. He has told me since, that he was undecided what to do. As it was, taking into consideration the lateness of the hour and the perils through which we were all passing, he slowed up the Crossley and called out to the man.

"It's all right, Mr. Bathurst," came the most surprising and unexpected response. "Miss Cameron has told me that you drove a Crossley. I recognized you. It's Nigel Strachan. I came back about an hour ago. And from what I've heard from Miss Cameron of the goings-on here, I don't think I'd better trouble bed for an hour or so yet. What do you think yourself?"

Bathurst eyed him shrewdly. "Sleep in the room that holds Colonel Cameron's body, Mr. Strachan, and if you're still alive in the morning, I'll have a few words with you. Good night." The car gathered pace.

Nigel Strachan watched it disappear in the distance. Somehow, the advice that he had just received was far from palatable to him. There is much virtue in an "if".

# CHAPTER XX
## THE MISSING WITNESS

WE WERE at breakfast when Anthony Bathurst came in next morning. He gave us a quick, almost curt greeting, and got down to strict business at once.

"All right last night, Mr. Strachan, after I wished you that last *au 'voir?*"

Nigel nodded brightly. "Absolutely! There was nothing doing at all. I took no risks but waited till dawn began to break through, before I closed my eyes. Then I went to bed just to get in an hour or so's sleep before breakfast. I didn't do too badly considering. I'm a bit tired and sleepy, but otherwise pretty fit."

Bathurst lit a cigarette with an almost studied deliberation. "I'm sorry then, that I can't report as clean a bill of health from our end as you are able to from here." He paused to notice better the effect of his next words. "I have very bad news in fact. My landlord, Hoad, of the 'Red Stag', was murdered some time last night."

The news chilled and amazed me. I was absolutely thunderstruck at it. I couldn't see sense or reason in it. To me it was all wrong and failed to fit. How could the affair touch Hoad? In what way could a landlord of an obscure Sussex inn be connected with it all? For I knew that was what Anthony Bathurst meant me to understand from, and read into, his statement.

"This man Hoad was killed, Miss Cameron, by the same agency that murdered your uncle. There was this difference, however. The mark was on the side of the left-hand jaw, instead of on the right, as in your uncle's case. For which, I have satisfied myself since, there was abundant reason. I have examined the dead man's overcoat this morning. He was wearing it when I found him last night in the inn-yard. The coat has—rather unusually—two breast pockets inside—one right, one left. From the left-hand pocket, the one that we don't ordinarily find in a coat of this kind, there are still slight indications of the same loathsome odour that we detected in your uncle's coat pocket." Very rapidly, without waiting for me to reply, he turned to Nigel Strachan. "Now for your news, Mr. Strachan. I think it extremely likely that you will be able to help me. Where's Mr. Douglas Cameron, do you think? Kidnapped by the same people that tried to get you—eh?"

Nigel's reply was disarmingly frank. "In my opinion there isn't the shadow of a doubt about it. But I'll tell you the whole story and you will be able to judge for yourselves."

"That's just what I want you to do, Mr. Strachan. There's nothing so valuable as first-hand evidence in cases of this sort. Proceed, will you?"

Nigel leant his two arms on the table and with an intent look in his eyes, commenced his story. "You will remember, Cecilia, and you too, Mr. Bathurst, that the telegram that took me back to Town purported to have a bearing on the Yorke-Singleton forgery case."

"I remember you *telling* us that—yes," commented Bathurst.

Nigel looked at him as though about to launch a remark; evidently, however, other counsels prevailed to make him change his mind, for he continued his story. "Now the facts of the case are these. I have been briefed for the defence in the Yorke-Singleton case and am appearing on behalf of the junior defendant, Mrs. Lydia Singleton. Sir Avery Hopkinson has been briefed for Crawford Singleton. My client has a very strong case and if I am only able to get into touch with a certain East End character who was in Dr. Yorke's employment several years ago she will have a very much stronger one. This fellow, however, seems to have flitted through the earlier history of the contesting parties and then completely disappeared. We aren't even sure of his name. Three times we have been within an ace of running him to earth, but on each of these occasions something has gone wrong at the very last moment, and the man has eluded us. I have always maintained to Mrs. Singleton that it is vital for us to put this man in the witness-box. Sir Avery Hopkinson, I may say, is in complete agreement with me, and during the last week or so our activities towards tracing him have been redoubled. Now listen to this, Mr. Bathurst, and see what you make of it! The telegram that came to me here, and which I opened in your presence, stated that the man had been discovered and was in Town at my chambers awaiting an urgent and immediate interview."

Bathurst extended his hand. "Have you that telegram now, Mr. Strachan?"

Nigel shook his head. "No. Unfortunately, I destroyed it soon after it came. One wouldn't naturally hang on to—"

"Tut—tut. What a pity. It might have helped us a good deal. Go on, Mr. Strachan."

"There isn't much more to tell," remarked Nigel Strachan quietly. "I hurried away, as you know, and went straight to my chambers to interview this piece of good fortune. When I got there, my clerk—his name's Coleman, by the way—informed me that a man had been waiting there some time for me, but had grown tired of waiting and had gone about an hour previously. He had left an address. 'Paradise Villa, Jubilee Street, Stepney'. Would I make it my business to call there at my earliest convenience? If I did, I would be in a position to lay my hands on the man I wanted. Or, in other words, I should have something to my advantage." Bathurst, his eyes alight with interest, interrupted him. "One question, Mr. Strachan. Had your clerk Coleman ever seen this man before? Did you think to ask him that?"

Nigel nodded his acquiescence. "I did. It was the first question that I put to him. And I will confess here and now that his answer rather startled me."

"Go on," repeated Bathurst encouragingly.

"My clerk said that the man had called once before. I asked him when that had been. He told me and I worked it back in my mind. The date—I mean. The answer to my calculation surprised me. The afternoon on which the man had called before *was the very afternoon that Douglas had disappeared.* Is it a coincidence, or what?"

Bathurst bestowed upon him a nod of approval. "What did you do then, Mr. Strachan?"

"Sent my clerk to fetch me a taxi and when it came, tootled off down to Paradise Villa as fast as its wheels could take me. When we came to the Jubilee Street corner, I got out and paid the chauffeur, intending to walk the remainder of the way. I had scarcely taken half a dozen steps down the turning when a couple of men appeared, seemingly from nowhere and without saying a word, fell in, one each side of me. I wasn't too pleased at this, and began to ask myself one or two serious questions. Had I been a fool and walked head-first into a trap? When I came to Paradise Villa, which I assure you in no way lives up to the promise of its name, I knocked rather gingerly. Half a dozen roughs were lounging outside to render the place more unattractive than ever, and I definitely began to regret even more my decision to come here. Suddenly, to my surprise, the two men who had been shadowing me, sheered off, and a woman who opened the door with a forbidding and eminently hostile frown, melted into a sort of beatific radiance. Nobody could have been more affable. But the man I asked for was not at home, she said, and mightn't be back till the morrow. I'm afraid I received the news with more pleasure than sorrow, and I confess, that as she shut the door in my face, I turned away from it with feelings of distinct relief and at the same time, bewilderment." He removed his arms from the table and looked Anthony Bathurst full in the face. "What do you make of it, Mr. Bathurst? What caused the sudden change of attitude? Is it to do with this business here and Douglas? Or have they gone—?"

He paused. Bathurst filled in the gap. "Gone where, Mr. Strachan?"

Nigel bent over towards me and whispered. "Gone as far as they *dare*."

"Don't think that," replied Bathurst, "don't think that, for a moment. You'll be dwelling in a fool's paradise if you do. You owe your sudden salvation in Jubilee Street to me. You were shadowed by friends as well as by foes directly you left your chambers, for which you can thank your lucky stars and me. I saw to it, for I may as well admit that I doubted from the first the bona fides of your telegram. In which, I may say, Miss Cameron here shared my misgivings. Your half-dozen or so loungers outside Paradise Villa, were under the command of an old friend of mine, Inspector Baddeley, of the Sussex Constabulary. And believe me, Mr. Strachan, it was as well for you that it was so."

A strange expression came into Nigel's face and he stared at Anthony Bathurst with a kind of fascinated incredulity.

"Inspector Baddeley?" he gasped. "Do you mean to tell me that he was one of the chaps outside the house in Jubilee Street?"

"I don't know for certain that he was there himself; all the same I'd be prepared to lay odds on it."

"And you'd win, Mr. Bathurst," said Baddeley, as he pushed open the door and entered the breakfast room, "hands down. Good morning, Miss Cameron. Good morning, Mr. Strachan." His entrance was so well timed that I wondered if the arrangement were deliberate.

## CHAPTER XXI
## THE INQUESTS

I HAD BEGUN to watch for those smiles. They were comparatively rare; but they were worth watching for, because when they came they lit up his whole face. It was characteristic of Inspector Baddeley that he could make himself at home in any company. Also, he had the happy knack of being on the spot when he was wanted, and these two qualities made up in no small degree for his relative deficiency in one or two other directions.

"Good morning, Inspector," returned Bathurst. "You are very welcome, for you will be able, I take it, to supplement Mr. Strachan's story."

"I will that, Mr. Bathurst," answered Baddeley, "that is to say, if you'll give me a minute or two's grace beforehand. I've one or two things that I must get off my chest first. To commence with, Miss Cameron, the inquest on your uncle has been arranged for to-day at noon. It will take place in a room at the 'Red Stag'. The Coroner will also hold an inquest on poor Hoad at the same time. In his case he'll be close to home, poor fellow."

"Who is the Coroner down here now, Baddeley? Anselm's retired, hasn't he?"

"Yes. Dr. Anselm went eighteen months after now, Mr. Bathurst." The Inspector turned to me again. "I've made arrangements for removing Colonel Cameron's body, Miss Cameron, and I've also had a word since I returned from London with your Dr. Emery."

"Has he come?" I asked. "He hasn't advised me."

"He arrived at the 'Red Stag' late last night, Miss Cameron. Too late, he considered, to trouble you. From what he tells he, however, Mr. Bathurst here has already made his acquaintance. Instead of carrying out his autopsy here, as his first intentions were, he'll do it at the 'Red Stag' in conjunction with Dr. Elliott, the Divisional-Surgeon. Dr. Elliott himself and Dr. Vallance also are quite agreeable. It's a bit out of the regular routine, but I've seen to it and fallen into line considering the special circumstances. That's about all, I fancy, with regard to the inquest. Now for this other business." He seated himself in the box-seat by the window and his alert eyes twinkled. "Lucky for you, Mr. Strachan, that Mr. Bathurst delivered you into my hands. Marked 'fragile—with care' as you might say!" He chuckled at his sally.

Nigel flushed and the Inspector noticed it. A broad smile illuminated his features. "There, there, Mr. Strachan, you needn't feel sore about that. You mustn't be thin-skinned, you know. Mr. Bathurst's held my hand in the past. I'm not ashamed to own it. And more than once, I can tell you. So there's no cause for *you* to feel peeved. Anyhow, when I got Mr. Bathurst's message, I was following up a little line of inquiry in connection with the disappearance of Mr. Douglas Cameron. I promised Mr. Bathurst that we wouldn't let you out of our sight and your car was well policed all the way down the road when you motored down to Jubilee Street. We were just a few yards behind you, that's all. Inspector Willmott, who was working the job with me, has had his eye on Paradise Villa for some time now, for more than one reason, and when he saw where you got off, he tumbled to it that

Paradise Villa was probably your destination. So he and I and four other plain-clothes men, well disguised, pushed on ahead of you, and as a result, were there when you arrived and knocked at the door. Did you notice the old woman's face when she opened it?"

"I saw it change pretty quickly," affirmed Nigel. "What was the cause of that?"

Baddeley chuckled. "She spotted old Willmott's dial through his disguise and twigged that the house was well watched. That's why she didn't invite you to walk into her parlour to look at the family album. For you had been intended to in the first place, take *my* word, Mr. Strachan."

"What is this Paradise Villa, Baddeley?" queried Bathurst, "ostensibly, that is? An ordinary house or what?"

"It's a common lodging-house, Mr. Bathurst, and some pretty rough characters get inside it, I can tell you. Limmer, the train murderer, was arrested there, if you remember."

Anthony Bathurst rubbed his hands. "It's my turn to give you a piece of information, then, Baddeley, concerning Paradise Villa. Information that will also interest you, Mr. Strachan. That lodging-house is kept by a Mr. and Mrs. Luke Morton, and an old lag named Trout died there somewhere about a month ago. Rather an interesting character that man Trout and incidentally the author of the Trout cryptogram."

This time it was Nigel's turn to stare.

Bathurst gave the stare quick interpretation. "Getting warm, aren't we, Mr. Strachan. Surprisingly warm! But not too warm, eh?"

Nigel was speechless at the turn affairs had taken.

"Remember the name of Morton, Miss Cameron?" continued Anthony Bathurst swinging round on to me. "Heard it before, haven't you?" I nodded. "Only too well."

"A member of 'Flame' Lampard's self-conducted touring party, Mr. Strachan, and the next thing is we find him running an 'at home' in Stepney. 'Curiouser and curiouser', to quote Alice. Ah, well, when we get all the pieces together we shall assemble the pattern and solve the puzzle."

*　*　*　*　*

The inquest at the "Red Stag", unlike most affairs of its kind in country districts, attracted but few people. There were, however, good reasons for this. My uncle, Colonel Cameron, had come to Dallow Corner so very recently that he, like all of us, was known but to the few, and the death of Stephen Hoad, the landlord of the "Red Stag" was of such recent date that the news of it was by no means common property yet. As I entered the room with Mr. Bathurst and Nigel, I caught sight of Major Neale, but beyond him I could see nobody whom I knew. Dr. Winnington, the Coroner, was a stout, bald-headed, florid-faced man who looked more like a country farmer than what he represented. But he speedily dispelled this illusion of his appearance. After grumbling most audibly about the draught, which he complained was pouring down on his head, and criticizing the room generally, he furraged in a pocket and produced an old-fashioned black velvet smoking-cap embroidered all round. This he placed defiantly on his head and wore throughout the entire proceedings. I shrewdly suspect that it was to cover his baldness and not to protect his cranium that he donned the cap. He took the inquest on my uncle first. Somewhat to my surprise, I was called immediately after Major Neale, who had described, very simply, how he had found the dead man. "Cecilia Mary Cameron."

I gave formal evidence identifying the body, and in reply to the Coroner explained my uncle's general position and antecedents. I was then subjected to a number of questions by Dr. Winnington and I will attempt to summarize them below.

The Coroner: "Had your uncle any worries, Miss Cameron? Financial or otherwise?"

Answer: "To my knowledge—none at all. Of any importance that is."

The Coroner: "Was he in good health? Didn't ail?"

Answer: "Good for his age. He had attended his own doctor some little time back in connection with his heart. But Dr. Emery—that's the doctor in question—is here and will be able to tell you about it much better than I can."

The Coroner: "Under medical attention—eh? That's important. Thank you, Miss Cameron. He never expressed any intention, I suppose, of taking his own life? You never heard, I suppose, of anything of that kind? I have no wish to distress you, Miss Cameron, but I feel that it is imperative that I should ask the question."

Answer: "Never! My uncle was a very distinguished soldier. He would never have considered such a thing." (Very firmly and with the proudest look on my face that I was able to summon.)

The Coroner: "I see. Thank you. Thank you. For the present, that is all. I may recall you, however, Miss Cameron, later. It all depends. Call Dr. Vallance."

Dr. Vallance's evidence was short and simple. He repeated what he had said when he first examined the body. "Call Dr. Elliott."

The Divisional-Surgeon stepped briskly on to the improvised platform that did duty as a witness-stand. He gave evidence as to his examination of the body when he had been notified by Inspector Baddeley, and after Dr. Vallance had stated that Colonel Cameron was dead, from cardiac weakness. When he first viewed the body, he explained in a rather slower voice, his attention had been drawn to a curious mark that was visible under the right jaw. But after mature consideration and reflection, he had come to the conclusion that this had really nothing to do with Colonel Cameron's death. It was, he thought, a question of cause and effect. What looked something like the mark of an injection of some kind, in his opinion had been caused *after* the Colonel's death—very likely, in fact, was the result of the dying man falling. Possibly brought about by a piece of grit on the surface of the road. He agreed with Dr. Vallance. He gave it as his opinion that death was due to cardiac failure aggravated by a certain amount of fatty degeneration of the heart's muscles. There was, he continued, a fair-sized patch of the heart's substance affected in this way. The soft fibres had given way under the influence of a strain—the Colonel had very probably been hurrying home—and as a result, he thought, the blood had passed into the surrounding pericardial sac. Dr. Winnington listened attentively and asked no questions. Dr. Elliott stood down and as he did so, I heard a constable at the end of the room call "Dr. Emery". I turned to look, and I saw that Mr. Armstrong had entered the room and was chatting with Inspector Baddeley. He waved to me encouragingly and Nigel half-waved back. I found myself wondering what Dr. Emery had to say in evidence, for I remembered what Baddeley had told us about him being called, and, quite frankly, Dr. Elliott's testimony after his earlier conversation with Anthony Bathurst had surprised and somewhat annoyed me.

Dr. Emery was brisk and brusque. There was this to be considered—his address was Wimpole Street and he intended that Winnington should realize it. He admitted that he had attended Colonel Cameron fairly recently. Although, to be precise, the Colonel had called upon him for advice which was rather different, if you came to look at it carefully. What he meant was this. He had never attended the Colonel at the Colonel's own residence. The Colonel's heart was not strong, it was true, and he was perfectly aware that there was present a certain amount of brown fatty matter between the muscles. But—the "but" was heavily laboured and burst in the small room like a bombshell—Colonel Cameron had not died from anything to do with that. He would stake his medical reputation, and he glared round at us all in emphasis of the voluminous nature of the stake, that Colonel Cameron had been poisoned! Murdered! His announcement created something akin to a sensation. The Coroner, in great excitement, pressed him for greater detail.

"I am not prepared to name the poison, sir," replied Dr. Emery. "For the simple reason that I can't. I should put it down as one of the more obscure vegetable poisons, but it was administered in some way under the deceased's jaw. That was the mark to which Dr. Elliott referred, and from which that gentleman has drawn an incorrect inference. In fact, I completely disagree with Dr. Elliott."

I could see that the latter shifted rather uneasily in his chair. The Coroner asked Dr. Emery one or two more questions which that gentleman adroitly parried, rather than answered, and then recalled me. Only, however, for a very brief period.

The Coroner: "You said in your previous evidence, Miss Cameron, that your uncle went out rather late on the evening of his death. Where was it you said that he went?"

Answer: "He walked up to the house of a neighbour of ours, a Mr. Ralph Armstrong."

The Coroner: "Did he tell you why he was going there? Give any special reason?"

Answer: "No—not in any detail. He said he wanted to see him—that was all."

The Coroner: "Thank you again, Miss Cameron. That will do. Call Ralph Armstrong."

Mr. Armstrong flashed me a comforting smile as he made his way to the little raised platform. As he took the oath something like an expectant hush fell upon the company of listeners. After a few preliminary questions of no special interest or importance, the Coroner came to what he evidently considered was the crucial point.

"On the night of his death, the late Colonel Cameron visited you at your house, did he not, Mr. Armstrong?"

"Yes, that is so."

"What was the nature of the Colonel's call? Will you please tell me?"

For a brief moment Mr. Armstrong hesitated. Dr. Winnington became aware of it. "I hope that you will help this inquiry as far as you can, Mr. Armstrong. For we need, it seems to me, all the help that we can obtain, from every—er—possible quarter. I place myself in your hands, of course."

The fine lines of the face of the man addressed grew even finer as he nodded agreement with the Coroner's last remark. "I understand, sir. There isn't the slightest mystery whatever about Colonel Cameron's visit to me on the night of his death. It was a purely conventional call on purely conventional lines. He called to see me about his fishing. The Colonel, I should say, was a keen angler. I had previously told him, in reply to an earlier question that he had put to me, that there was no stream near of any size. But he seemed to persist in what was an entirely erroneous idea, for on the evening about which you speak, he returned to the subject again. For some reason or the other, of which I am entirely unaware, he was very keen to find out all he could with regard to all the stretches of water in the vicinity."

"Very natural, after all," commented the Coroner, "if the Colonel were an enthusiastic angler. As he no doubt appears to have been!"

I knew, as I listened, that this was far from the truth, and that the evidence was so much ploughing of sand. I realized that my uncle had merely been seeking information with regard to the Trout cryptogram, and the strange conversation that we had overheard on the evening on which we had come down to Dallow Corner. I began to tax myself. Was it fair of us to withhold all this information and yet expect fruition of Justice?

Dr. Winnington continued. "What time did Colonel Cameron leave you for home? Be as precise as you can, Mr. Armstrong."

"About twenty minutes to eleven, sir."

"In normal health and spirits, of course?"

"As far as I could judge on a very recent acquaintance—absolutely. Colonel Cameron talked rationally, walked rationally, and altogether left me in the most jovial of moods."

"Thank you, Mr. Armstrong. It would be wrong of me if I omitted to say that you have been very helpful, very helpful, indeed. I will now attempt to take the long view of the matter and whilst remembering that it is my duty to—" He stopped and bent his head towards the sergeant of police who had, at that moment, come and stood at the side of his table. I heard him say, "tell Inspector Baddeley that I should like a word with him."

Baddeley obeyed the summons almost instantly. His brisk step resounded throughout the room and the two men conferred for a few moments in low tones, the sergeant taking up his position a pace or two in the rear. Then the Coroner pushed his smoking cap farther back on his head, raised his voice, and addressed us. "In view of what I have just been told, I have decided to adjourn the inquest on Colonel Cameron for one month from to-day. With regard to the second inquest that is occupying our attention to-day—that on the body of Stephen Clowson Hoad, late licensed victualler of these—er—premises—I propose to take formal identification of the body, and then adjourn that also, for the same length of time. I am taking this step in order to conform with the wishes of the police."

As he spoke, I saw his eyes dwell on something or somebody at the rear of the room and rest there for a moment or so, as though he felt himself attracted thereby, against his will. I found my eyes following his, and as they did so they were suddenly, as you might say, jerked, to a precipitate standstill. For I could scarcely believe what I saw. For, leaning nonchalantly against the old wainscotting at the very back of the room, stood a figure that I had hoped never to see again. It was the figure of "Flame" Lampard, and I pulled at Nigel Strachan's sleeve in my agitation. Then I remembered Anthony Bathurst, and looked across to the place where I knew he was sitting. I saw his eyes meet those of "Flame" Lampard and in the latter's there came a gleam of hatred mixed with consummate contempt. Bathurst's, however, were relentlessly unwavering, and I knew that when the final clash did come between these two, each man would find therein an opponent well worthy of his own steel.

"Look, Nigel," I whispered, "at the back there. Do you see whom I mean?"

He frowned, seemingly mindful of something unpleasant, and then deliberately averted his glance from the flaming-haired giant who had crossed our lives in such sinister fashion. As we filed from the room, I saw Anthony Bathurst in deep conversation with Mr. Armstrong. Major Neale noticed it too, for after a second or two's hesitation, he turned on his heel and limped away.

<h2 style="text-align:center">Chapter XXII</h2>

# MR. BATHURST DIGS DEEPER

As I HAD not seen the coming of "Flame" Lampard, so neither did I see the manner of his going. I suppose my eyes must have been following the form of Major Neale and during the period I was thus occupied, the giant slipped away. Anthony Bathurst left Mr. Armstrong at once, and came over to me. "I'm going along with Armstrong, Miss Cameron, up to his place; there are several points about your uncle's last interview with him that I should like the opportunity to discuss. I've told him that and suggested that I went along with him now. If you and Mr. Strachan go back to the bungalow I'll hope to join you later."

I nodded my acceptance of the position as he outlined it. "Mr. Bathurst," I proceeded, "did you see who was at the inquest?"

He nodded. "'Flame' Lampard, do you mean? Yes, I saw the beggar come in. He's got an almighty cheek, but I wasn't altogether surprised, Miss Cameron."

I intervened hotly. "He's audacious, if he's nothing else. And in no way deterred by your warning to him. I'm pretty confident, too, we haven't seen the last of him."

"He's all that you say—and then some, as our cousins put it. But he's not quite so confident as he was, and every step he takes now, he'll take very warily." He lowered his voice. "On no account, Miss Cameron, let anybody know of the message from your uncle's diary. The murderer doesn't know that we know so much. That's going to be our trump card. I'll see you later." He raised his hat and I saw him walk across the room and rejoin Mr. Armstrong. The latter entered the primrose-wheeled Crossley and Anthony Bathurst drove off. Arrived at Armstrong's home, he was made tremendously welcome.

"The occasion, Mr. Bathurst, calls for a glass of a really excellent brown sherry that I keep in my cellar and of which I am inordinately fond. It is perhaps my only weakness. You will join me, of course?"

Anthony expressed his willingness.

"I am a lover of good wine, Mr. Bathurst," went on his host. "With the exception of the very finest rum, spirits make small appeal to me." He smiled appreciatively. "But you may disagree with me. Yes?"

Anthony shook his head. "No. Not at all."

"I'm afraid that this particular brown sherry of mine is going too fast for my liking and I doubt whether I shall ever adequately replace it. I decant a bottle every other day, and my stock is running low." He indicated the decanter and the funnel as he handed his guest his glass of wine.

Anthony smiled at his host's enthusiasm, but the wine was good and well merited the praise that had been accorded it.

"What was it that you wanted to ask me, Mr. Bathurst?"

"Going back to the night of Colonel Cameron's death, Mr. Armstrong, were you surprised to see him here as your visitor?"

Armstrong took a chair opposite to his questioner.

His leg was still painful from the recent episode at the bungalow and he moved awkwardly. "Yes—and no. That answer may appear to be contradictory. All the same, it's the best that I can give you. Let me put it to you like this. When I answered the door, after the Colonel had rung the bell, I never expected to see Colonel Cameron there. At the same time, from my previous knowledge of him, small though it may have been, and of only a few days' standing, I had formed the conclusion that the Colonel was the kind of man who might be *expected* to do unexpected things. Do I make myself clear?"

"Perfectly, Mr. Armstrong. I've felt the same way myself before now, about people, and first impressions are by no means the worst. Now when Colonel Cameron came in here, did he at once raise the question of fishing?"

"Not at once, but *almost* at once. Within, I should say, half an hour of his entrance."

"I see. So quickly, we will say, as to leave no doubt in your mind that it was the real object of his visit?"

"Undoubtedly."

"Now tell me this. Did he inquire about any particular *kind* of fishing?"

Armstrong smiled. "You're a wizard, Mr. Bathurst. He did. He made very particular reference to salmon."

Anthony looked up quickly. There was sound sense here and the answer gratified him. "Were you able to help him in any way?"

"Not in the least. That is to say, of course, from his point of view. I simply told him what I had already told him. What I told the Coroner to-day. That this little corner of Sussex was hopeless for what he apparently wanted. I told him that he had come to the wrong shop." Armstrong laughed, and Anthony fell to hard consideration.

"Was he terribly disappointed?"

Armstrong furrowed his brow. "A bit, perhaps. Not a lot, though, and he'd quite recovered when he eventually got up to go.

By that time he was in splendid spirits, as I told Miss Cameron. My big regret is that I didn't accompany him part of the way as I had intended. It's on the cards that I might have saved him." Armstrong shook his head in sorrow.

Mr. Bathurst tendered him sympathy. "I think not, Mr. Armstrong. Don't reproach yourself over that. You could not have frustrated the forces that were arrayed against him." He rose and regarded his host gravely. "I don't think that Colonel Cameron *was* disappointed when you told him what you did. Something tells me that he was in a mood of comparative exultation. He may have dissembled, of course. He may have hidden it from you to a degree. But I believe I should be correct if I said that his enthusiasm ran high."

Armstrong shook his head again, rather sadly and wistfully. "I don't know to what you refer, Mr. Bathurst. You have evidently more knowledge than has come my way—and I don't suppose you will tell me of it. So that I can't be expected to offer any comment."

Anthony broke fresh ground. "The landlord of the 'Red Stag', this poor devil Hoad—how does he come into the affair, do you think. What's the connection? Formed any idea?"

Armstrong showed signs of surprise. "Are you certain, then, that the two deaths *are* connected? I didn't know that—"

"Colonel Cameron and Stephen Hoad were killed by the same devilish agency, Mr. Armstrong. I could establish that fact beyond the scintilla of a doubt. Tell me—you've known him some time. What sort of a fellow was this Hoad?"

Armstrong replied with some warmth. "A very decent man indeed. Eminently trustworthy, courteous, and always very willing to be obliging. I've never heard a whisper against his good name. A splendid example of an English innkeeper. The last man in the world I should have thought to be mixed up in an affair of this kind. I think that he must have stumbled on something, unwittingly, and—"

"Paid for his knowledge—eh?" suggested Bathurst.

"Exactly. Dead men tell no tales. History tells us that and it's constantly repeating itself. There was a namesake of yours once who learned the truth of it. A certain Benjamin Bathurst, wasn't it?"

"Quite true. The traveller in the fur cloak. He was an ancestor of mine, as an actual fact. His eldest brother was a cousin of my great-great-grandfather. It may amaze you, but I've thought more than once of running over to the Continent and looking into the case."

Armstrong smiled and nodded. "It has always interested me. If my memory serves me correctly, he was the fourth son of the Bishop of Norwich, and he disappeared from an inn-yard at Perleberg in the spring of 1819. Am I right?"

"Not altogether. Nearly. He was the third son of his father and the year was 1809."

Armstrong's keen old face flashed into admiration. He felt as the Rector of Kirve St. Laudus had upon a memorable occasion in the past. "You have an excellent memory, Mr. Bathurst, and I'm somewhat humiliated. I will accept your corrections of my statement because I can see that you feel certain about their accuracy. Allow me to congratulate you."

Anthony waved a deprecating hand. "I'm afraid that my memory would not stand a very severe test, sir, judged from the highest standards. After all, values are relative and only relative. Consider what the giants of the past have done. Morton, an Englishman, could repeat from memory the exact words of a lecture delivered to him just previously. Claudius Menetrier could repeat three hundred arbitrarily connected words which he had heard *once* in the exact order in which he had heard them. A pupil of the famous Schenkel (inventor of one of the 'arts of memory') could repeat two hundred and forty sentences in the same order in which he had once heard them. And there were others." As he warmed to his subject, Anthony waxed more enthusiastic. "Men of terrific powers of remembrance. Look at Pica della Mirandola, who could repeat two thousand names after a once-heard discourse; Cineas, the ambassador of Pyrrhus, who could repeat verbatim a poem which he had heard but once *in a language that was foreign to him*; Maglibecchi, the Florentine, the greatest master of memory-detail the world has ever seen; and finally, the colossal Joseph

Scaliger, who learned by heart the whole of Homer in a little matter of twenty-one days. Consider the task, sir, Homer by heart in three weeks!" Anthony turned and picked up his hat preparatory to departure. "It is when I think of these mighty memories that I'm appalled at the puniness and feebleness of my own. Goodbye, Mr. Armstrong. Thanks for all that you have done for me."

Neale was in the coffee-room of the "Red Stag" when Anthony Bathurst looked in the door. "Sorry to disturb you, Neale," said the latter, "but I'd like a chat with you about one or two little matters. Can you spare the time now?"

"Delighted," said the Major. "What's worrying you now?"

Bathurst came to the point at once. "Carry your mind back to last night. After we'd played host to friend Lampard and his merry men. You went from Dallow Corner about an hour before Armstrong and I did. You remember, don't you?"

Major Neale shook his head. "I can't say that I do, Bathurst. I certainly left you and Armstrong there. But, you see, I don't know when *you* came away. So that on the question of actual time, I can't—"

"We were a good hour behind you. A bit more if anything. Did you walk up here?"

"Yes."

"All the way?"

"Every step. Why?"

"See anything of anybody on the way?"

"Can't recall that I did. Don't believe I either overtook or met a soul."

"Any car or motor-cycle pass you—going either way, I mean? Car for preference."

Major Neale reflected over this last query. "That question's not so easy to answer as the others, because cars, fast cars particularly, sometimes flash by and one hardly notices them. They make but little impression on the mind. But I don't think I can remember one."

"You didn't happen to notice Hoad anywhere about, did you?"

"Anywhere about where?"

"Well—did he let you in?"

"No—I came round the back entrance. The way that you usually use yourself. I always do at that time of night."

"And you're quite sure that you saw him nowhere on the road between here and Miss Cameron's, at Dallow Corner?"

"Absolutely certain, Bathurst. Why are you so persistent?"

Anthony paced the room in consideration of Major Neale's reply. Then another thought appeared to strike him.

"After you came in here to write your letter, did you come out again?"

Neale shook his head in a suggestion of impatience. "No. What reason had I for coming out again? As I told you, when I left Dallow Corner, I came up here to write a letter. There was not another evening post; I simply wanted to write it so that I could catch the first post out this morning. I knew it wouldn't get written if I left it till the morning. After I wrote the letter, I went to bed, where I remained until you came and lugged me out in the early hours of the morning."

"I see. Was there any sign of life about this place when you came in?—Anybody moving about, for instance? Mrs. Hoad? Or any of the servants?"

"If there were, they didn't cross my path. But what on earth are you driving at Bathurst?"

This time it was Anthony Bathurst's turn to show manifestations of impatience. He swung round on Major Neale in the heat of his explanation. "I want to find out why Hoad went out at that time of night. What it was that took him out. Ask yourself and see whether you can find a satisfactory answer. Whom did he go to see? Whom did he go to meet? Or, alternatively, who summoned him? What has Lampard, for instance, to do with Hoad? What has Hoad in common with Colonel Cameron? If he knew something, and knew where he could find Lampard, for example, to have it out with him, what was the strong incentive that made him put himself into Lampard's clutches? When I know that, assuming my premises to be accurate, I shall hold the whole truth. But, on the other hand, if my premises be wrong and I'm forced to revise my view of the case, if Hoad merely suspected some part of the truth, and went out to—" He stopped his sentence abruptly and fell to pacing the room again in silence. Major Neale watched him quietly and shrugged his shoulders.

"It seems to me," he declared, "that the outlook at the moment is pretty hopeless. Take the medical evidence at the inquest to-day. To say the least of it, it was conflicting and contradictory. Elliott and Vallance said one thing. Emery flatly contradicted it. If skilled opinion such as that finds extraordinary difficulties about the case, there must be correspondingly less likelihood for people like you and me to arrive at the true solution."

Anthony Bathurst grinned at his companion for the first time that afternoon. "All very true, Neale," he observed, "and thanks for the compliment. But true only as far as it goes. Which isn't a great way. You and I have one or two cards in the shape of actual evidence up our sleeves. We hold an advantage, therefore, over more than one person who gave evidence at the inquest. Don't you see? I don't mind telling you, Neale, and you may be very much surprised, that I'm far from pessimistic. In fact, I'm very closely bordering on what you would term unfounded and confounded optimism." Bathurst grinned again.

Neale looked across at him and his face registered surprise. "You amaze me, Bathurst," he exclaimed, "when you talk like that. I had no idea that you were anything like so confident." The Major rose and came to the point. "If I may be allowed the privilege of trespass, when do you hope to have your man?"

Mr. Bathurst was silent for the space of a moment or so. "That question, Major, is perhaps a little difficult to answer, as it isn't yet a clean-cut issue. I have to reckon, you see, with such considerations as weather, individual opportunity, and my own good fortune, shall we say, in wringing the truth from a certain dark secret." He paused as though in the process of a mental calculation. "However, with your assistance, Major, I am confident that I shall have my man, as you say, within a matter of forty-eight hours. You shall know of my last plans directly I decide upon them."

Major Neale's eyes followed him as he crossed to the door of the coffee-room and made his exit, and had Bathurst turned, he would have seen that those same eyes held a look of complete incredulity. It was evident that the Major by no means shared Mr. Bathurst's optimism.

# CHAPTER XXIII
## MR. BATHURST AND THE CRYPTOGRAM

BATHURST went straight from Neale to the privacy of his own room and locked the door. Taking a sheet of notepaper from his pocket, he removed the top of his fountain-pen and deliberately committed the lines of the Trout cryptogram to the paper. He had decided half an hour ago that it was imperative for him to make this his next job. As he had informed Nigel Strachan on the day when he had first heard the story of the man Trout, he was a quick study, and was able to reproduce the words and figures of the cryptogram without the slightest difficulty. From the first line to the last, he surveyed the entire message with the utmost care and the intensest application.

> "No Dancers need apply"
>
> First find the Bulb, that flowers more bright
>   than Daffodil or Crocus white.
> Look neer for Sun, but seek the shade
>   from Sky they came, on the Death Parade."

$$16 \, P - \tfrac{146}{122} + \tfrac{19}{234} + \tfrac{19}{132} + \tfrac{19}{74} = 50{,}000 \, L$$

Taken on the whole, it was comparatively simple. That is to say, unlike most messages of a similar nature of which he had heard, it was couched in moderately ordinary terms. There was no abstruse classical allusion, for instance, to veneer the doggerel and give it a false identity. All the substantives might reasonably be taken to stand for things of everyday use and reference. Similarly to Nigel Strachan, who had preceded him in the attempted elucidation, he first turned his attention to the row of figures that finished the unambitious effort. Before very long, and by exactly the same process of reasoning, he was able to elucidate the hidden kernel of "Dallow Corner". The 16D or 16P—whichever it might be in the end—he decided to leave for the time being, whereas the 50,000L he took temporarily to stand for £50,000. That fitted and seemed eminently reasonable. Certainly, it was a prize to stir the depths of cupidity in many a mind, and turn those minds to the mazes of murder and the channels of crime. From the row of figures at the bottom, he went back to the line with which the cryptogram began. "No Dancers Need Apply." After turning over the possibilities of this in his mind for a comparatively short while, he came to the conclusion that there was a very strong likelihood that the plural substantive did not refer to devotees of the art of Terpsichore. "Dancers", it seemed to him, must have another and probably quite different significance from that of the light, fantastic toe. Suddenly, like a flash of lightning from a summer sky, the solution illuminated his mind. *Of course*. Trout was an old "lag" and was using a well-known word in the "argot" of the criminal class. "A dancer" was a stair. As he considered it, Bathurst remembered the famous old line of the "Flitterbat Dancers" that had troubled the astute Martin Hewitt. "Over the coals the fifth *dancer* slides, says Jerry Shiels the horney". "No dancers need apply" obviously meant some place "without stairs"—a not inaccurate description, to a man of Trout's mentality, of a bungalow. The particular residence bearing the name of Dallow Corner itself must therefore be the actual place that was indicated by Trout in his cryptogram. Progress! Definite progress! So far, so good! Mr. Bathurst rubbed his hands, and with increased zest turned his immediate attention to the four main lines of the doggerel.

The last line of the four puzzled him intensely, and the more he cudgelled his brains, the more utterly meaningless it seemed to him to be. "From Sky they came, on the Death Parade." What? Who? The more he considered it, the more certain he became that this particular line, when properly understood, would explain almost all. It seemed to him that the searchlight of inquiry needed to be turned on to the operations of Trout just prior to his last arrest; there had been scarcely any time to speak of, between his last release and his death, for anything important or startling to have happened. Therefore, the occasion to write the cryptogram should have occurred before either of these. Anthony Bathurst leant back in his chair, lit a cigarette, and puffed at it reflectively. What possible connection could Sam Trout, the old "lag", have had with Dallow Corner, the residence of Colonel Cameron and Cecilia Mary Cameron? How could it and he have ever been connected? Whatever the connection was, he argued, it could only have been fugitive, fleeting, almost accidental. Something that surely must have occurred by the chance trembling of Fate's finger. He knew, from what I had previously told him, that our predecessors at the bungalow had been a Mr. and Mrs. Christie, who had packed up, as it were, very suddenly and gone abroad. The bungalow had been offered for sale exactly as it stood. Mr. and Mrs. Christie had lived in the bungalow since it had been built, so that there was no question of previous occupation operating.

Anthony therefore proceeded to develop a definite theory, and cigarette after cigarette was smoked in its contemplation and the end tossed away. Assuming that something was buried, or hidden, in some way in the bungalow at Dallow Corner, it was surely sound reasoning to argue that Sam Trout was the person who had buried or hidden it. It was long odds on it. Carrying on, then, from that established position, the next question that arose concerned the element of time. *When* had Trout been able to enter Dallow Corner and *cache* his treasure there? Obviously, the soundest and surest answer to this last query was that Trout had done this during the interregnum that had existed between the departure of the Christies to South Africa, or wherever it was, and the taking over of the bungalow by Colonel Cameron and his people. How long had the bungalow been empty? The answer to this was not too encouraging, for six months is a long time. Half a minute! Anthony Bathurst's reason asserted itself. Trout had been in "jug" since somewhere about the middle of May, and he remembered that I had told him that the Christies had gone on May 4th! Better and better! A mere matter of about a week at the most. He must find out what Trout was up to during that week. Things, after all, were working out splendidly.

Mr. Bathurst settled down to another process of intensive thought. He reasoned to himself that Trout might have used the bungalow as a hiding-place as a last resource, or, better still, that the time had come to him when he was absolutely forced to use the first available place that he could find. Or even better still than that, as an harmonic progression in mental gymnastics, that the treasure, or the wealth, or whatever it was that had come to him, had dropped into his lap *suddenly*. Entirely unexpectedly! So suddenly and unexpectedly that he was, as it were, taken mentally unawares and compelled to employ the first hiding-place that came to hand. Then had come his arrest. He was laid by the heels, unable to pass the word on, powerless to retrieve his hoard, and had come out of prison—not to salve his fortune, as he had no doubt hoped, but to die in an ignominious lodging-house in Stepney. And before his death, realizing that he had no chance of life to send out two copies of the now famous cryptogram to the only two friends he had in the world. That raised a further question. When had he been arrested? A trunk call to Sir Austin Kemble at New Scotland Yard would give him that information at once. He decided to put one through to him. He rose, unlocked the door, descended the stairs rapidly, and went to the back of the inn for the Crossley. Ten minutes' run brought him to the telephone booth, and after a reasonable interval, he got through to the Yard and asked for the Commissioner. Sir Austin listened attentively to Bathurst's request. "Didn't I send you that information in my report on Trout? I thought I forwarded everything."

"No, sir. Your report states that Trout was arrested 'in the spring'. That's pretty elastic, isn't it? What I'm asking from you now, sir, is the *exact* date. The day and the time, if possible."

Sir Austin's reply was curt and crisp. "Hold on, then."

Mr. Bathurst wrapped himself in a mantle of patience. After what seemed an interminable wait, the Commissioner's voice was heard on the line again.

"Are you there, Bathurst?"

"Right-o, sir."

"I've obtained the information that you want. Luckily for you, MacMorran was in and he was able to get it at once. If he hadn't have been in, you'd have been unlucky. Trout was arrested by the police late in the evening of the eighth of May. Where? Oh—let me see—at Worthing, I believe, or at least near there. One of the south coast seaside towns. I'm certain. Is that all you want to know? . . . What? . . . Yes . . . a search-warrant is being put into effect almost at once. Baddeley's on it, I believe. Personally, I don't think we should waste a moment."

"Well, I'm convinced you'll find him there, sir. What? Oh—undoubtedly! A very clever customer indeed. There'll be a few scratches possibly, and perhaps a bruise or two. Nothing beyond that, I'll be bound. It's been a very clever game, but not quite clever enough. I fancy I'm nearly home all the way through. You're surprised? . . . No—not altogether . . . I'm not. I've found where the weakness of the story lay, and I'm moderately certain that my conclusions are right. . . . Yes, yes, of course. . . . Good-bye." Anthony Bathurst hung up the receiver and entered his car. "May the eighth." He repeated it to himself more than once. What the blazes was familiar to him with regard to the date? He sat in the driving-seat, making no attempt, for the time being, to start the Crossley. "May the eighth." It was a Wednesday, wasn't it? Where the devil had he been that afternoon? With whom had he been? Wasn't that the afternoon that he had turned from Henrietta Street into Southampton Street and had bought a so-called evening paper just outside the establishment of Samuel French, Ltd.? What the deuce had been the excitement?

In the hope of success, he resorted to his habit of mental visualization; the habit that had served him so well so many times in the past. The process of "mental photography", as an offshoot of the power of visual remembrance, was one that he cultivated assiduously. Bathurst had understood from his infancy almost, that the memory needs development like every other human attribute. All gifts and powers are given to us in a state of imperfection, and their growth is brought about by education and training. Memory is no exception to this rule. It wants work. It atrophies from want of use. He closed his eyes and thought hard. After a little time of intense concentration he brought the scene back to him.

The youth from whom he had bought the paper had carried a contents bill in front of him. Its yellow colour and heavy black type gradually strayed back to the retina of his mental visualization. Almost immediately with the success of this reminiscence, the actual words of the type were revived. Alas—completely unsatisfactorily! The words on the placard had been nothing more nor less than "Chester Cup! Result!" Anthony shook his head in impatient annoyance. This was all wrong!

There was a link missing from his chain somewhere!

He felt certain of that fact. What was the association that so persistently eluded him? If he could only come to it, and thereby wrest the marrow out of that last line, he was confident that the other lines would present a much easier problem. He leant forward and restarted the car. For he knew now that the association that he sought so eagerly would refuse to come to him as the result of prolonged effort. The tricks of his own memory were like that. When the association did come (as he knew it ultimately would), it would come wantonly and whimsically. It would float or frolic to him on a stray fugitive wind, or on an unexpected breeze from an entirely unlooked-for direction. Sooner or later? That was the question, and unhappily much depended on the answer thereto.

The car made its way down the hill. The way was clear, and Anthony Bathurst trod on the juice and allowed it to gather healthy speed. As he rounded the corner, just before the approach to the "Red Stag", he came upon a small knot of people who had stayed their respective steps at the cross-roads to gaze earnestly upwards.

Anthony Bathurst's ear caught the words of one of the men as he slowed down the pace of the car to take the turn with care and comfort. For a moment his mind tossed the words over carelessly and lazily, as it will do when it is semi-receptive. Then, in a staggering, blinding second, his whole mental equipment tautened and held fast. He could see—not the placard that the seller of papers had carried in front of him on the eighth of May last but the staring headlines of the front page of the paper itself. And in that precious second the sinister meaning of the phrase, "the death parade", was at once made clear to him! Of course! He pictured the scene in all its changes. Trout, flying from justice on the way to Worthing, and by a trick of fate made intimate with the whole ghastly tragedy. Trout—with no time to spare! Trout, at his wits' end for a suitable hiding-place! Anthony Bathurst peered closely into the picture, and the shades of the various colours thereof were seen, recognized, and understood by him. As a consequence, the "Red Stag" seemed a far pleasanter place to him than it had done an hour previously.

# Chapter XXIV
# THE HOUSE IN JUBILEE STREET

WHEN THE indefatigable Baddeley, armed with his warrant, turned his attention to the house in Jubilee Street, Stepney, that he had favoured with his esteemed patronage on a previous occasion, he was in distinguished company. For the wisdom of the Commissioner, Brigadier-General Sir Austin Mostyn Kemble, had decreed that it should be so. Chief Inspector MacMorran, in charge of the party, accompanied Baddeley, and the two other plainclothes men who made up the personnel of the adventure had been specially picked for the purpose. Two fast cars from the Yard, detailed from the Flying Squad, slithered into the Mile End Road and sped relentlessly on their journey. It was early in the morning when the job was done, and London was only half-awake. I remember the morning ever so well. The white fog, that had been threatening for some days, had come into its own, gathered in force, and closed hungrily round the city. It was particularly aggressive in the vicinity of the London Hospital, and the Yard cars were obliged to diminish their pace as they passed the hospital itself. MacMorran had decided upon a morning raid in this instance because he considered that he had more chance of preserving the "surprise" element during the early hours than during the late. It was bitterly cold, for the white fog had a powerful ally in a keen white frost. How often the two hunt hand in hand!

"Baddeley," said MacMorran, "there's more in all this than meets the eye. Sir Austin Kemble, on his own admission to me, has spent more than one sleepless night over the business. When I hear the old man quoting advice about 'delays being dangerous' and 'procrastination being the thief of time', I ask myself, 'are things what they seem, or is visions about?'"

Inspector Baddeley fingered his neat little moustache. "Yes, sir. I understand your point of view, sir. But I guess Mr. Bathurst's been prodding him for a day or two now. The Commissioner knows well enough that when Bathurst sings out 'action', he's well advised to show a leg and get busy. I'm pretty certain in my own mind that Mr. B. doesn't like the affair a little bit. You can understand the hole a bullet makes, or a proper fourpenny dent in a bloke's head, but when it comes to such things as teeth-marks that are hardly visible to the naked eye and—" Baddeley shrugged his shoulders in eloquent resignation.

Chief Inspector MacMorran caressed his chin in consideration. "This 'Flame' Lampard's been asking for it for a long time. That's all it comes to in the long run, you know, Baddeley. Reminds me of the hymn I used to sing when I was a choir-boy. 'The cry goes up how long.' This Lampard's been screaming for a few years now. If it hasn't been 'snide', it's been other things."

Baddeley nodded. "So I've heard, sir. What do you make of Willmott's report? Anything in it, do you think?"

"How do you mean?"

"Any truth in it?"

"Depends how you look at it."

Baddeley looked puzzled. "Sorry, but I don't—"

MacMorran smiled the slow, exasperating smile that had been known to annoy Sir Austin Kemble. "Well, the source is authentic, you can bet on that. Willmott's a thundering good man, and if we get a 'squeak' that comes directly through to him, I can tell you, Baddeley, we listen to it. There's more than one 'nose' who supplies him. As to this story of the strange noise that is supposed to be coming from Luke Morton's place of a night—well, it seems to me that it might be anything."

Baddeley leant over to him and spoke very quietly. "How about an animal of some kind? Has that possibility struck you?"

"Thinking of 'Flame' Lampard's past—eh?" Baddeley nodded. "Perhaps. But I should be inclined to doubt it. Don't think the place is big enough, for one thing. There's not a lot of room down there." MacMorran paused, to proceed almost immediately. "No, Baddeley, I shall expect to find that the explanation is a simple one. And I'll bet you, you'll find that I'm right." As he spoke, they felt the car swing on the turn. MacMorran leant over a little and rubbed the moisture from the window with the back of his hand. "Here we are, Baddeley. Jubilee Street, as I thought. See that little shop over there?" He pointed across the street, and his companion nodded. "That's where half the girls of the East End hire their wedding-dresses. Trust them not to throw money away if there's half a chance not to. And it's a Scotsman that's telling you—remember that. God! what a testimonial! Stick your head out of the window and wave Raddon's car to slow down behind us. I don't want the news to get round that the 'busys' are about."

Baddeley did as he had been directed, and an answering hand indicated understanding and obedience. A minute later the two cars slunk almost silently to the kerb; Baddeley looked out, and the prospect pleased him, although more than man was vile. There wasn't a soul to be seen outside Paradise Villa, which was, to him, on this errand, entirely as it should have been. He slipped out of the car in the wake of the Chief Inspector. Raddon and Thwaites, the two other men, ranged themselves at his side. MacMorran raised Mr. Luke Morton's knocker and pounded on the door, and the noise that he made resounded throughout the squalid street, loud and vibrant on the sensitive winter air. "At the gates of Paradise," thought the tactful Baddeley to himself with a strange mental twist, "and St. Peter a heavy sleeper, who requires no reference to the excellence of my Rhode Island Reds."

A wait of twenty seconds produced no answer whatever to MacMorran's knock. Stepping resolutely to the door again, the Chief Inspector pounded a second time with the ugly knocker.

"What about the back?" whispered Baddeley, cautious as ever. MacMorran shook his head.

"There's no get-away, if that's what you're fretting about. There's a blank wall at the rear that runs along for some considerable distance. It's high, too. A cat couldn't scale it." He went close to the door, put his ear to it and listened for any sounds of movement or reply.

Baddeley watched him anxiously. Judged by his face and general attitude, he could hear nothing. MacMorran stiffened and jerked his head towards Thwaites.

"Thwaites—and you, Raddon! Put your shoulders to this door. With me. Altogether."

As he spoke, a strange impulse came to Baddeley, for which, had he been asked there and then, he would have been unable to account. The door had a big black knob, just below its middle, and an unusual mental prompting caused Baddeley to extend his hand to it and grasp it before Raddon and Thwaites found time to move to MacMorran's side. To his utter astonishment, the door opened as his hands held the knob and gently pushed it.

A dirty and by no means sweet-smelling passage was before them, and MacMorran looked at Baddeley, his eyes full of surprise.

"Who'd have thought it, Baddeley? The place is as empty as an Irishman's money-box. I'll bet a packet that our birds have flown. Still—we'll see. Follow me, men. And close the door. Although I had to run the risk of it just now, I'm not exactly clamouring for a crowd."

The Chief Inspector entered with Baddeley at his heels, and Thwaites and Raddon followed just behind. No sound whatever came to greet them from the recesses of the establishment. The empty front room had evidently been used at some time in the past for the purpose of meals, for its general arrangement, with wooden pew-like compartments, was similar to that of a fourth-rate eating-house. There were no obvious traces, however, of anything like a recent meal. At the back of this room was a dirty kitchen that communicated with an even more squalid scullery. In these two rooms, no doubt, the various meals had been prepared and cooked.

"Be careful," cried MacMorran, "we're going upstairs. Be as quiet as you can. I think it's empty, but you never know in these places."

The four men ascended the rickety stairs. The upper part of the house had been turned into a number of small cubicles. They were all empty. Thwaites and Raddon went through them carefully and methodically. "It's a doss-house, Baddeley," explained MacMorran, "and they probably made money out of it, too. 'A tanner a night' touch, I expect. That's what it looks like to me."

Two of the bigger cubicles showed signs of fairly recent occupation, for in one a newspaper that wrapped up two dirty and threadbare soft collars, lay on the bed, and in the other, tossed on the floor, lay a pair of very muddy and almost worn-out brown shoes.

"You're quite right about the birds having flown, sir," observed Baddeley. "It seems to me that there's been another 'squeak' besides the one that fell on your ears."

MacMorran grunted. The grunt was non-committal—almost evasive.

Baddeley, mildly reproachful, continued his effort. "What is there here, either, for a man to get his hooks into? There seems to be nothing in the nature of a private room where there might be papers and such-like. Where's the H.Q.? The confidential part? See my meaning?"

MacMorran crossed over to the bed, took the two soft collars from the newspaper and looked at them. "I see your meaning all right, Baddeley. But whatever was here of the like you mention—papers and so on—went with the birds. You can bet on that quite safely." He turned to Thwaites, who had appeared in the doorway behind them. "Well, Thwaites, got anything?"

"Nothing in any of the cubicles up here, sir. Not a sign of life anywhere. Raddon and I have been all over the top floor."

MacMorran pushed past him and beckoned to Baddeley to follow. "We'll see what's in the lower regions, then. It's just possible we might hit up against something down there. Thwaites! You and Raddon come down with me and Inspector Baddeley, and watch out."

The four men descended the stairs. Two steps from the bottom, Baddeley stopped and caught MacMorran by the arm. "What's that?"

"What?" demanded MacMorran. "For Heaven's sake don't get jumpy."

"I heard a noise of some kind. Seemed to my ear to come from under these stairs somewhere."

"I heard nothing," declared MacMorran curtly. Thwaites, however, ranged himself with Baddeley. "Begging your pardon, sir," he announced to his own immediate chief, "but I fancy I heard some sort of a noise, sir. So did Raddon, sir."

Baddeley held up his hand and made a suggestion to MacMorran. "Let's keep quiet, sir, for a second, as we are. Stop here on the stairs. We may hear it again. If we do, it will settle the argument once and for all."

The four men stopped on the stairs, MacMorran with one foot on the last stair and with the other foot in the passage itself. With their heads half-inclined they listened. The seconds went by, and MacMorran was just about to shake his head in final dismissal of Baddeley's contention, when the latter clutched his arm again.

"There you are. There it is again. Didn't you hear it that time?"

There was no mistaking the truth of Baddeley's statement, and the Chief Inspector nodded his head in curt agreement. A heavy dragging sound came to them from somewhere below the stairs. It was as though a heavy body was either moving or being moved with some degree of difficulty. Simultaneously with the noise reaching him, Baddeley felt the cold clutch of fear at his heart. He was not a nervous man by any means; on the other hand rather, he was a man with a strong fund of courage and a very resourceful brain. When he saw a difficulty or danger, it was his habit to face it with determination and resolution. At the moment, however, his imagination took possession of him, and for a half-space of time, rode rough-shod over his fortitude and dominated him with its tyranny. The story of the strange noise that had been reported to have been heard coming from Luke Morton's place at night, and the association with an unknown animal that he himself had suggested, came flooding back to him and engulfed his brain. He has since confided to me that he thought of Anthony Bathurst, of me, of my uncle's murder, of the death of Hoad, and of the ghastly "triple bite".

MacMorran's voice roused him to action, however, and the clouds of Baddeley's misgivings were instantly blown away. "Make sure the yard's clear before we go down anywhere, Raddon, will you? You and Thwaites look round there, and then report to me. I'm taking no chances. Jump to it, men."

The two men named dashed off to their task.

Baddeley edged towards MacMorran and whispered what was in his heart. "What about that yarn now, sir? There's something down there somewhere, dragging itself about. I'm certain that's the sound I heard. I don't like it, Chief."

"I don't like it any more than you do, Baddeley. But I've a revolver here that talks the same language to anything or anybody. As soon as Raddon and Thwaites come back, I'm going down. So get ready to—"

"To what? I'm coming with you." As he spoke the two other men returned.

"It's all clear out there, sir. Nothing to worry about. The yard's absolutely empty."

MacMorran nodded and advanced, revolver in hand, to what evidently was the door that led to the cellar. Baddeley followed him. The senior man opened the cellar door and turned to Thwaites. "You and Raddon stay here. There's no room for more than two of us at the top of these stairs. If we want you, we'll call. If we have time, that is," he concluded grimly.

MacMorran and Baddeley descended the stairs with every care. Unfortunately, neither had brought a torch. Each had considered that he would be acting under conditions of daylight, and had in consequence carelessly neglected the obvious precaution. The cellar, however, was fairly wide and spacious, and a broad stream of light was by now filtering through to it from an opening above. Baddeley, from his position behind MacMorran, could see an old broken table in front of him, and when his eyes got more accustomed to the comparative absence of light, they were able to pick out an untidy heap of coal that lay in the extreme left-hand corner of the cellar. In the other corner was piled a heap of broken chairs that seemed, any minute, to be on the point of toppling over. As he looked, he heard the dragging, shuffling sound again, and his heart seemed to stand still. But MacMorran's burly form was still in front of him, and he was unable to see perfectly the precise spot from where the noise came.

Suddenly, however, a cry from the Chief Inspector brought him reassurance. In this reassurance, courage was born again. For the cry, sharp though it was, was a cry of understanding, relief, and sympathy. There was no note of fear or dread in it, and Baddeley, seeing MacMorran dash forward, followed suit at once, willingly and hopefully. An iron staple had been driven into the floor of the cellar, and a man sat there lashed to it. The ropes that held him were bound round his body, but his hands, although the wrists were tied together, were in front of him and had not been tied behind his back. This had been done, obviously, that he could drink from an enamel jug of water that had been placed in front of him, and eat when he wished from a tray of bread and cheese that was at his side. As he shuffled his legs back from the latter, Baddeley heard again the noise that had first attracted his attention. MacMorran rushed to the man's assistance and rapidly and skilfully cut through the bonds that had held him. This done, he sought explanation.

"Who are you?" he cried. "Are you all right? Not hurt or anything?"

A tremor ran through the man's frame as he rose to his feet to reply to MacMorran's questions. He looked wildly round and passed a trembling hand across his forehead. "My name is Douglas Cameron," he replied. "I'm the nephew of the Colonel Cameron who was found dead at Dallow Corner in Sussex. The woman here has shown me the newspapers. I've been here weeks, I think—at any rate, it seems like weeks. I was tricked and brought here."

"Are you all right?" Baddeley heard MacMorran ask again.

"I think so," replied the young man as he staggered to his feet and weakly tried to square his shoulders. "Except for a few scratches, perhaps, and a bruise or two."

Chapter XXV
# THE HAND ON THE SILL

AT A quarter-past eleven that same night (or rather, on the night of the same day) I was awakened by a peremptory tapping on my bedroom door.

"Who is it?" I asked.

The answer came at once. "Me, Lois. Put something on, Cecilia, quick, and open the door. Don't make a noise. I want you."

I obeyed. I slipped on a *négligée*, and trembling a little, I opened my bedroom door to let her in. "Whatever's the matter?" I gasped.

Lois slipped inside the room noiselessly and put her finger to her lips. "Ssh, Cecilia! Don't make a noise, whatever you do. I think we're in danger again."

I went still colder at her words. Already cold, I positively shivered. Nigel had gone back to Town directly after tea, on business which he said couldn't possibly wait; Hardy was on a day's leave again. We were four women in the bungalow, and two of us old, at that.

"Tell me, Lois," I said with urgent emphasis. "What's going on?"

She came quite close to me. "There's a man or men outside the bungalow. I heard him—or them. You know what quick ears I've got, Cecilia. I was lying awake, you see. I heard the noise of a car first. Then I heard a man's footstep. He came up the road, I'm certain, and then turned in the front gate. He was trying to make as little noise as possible, but being awake, I heard him. And I'm almost certain he's worked round to the back of the place. I think he'll try to get in by what's happened previously."

I didn't like the sound of this a little bit. "How long ago was this, Lois?" I demanded of her. "Five minutes?"

"Hardly that. I slid straight out of bed, Cecilia. Didn't waste a second."

I reflected. "The back of the place"—the phrase that she had used—seemed to me to hold an ominous sound. "He may be inside by now," I said fearfully.

She nodded. "I know."

"Where's Aunt Elspeth?" I asked.

"Asleep—or at least she was when I left her. Don't let's wake her."

I plucked up the sorry remains of my mangled courage. "Well, there's nothing for it, Lois," I declared. "It's up to you and me."

She nodded again. Although I was trembling like an aspen leaf and my hands definitely shaking, I walked across to a drawer in my dressing-table. I had put Uncle Ian's revolver in there the day previously, little thinking that I, of all people, should need it so immediately.

"Stand by me, Lois," I said, "and don't scream if I have to fire. And may God have mercy on us born."

We stole out of the room—a craven couple, I fear—and before we had gone two paces I realized how helpless we were without a light of some kind. To switch on the electric light might court disaster, and yet, if our antagonist commanded the use of light, and we were without it, we were equally badly placed. It was too late, however, to turn back, even if I had known where to lay my hands on a torch, so we crept forward along the corridor. Lois kept a foot or so behind me, and seeing the position, I don't know that I blamed her. Gradually, step by step, stopping at the slightest whisper of a noise, we came to the room that Mrs. Veitch used for cooking, and which was the end room on this side of the bungalow. No sound came from it, and Lois plucked the growth fear from both our hearts and impulsively pushed down the switch of the electric light. The room was empty and the window shut and fastened. We gazed at each other, trying, I think, to read each other's thoughts. Had our visitor effected an entrance at the back of the bungalow, he must use the window at which we were looking. There was no other that was either convenient or practical. My bravery, such as it was, returned to me.

"You were mistaken, Lois," I declared, with a fine show of courage. "If you heard anybody, he didn't come round this way. Now what do you say?"

She wrinkled her brows in an attempt to readjust the conditions. "I heard him, Cecilia. And I'm certain he came round here.

It's possible, you know, even now. Perhaps he tried to force this window and failed."

It was my turn to shake my head. "If he had wanted to get in, Lois, that window wouldn't have prevented him. I'm inclined to think that you may have been—" Before I could finish what I had been about to say, Lois held up her hand to me authoritatively.

"Hark," she cried softly. "What was that?"

It was quite true that there had been a slight sound. I had heard it, as she had. But I couldn't have said what it was, what had prompted it, or where was its exact location. My nerves began to get the better of me again, but before they had time to overwhelm me, a flash of intuition lit up my brain and galvanized me into action. I suddenly remembered the room where my uncle's body had lain. I remembered the importance with which Anthony Bathurst had invested the changed position of its furniture. And Nigel Strachan had told me what Bathurst had said to him on the night that he had run into him in the darkness. If anybody got into the bungalow, surely it would be that room to which he or she would go. I made up my mind and pulled Lois's sleeve.

"The lounge," I whispered. "You were right, after all. He's gone round to the front, whoever he is."

Before she could answer me, I began to creep my way back, and as I turned, I could hear Lois following me. When I reached the objective, I opened the door, and the strange idea possessed me that my uncle was inside waiting to greet me as I stepped across the threshold into the darkness. His body had lain therein, and although it had been taken away, it was as though his spirit had shaken off its earthly garment and refused to leave the place where he had been.

"Get against the wall, Lois," I whispered as we entered, "one of us on either side. We shan't be seen so easily."

She obeyed me instantaneously, and we each flattened a trembling self against either wall. It was a little lighter at the front of the bungalow than it had been at the back, and I dragged a crumb of comfort therefrom. Suddenly I heard the sharp intake of Lois Fletcher's breath. She had slipped round to the left-hand wall in order to take up her position, and, in consequence of this, commanded the right-hand window, whereas my better view was of the window on the left-hand side. The noise of her breathing caused me to look sharply in her direction, and I was amazed to see her right hand outstretched and pointing towards the window that of the two she could the better see.

"Cecilia," she whispered almost inaudibly—"quick, dear, your revolver. There's a man there. Look by the window. I saw his figure crouch there, and I saw the shadow of a movement as he turned towards this way."

The hand that held my revolver shook horribly, but I took two paces forward and craned my head to see. What I saw in the darkest patch beneath the window set my pulses racing and my heart thudding like a hammer. And when my eyes looked again, they lit on something even more terrifying. There was a man's hand on the edge of the sill. Its fingers were long and lean. Then I flung caution to the winds of heaven.

"Who's there?" I cried defiantly, but the defiance, I fear, was rooted in timorousness, and if ever a girl was craven, she was Cecilia Mary Cameron at that moment. For the infinitesimal fraction of a second there was (to me) a paralysing, stupefying silence. I don't know what I expected to happen, but I know that I was prepared for almost anything. Then a well-known and gloriously welcome voice said: "Don't shoot, Miss Cameron—and a thousand apologies for disturbing you," and Anthony Bathurst vaulted over the sill into the room in front of me.

## Chapter XXVI

## MR. BATHURST TOASTS
## SOME CHEESE

"You frightened us," I gasped. "I know it's perfectly silly of me, but—"

"The boot's on the other foot. It was silly of me, Miss Cameron, but I hoped to get in without you knowing. I had to risk it, you see, and I've failed. Good evening, Miss Fletcher. I owe you an apology, too. Please accept it."

Lois bowed rather distantly, I thought, and I walked across to the wall to switch on the light. An imperious gesture, however, from Anthony Bathurst checked me.

"No, Miss Cameron, please. Not for a moment. No more light than we have, if you please. I'm practically certain that there's no danger for the time being, but in spite of that, I don't propose to take any risks."

"Lois heard you," I explained. "It wasn't I. She has better ears than I have. She came to my room and woke me up."

Anthony Bathurst frowned at my explanation. "Where's Strachan, then? Isn't he here?"

"He had to return to Town on urgent business."

"What an ass I am," he muttered. "I thought he was still here at Dallow Corner. Miss Cameron, I ought to be kicked. I would never have risked coming here as I did had I known that you ladies were, to all intents and purposes, alone. You must forgive me my miscalculation. Particularly you Miss Fletcher."

"Why particularly me, Mr. Bathurst?" flashed back Lois with frigidity in her voice.

Anthony Bathurst's face lit up with one of his irresistible smiles. "For disturbing your night's rest. You disturbed Miss Cameron yourself."

"Because of you," she retorted.

"You weren't to know that it was I." He turned to me. "Take me into the other room, Miss Cameron, please! I want to talk to you. We can have a light in there."

We all three went to the dining-room and I put the screens in position. Anthony Bathurst sought a comfortable chair, and seating himself in it, leant forward to me with an earnestness that was unmistakable. "Has it struck you yet how I managed to get in, Miss Cameron?"

I stared and realized my abject foolishness. "Why—no. But of course, the window should have been—" I stopped and looked helplessly at Lois.

"If you look at the window through which I came, you will see that the handle of the catch inside has been unscrewed. It is a comparatively simple matter to insert a knife from the outside and gradually ease the window open."

"How did you know that, Mr. Bathurst?" asked Lois with an almost ominous quietness.

He smiled at the probe. "I happened to notice it when I was here on a previous occasion, Miss Fletcher. Quite a simple explanation, isn't it?"

But it all left me amazed and wondering. "Did you say 'unscrewed' on the *inside*?" I demanded of him.

"On the *inside*, Miss Cameron," he repeated with insistence. "That's just the point."

"Then it must have been done by somebody in this bungalow. Which is absolutely absurd. Don't you see? It can't be any of—"

"It is tremendously helpful. It establishes a definite position. It was unscrewed by somebody inside this bungalow. Believe me, of that fact there isn't the shadow of a doubt. We will, however, let it pass at this stage of the case, for a very good reason. We shall be in a position to discuss it more fully when we lay our hands on the guilty person." He spoke very quietly, but there was a ring of sincerity and truth in his words that Lois recognized as well as I. Anthony Bathurst went on. "I wanted to see you about three things, Miss Cameron. They are, all three of them, almost equally urgent." He looked at me queryingly.

"Yes," I answered, "tell me what they are."

"The first is excessively ordinary. I am leaving Dallow Corner— the 'Red Stag'—as soon as I leave here to-night. I'm just going up for my traps and then I'm clearing. Understand?"

"You mean that you are going away?"

"Exactly. That's just what I do mean. I've told the 'Red Stag' people. Mrs. Hoad knows. She'll have everything ready for me. And you will tell all your people to-morrow. All the people with whom I've come into contact. Tell everybody concerned that I shall be away for a day or two. Perhaps for a week. Is that clear?"

"Perfectly," I replied. "I will do exactly as you ask me. What else do you want to see me about?"

"Point number two is more simple even than point number one was. Is there a florist's near here? Think hard, Miss Cameron."

I wrinkled my brows in an attempt to remember.

"A shop that sells flowers, do you mean?"

"Not necessarily. A nurseryman, for instance, would fill the bill just as well."

Lois came to the rescue. "Of course," she contributed. "There's that big nursery on the left of the Quoynings road. Don't you remember, Cecilia?" Anthony Bathurst seized on the information with avidity. "I thought so, Miss Fletcher. I fancy I remember passing the place you mention in my car only yesterday. It looked like a nursery to me as I careered by, but you can't always be sure of these things!"

"And the third matter that you came about?"

He was silent for a little while. When he found words they were gravely and quietly spoken. "I want you to go back to bed—you and Miss Fletcher. When you've done that, I want to spend—say half an hour—in the room that we've just left. I don't think it will mean more than half an hour." As he concluded, he smiled at us rather whimsically. "I assure you, Miss Cameron, that I shan't do any damage. Irreparable damage, that is."

"I am sure of that," I answered him, "and it shall be as you say. Come on, Lois. We will leave Mr. Bathurst to the devices and desires of his own heart."

"Thank you. And I will undo one or two things that ought to be undone. Stay, though. Before you go, Miss Cameron."

"Yes?" I queried.

"Tell me this, please. Did Strachan say anything definite about coming back?"

"No. Just that it was necessary for him to go to Town—that was all. Why?"

He ignored the question, and his general appearance gave me the idea that he was endeavouring to solve something that had been perplexing him. His next remark, however, caused me a considerable amount of surprise. "It's quite on the cards, Miss Cameron, that you will hear something of your cousin in the morning. At any rate, I have high hopes. I'll leave it at that."

"Douglas?"

"Douglas."

"Is he safe, then, and well?"

"You must remember that I know nothing. I am merely basing my statements on the science of deduction and giving colour to certain suspicions. But if you will allow me the privilege of prophecy, I will venture to assert that he will be found to be safe and comparatively well." He came over to the two of us and extended his hand. "Good night, Miss Cameron. Good night, Miss Fletcher."

I took the hand that he held out to me and Lois did likewise. "Good night, then, Mr. Bathurst," I heard her say, "I'm cold, tired, and only just recovering from what was close to sheer fright, so I'll gladly accept your instructions and go to bed. Good-bye—or should it be *au 'voir*!"

"It will most certainly be *au 'voir*, Miss Fletcher. With the goodwill of the gods, that is, of course."

She waved her hand to him as she made her exit, and I turned to follow her. But the voice of Anthony Bathurst called me back. He spoke very quietly, but with tremendous earnestness. "To-morrow morning, Miss Cameron, I want you to lock the door of the front room and keep the key. On no account whatever, allow that key to go out of your own possession. Understand me—on no pretext at all. Go to bed comparatively early to-morrow evening, and prevail upon everybody here to do the same. And don't 'panic' if you should hear noises in the night. I will give you my word of honour that if you obey my instructions implicitly, no harm will come to you. Please trust me. Now I must be off to that other room of yours. I don't want to be long. I expect my engine's too cold already to be good for it."

"Where are you going to afterwards?" I asked him. "To London?"

"Later on. I have an inquiry to make of our friend the nurseryman on the left of the Quoynings road, and a purchase to make at an establishment something like a toy-shop, perhaps. For you must understand, Miss Cameron, that I cannot shut my eyes to the one fact that stands out very plainly. Our antagonist is singularly clever, completely unscrupulous, and will stick at nothing to achieve the desired purpose. I am therefore forced to choose my weapons with the utmost care. 'Weapons' is certainly the word, Miss Cameron. Good-bye, and be brave."

He turned quickly into the lounge, and I walked silently and thoughtfully back to bed. Twenty minutes later, a minute's rapid thought brought Anthony Bathurst to the decision that he would spend the night in the Crossley, and after a run of approximately half an hour, he came to a side lane that he considered eminently suited to his purpose. As he turned the car and then brought it to a standstill, his thoughts mechanically reverted to the last occasion when he had spent a night somewhat similarly. He pulled the rugs round him, and remembered his drive from the Rectory of Kirve St. Laudus to the main station of Exeborough, to stage the last scenes in the matter of the Walsingham inheritance, which ended so dramatically at the mouth of the abandoned "Talisman" mine. It had been touch and go then. Who knew that it might not also be touch and go on the night of the morrow? He had always possessed the invaluable gift of snatching sleep from the dregs of discomfort, and although the night was cold, with a sharp frost, the heavy rugs gave him considerable warmth, and the interior of the Crossley was far removed from such a condition as that just mentioned.

When he awoke, the hands of his wrist-watch showed the time to be ten minutes past seven. He reflected on things generally. What he had to do first, and then, what he had to accomplish afterwards. Breakfast, a wash, and a shave were at least an hour away, for in the meantime there was the nurseryman on the Quoynings road to be seen and—if the fates were kind—questioned. Nurserymen rose early—he would go there at once.

Mr. Bathurst reversed the car and travelled back swiftly along the Quoynings road. The nurseryman, according to his advertisement on a board that showed in the front garden, Robert Croft, was up betimes in scrupulous attendance upon his hot-water pipes. Mr. Bathurst took out his pocket-book, and from there his visiting-card and a slip of paper. He had taken the precautions to write his message beforehand. The nurseryman took the card that Bathurst offered him, and his face wrinkled itself in surprise.

Then he wiped his hands on the corners of his apron and said simply: "I am at your service, sir. What is it that I can do for you?"

"That's very good of you, Mr. Croft," replied Mr. Bathurst. "Let me tell you that I appreciate your kindness. First of all, am I right to assume that you are the nearest nurseryman to Dallow Corner?"

"I'm more than that, sir," answered Croft sturdily. "I am the only nurseryman within five miles of Dallow Corner. And thank God for it. If there was another, there'd be one more to add to the ranks of the unemployed. As things are—the cost of 'em and so on—there's only a frugal living here, sir. Beyond tomatoes and—"

"I'm sorry," returned Bathurst. "Times are bad, I know, and I hope things will improve. It's always the darkest hour before the dawn, you know. Anyhow, you've told me what I wanted to know. Now tell me something else, if you can. I'm seeking information concerning the 'Florence Iris'. If you prefer it, *Calamus Aromaticus*. Know anything about it?"

Croft grinned at his questioner. "Don't recognize it by its highbrow description, but I'm fairly well acquainted with what you called it at first, the 'Florence Iris'."

"Good," rejoined Anthony Bathurst. "Now to dig a little deeper—got any on the premises?"

"I have."

"Better still. Sold any recently?"

"I have. More than one lot, too. I grow and keep things to sell 'em."

"Best of all," returned Bathurst. He held the slip of paper, that he had previously taken from his pocket-book, for the nurseryman to read. "What have you to say about that, Croft?" he asked. Anthony Bathurst waited for the nurseryman's answer with an anxiety the equal of which he had seldom felt. For, out of it, the edifice that he had erected either stood gloriously or fell ignominiously. Croft read the words that Bathurst had written, and turned to him to give his answer.

"Only one thing, sir. You're absolutely right. But I don't know how you know. The second lot was sent early this month, sir."

"Perfection, Croft." Mr. Bathurst slipped a currency note to the value of ten shillings into the man's hand. "A little alleviation of the cost of living, Croft, and may all other nurserymen respect the five-mile limit for ever. Many thanks for your information."

The primrose-wheeled Crossley gathered speed in the near distance, and Robert Croft, nurseryman, looking after it, and then at the note in his hand, shook his head wonderingly.

*　*　*　*　*

The day that followed Anthony Bathurst's departure from Dallow Corner was the longest, I think, that I have ever spent. My uncle was to be buried on the morning of the day after and, so far, despite what Bathurst had told me, I had received no further word from either my cousin or Nigel Strachan. Major Neale and Mr. Armstrong called in the morning, and to my astonishment informed me that "Flame" Lampard, with his two associates and consummate audacity, had once again arrived at the "Red Stag". Neale had seen him enter the coffee-room and heard him give an order. "He has a curious wooden box affair with him," added the Major. "He hangs on to it like grim death, and won't let it out of his sight. Bathurst's gone back to Town, I hear."

"Yes," I answered somewhat listlessly.

"For what reason, do you know?"

"Not exactly, but it's to do with this affair down here, no doubt."

"Bit disappointing for you, isn't it?" persisted Neale. "How long's he away for?"

"Two or three days, I believe, and I'm *not* disappointed."

"I like to hear you say that, Miss Cameron," said Mr. Armstrong. "It shows loyalty, if nothing else. Give the man a chance, Neale. You can't expect him to work miracles in twenty-four hours."

"I wouldn't mind so much if he didn't expect to himself," replied Neale, a faint smile showing on the corners of his mouth. "There's one thing about our friend Bathurst—he's not lost for self-confidence." Neither of them would accept my invitation to lunch, and the day wore on through afternoon till evening. More than once I found myself wondering how long a day seemed to a murderer in the condemned cell. Somewhere about six o'clock a wind began to spring up, and it howled round the bungalow with always increasing ferocity. The evening dragged its interminable length, and its minutes seemed to crawl through my brain on hands of lethargy. At half-past nine I announced my intention of going to bed, and was successful at once in obtaining the cordial agreement of all the others. I went to my bedroom, and I hadn't been there two minutes when there came a ring at the bell. I answered it myself, and took the telegram that it had heralded, with eager hands. It was from my cousin Douglas. "Am quite well, don't worry. Expect me shortly."

So Bathurst was right in his conjecture, after all! Douglas was all right. Would Bathurst be as right in the other directions? I began to retrace my steps towards my bedroom. Suddenly I stopped, and acting on the impulse of the moment, I did a mad and foolish thing. Something for which I have never quite forgiven myself, and do not think I ever shall. Taking the key of the front room that I had kept to myself all day, I unlocked the door and entered the room. What prompted me to do this, I know not, except perhaps that I had a wild and overmastering desire to see this thing through off my own bat. I looked at my watch. The time was ten minutes to ten. The moon was high in the sky, and the wind was still whining through the trees like a banshee in pain. As I listened, the continual sough of it came into my ears. Then, for some inexplicable reason, I crouched in the corner of the room and waited. Waited for I knew not what!

## Chapter XXVII
## THE THING THAT FLEW

For half an hour at least, I suppose, I crouched there in complete silence, save for the sound of the wind in the trees, and the feeling was gradually coming home to me of the utterness of my folly. For all I knew, I had not only placed myself in personal danger, but I was also endangering the success of Anthony Bathurst's general plans. He had said that we were dealing with an antagonist that would stick at nothing to achieve success, and here was I behaving like a silly, hysterical schoolgirl. More than that,

I, a soldier's daughter, and another soldier's niece, was actually disobeying orders on the field of battle, as it were, spiritually if not literally. The thing was unforgivable, and I knew it. Was it too late for me to return to my bedroom and put matters right? I had just decided "no", and that I would go back there at once, when I realized with a sickening feeling of dread that it *was* too late. Almost coincidentally with my making up my mind, I heard a soft, light step outside. It was an unusual step. It was not quite normal. It seemed to drag a little, and I was far from sure whether I had ever heard it before. I thought of the window with the defective catch-handle, and began to wonder whether Bathurst had repaired it during the time that he had spent in here alone. I was soon to know, for the dragging step came close up to that very window of Bathurst's interest, and I heard the knife being inserted in the same manner that Bathurst had described to me. Had I not already heard that ominous step, I might have been able to persuade myself that it was Bathurst himself who had returned again to the bungalow, but the step contradicted that idea, and told me with eloquent and terrifying certainty, that there was no hope for me of that. I heard the creak of the window as it was gradually pushed open with something, I suppose, like a knife, and then, horror of horrors, I heard somebody step over the sill into the room. And there was I, crouching in the darkness of the corner holding my breath! All I could see was a shadowy form that crept stealthily and strangely into the middle of the room and then dragged the table to a certain position there. It was a man! I could tell that. He was dressed in very dark clothes and black hat and had a strip of black felt across his face with holes cut for eyelets. I saw him move a hand, feel in his pocket, and produce an electric torch. My knees trembled violently as the realization came home to me that I must be on the very verge of his discovery. What could there be to save me? But the Gods were kind, for, by a marvellous stroke of luck, he trained the light upwards towards the ceiling, and never attempted in any way to sweep the corners of the room with it. The yellow beam of light struck upwards and I saw it catch and hold the crystal shade that hung round and encircled the electric light. For a brief moment he stood there, with his light poised in one hand, and with his other hand clutching the side of the table. As I watched, I registered the impression that his body was under complete control, with perfect poise and balance, and within a second or so of my forming the opinion, it received very definite confirmation, for my visitor leapt lightly on to the octagonal oak table and reached above his head with his right hand. He grasped the glass pendants of the lustre-like crystal that I have just mentioned and pulled them towards him. The hand was predatory and the whole action seemed an apotheosis of avarice; I marvelled at what the meaning of it all could be. Then things began to happen in rapid sequence. I began to like my position less than ever. The man on the table evidently heard a sound of some kind from outside, for he slid from the table like a flash, extinguished his torch and made for the corner of the room diagonally opposite to the one that I was occupying. Within a second I knew the reason of this sudden change of plan. Somebody else was on the point of entrance. The window that had been previously pushed open, and only partly closed, was smashed open by a blow from a huge fist on to its wooden frame, and a great body vaulted into the room. I knew this new-comer to be "Flame" Lampard, by reason of his bulk, and the action of the man on the table, immediately preceding his entrance, told me that they were not allies, but that there was enmity and antagonism between them. Because of this, my heart beat high with hope. When thieves fall out. . . . Lampard wasted no time whatever and apparently thought that he knew all that there was to know. He addressed himself to the shadowy figure that crouched in the corner. Although the room was dark, Lampard had obviously been in time to watch the man's movement throughout its entirety. When he spoke, however, his words amazed me, and for a moment I began to wonder if I were awake or living through a fantastic dream.

"Come out, Bathurst," he cried mockingly. "Come out and take your medicine. Skulking there won't get you anything. You're cornered and covered, my fine cockerel. For two pins, I'd shoot you where you lie, but luckily for you there's a shortage of pins this evening. Don't move that right hand, if you've no objection. Thank you! I can see you perfectly well, you know, and if you moved sus-piciously, or one of your prying fingers strayed a little, this gun of mine would most assuredly go off. And effectively at that. Put your hands up, Bathurst. Come out from there, and hand over the 'sparklers'. And don't dawdle over it, my friend. I've a date."

The man to whom the sinister invitation had been addressed, came out of his corner with his hands above his head. Although he was doing his best to keep his fingers still, they were twitch-ing with convulsive emotion. I could see that it was not Bathurst, and I wondered why Lampard had made the strange mistake that he had. The figure lacked Bathurst's physique and athletic alert-ness. I realized, however, on after reflection, that I had seen the man's figure quite plainly under the light of his own torch, where-as Lampard from his coign of vantage outside, had scarcely had time for that. Lampard backed towards the electric switch which was directly above my head as I cowered in my corner. With his revolver levelled in his right hand, he came over slowly, step by step, and without turning his head an inch towards me. On the other hand, he kept his eyes fixed relentlessly and unwaveringly on the figure in the middle of the room. Two paces or so from me, he stretched out his great left arm behind him, fumbled for the switch, found it, and flooded the room with light. The figure of his opponent gave no sign that he had seen me or was in any way aware of my presence there. He stood there, the picture of silent and unruffled impassivity. But for the fact that he had his hands up, and they twitched occasionally, there was nothing in his appearance to show that he was in any way disturbed. Then I saw him shrug his shoulders ever so slightly.

"Perhaps you will allow me to get you what you want. I assure you that I am entirely unarmed, Mr. Lampard, and that you will be running no risk whatever."

I am positive that when he heard the voice of our companion, Lampard was as astonished as I was. Once again, too, I had to persuade myself that I was fully awake. Lampard went over to him and ran his left hand over his pockets. "You haven't a gun on you—so go ahead."

The man to whom he spoke, put his hand nonchalantly to the breast pocket of his coat. Lampard held out his hand greedily, and his whole attitude was pregnant with meaning. His opponent took from his pocket something which looked to me, from the little distance I was away, like a small glass tube, such as we used to work with in "stinks" lessons at school. Lampard eyed him covetously. The man whom we watched made a curious movement, as though he were shaking the tube, when I heard a shout of horror from the window that sent my senses leaping and tumbling from me beyond recall.

"Look out, Miss Cameron! For God's sake drop on your face!"

Somehow, I did as I was bidden, and simultaneously Anthony Bathurst leapt through the window and ran frantically to my side. In his hand, he brandished what looked like a very closely-meshed butterfly-net, and looking up fearfully, I saw come through the air, straight from the other man's hand, as it were, the darting horror that had killed my uncle. There, in the room with the four of us, was the red thing that flew!

## Chapter XXVIII
# THE TRUTH OF THE TRIPLE BITE

For a palpitating moment, it seemed to me to be darting towards "Flame" Lampard, and the red-haired giant stared helplessly and hopelessly as he faced the little devil of death. Then by some strange mischance, it turned in the air (or writhed perhaps would be the better word) and flew straight for Anthony Bathurst. For another semi-paralysing moment he faced it—his grey eyes shining with the light of battle, and the deadly earnestness of a definite purpose. Then, with a rapier-like stroke of his right arm, that spoke of the accomplished fencer, he flashed the net affair at the little red object, swept his other hand across the net, and there before us all, by the work of a second, lay the little horror, writhing and squirming, but helpless and impotent in a cage of firmly and very closely-woven net. At the same second the noise of a revolver-shot rang out and the man who had held the tube and launched the horror at us, fell to the floor—a bullet through his heart.—Late—but not too late, "Flame."

Lampard had forwarded his personal contribution to the drama of the room. The noise of the shot had scarcely died away, when I heard the voice of Inspector Baddeley at Lampard's elbow and I saw that the latter's wrists wore handcuffs.

"A beautiful shot, Lampard, and timed to the second. But I want you, all the same. Over a little matter connected with, say, a Mr. Douglas Cameron. There's no need for me to warn you, is there?"

Lampard's face flamed with frightful passion and his eyes darted from the Inspector to Anthony Bathurst.

"Douglas Cameron? So, I'm double-crossed after all, eh? Tell me, then, whose is the carcase lying yonder?" He pointed to the dead man on the floor. "I've a right to know," he continued, "because mine was the hand that helped him into hell."

As he spoke, a chill of agonizing horror struck at my heart for I had a sudden sickening revelation that the whole truth was going to prove very far from the lines of our previous imagination. Anthony Bathurst seemed to sense my apprehension. He gave my arm a pat of reassurance, however, and walked across to the dead man who lay in front of us.

"I appreciated your shooting powers, Lampard, a few moments back, quite as much as did Inspector Baddeley. So don't think that I'm ungrateful. For one thing, you've saved the executioner a job. But you've made two glaring mistakes in the carrying out of your campaign. The first was when you underrated your opponent, and returned here in defiance of the warning that I gave you, and the second when you supposed that you had been double-crossed. You haven't been double-crossed at all. All that's happened to you is that you've been frustrated." He bent down to remove the black covering from the dead man's face. "I don't suppose that any one of you here, with the exception of Miss Cameron, realizes the identity of the pleasant specimen whom we have here. I only hope that it will not prove too great a shock to you."

He stooped and tore the mask from the murderer's face. "Let me introduce Mr. Ralph Armstrong—one time 'host' to a gentleman of the name of 'Trout'."

Although I had been prepared for the shock, both by reason of the illumination that had previously come to me, and by the words that Bathurst had used a moment since, I had not had very long to assimilate the truth as it was now revealed to me. My senses reeled at it and dull stupefaction gave place to a kind of questioning bewilderment.

"Haven't the pleasure of *his* acquaintance," sneered "Flame" Lampard, "and I reckon he was damned unlucky to run across my path to-night. Strange, how these things work out."

"Not so strange as you may imagine, Lampard." Bathurst's reply came curtly and crisply, and Lampard winced at its mercilessness. "I rather fancy that he must have favoured you with a little correspondence. I'm not certain about it, but I don't think I'm wrong. Otherwise the coincidence of your arrival just now was nothing less than remarkable."

"Mr. Bathurst—please explain," I gasped. "Please explain some of the truth at least. I'm in a whirl. I can't think clearly. I feel that I am just awakening from the foulness of a horrible dream." I put my hand to my head. "I'm bewildered," I concluded rather lamely. I loathe making anything in the nature of a scene, but as I spoke, Bathurst looked at me and I could see that I had his sympathy.

"I'm sorry, Miss Cameron," he remarked, "but I never thought when I laid my last plans, that you would be forced to go through what you have endured to-night. I never contemplated that anything could happen that would make it necessary for you to come down alone to this room. I suppose, however, that I misjudged the position. My apologies for the lapse. What happened to entice you down here?"

But Cecilia Mary Cameron, humiliated now, and very penitent, shook her head shamefacedly. "Nothing did happen," I confessed. "It was all my own fault. I disobeyed your orders and I'm most frightfully sorry and sick with myself. I feel that I can never look you in the face again."

He was very grave when his reply came. "It was very wrong of you, Miss Cameron. Mr. Lampard has only himself to blame, but you placed yourself, and after yourself, me, in a very deadly peril." He walked across and picked up the net that held the little red thing that he had snared. "Baddeley," he cried, "and you, Miss Cameron! Here's something here that I think none of us has ever seen before." He held up the net and we gazed at the object therein, with something approaching awe. But my awe held a shiver of fear. "That little thing there, if I'm not very much mistaken, is a particularly fine and well-nourished specimen of the flying leech of Ceylon."

"I'm just as wise," said Baddeley tersely. "And I, too," I contributed wonderingly.

Anthony Bathurst rubbed his hands at our lack of knowledge. "You mustn't think that I know very much more of the flying leech than you do. It took me a very long time indeed to reach the light. It was only when I remembered the singular case of Crosby the banker that I began to move at all."

"Is the thing poisonous, then?" croaked "Flame" Lampard from the rear.

His voice brought me back from forgetfulness of him.

"Not in its natural state, Mr. Lampard," replied Bathurst sweetly, "but under Mr. Armstrong's special treatment, and remembering Colonel Cameron and Hoad, I should say that the answer is in the affirmative. Very much so, in fact."

"Just a minute," intervened the Inspector, "before you go any farther. What was that case you mentioned just now, Mr. Bathurst? I don't recall it. Who was Crosby?"

"The death of Crosby the banker was one of the cases of the great master Holmes, the details of which, for a very good reason, were never given to the public. His indefatigable chronicler, Dr. Watson, only just mentions it, and that, too, but once. It took place, if my memory serve me correctly, in the February of the year 1894, and to the whole affair, the faithful Watson attached the adjective 'repulsive'. I don't suppose that you ever heard of it, Baddeley."

"No, Mr. Bathurst, I didn't." Baddeley looked across at Anthony and then slightly inclined his head in the direction of Lampard, the prisoner.

Anthony Bathurst understood its significance and nodded. "I won't keep you very long, Baddeley. When I've finished, I'll run you and Lampard over to Lewes in the Crossley. It's not more than two hundred yards away from here and I've plenty of petrol. That all serene?"

"O.K., Mr. Bathurst."

"Right, then." Anthony resumed his recital. "Watson's mention of the case of Crosby the banker occurs in his account of 'The Adventure of the Golden Pince-nez', and its mention has always intrigued me and aroused my very keenest interest. All we are told by Watson, is that Crosby's death was 'repulsive' and that a 'red leech' figured in the affair. When my mind, in its initial investigation of the murder of Colonel Cameron, began to consider the possibility of such a thing as a leech having been employed in some way by the murderer, as the agent of death, the Crosby case came back to me and I wondered if it were possible for me to obtain details of it."

Here I couldn't help making an interruption. As far as I was concerned there was a link missing. "May I ask you a question, Mr. Bathurst?"

"Of course, Miss Cameron. Ask on."

"How did you deduce—that's the right word to use isn't it— the presence of a leech?"

It was obvious from his facial expression that my question pleased him. "I had two things that helped me, Miss Cameron. I had, first of all, your uncle's dying message. You remember it. Probably you will never forget it. Without it, I doubt if we could have ever emerged from the dark. He told us to mind, so we eventually decided, you and I, 'the red thing that flew'. Not much in that, perhaps, to indicate such a thing as a leech, but I had, in addition to that, a piece of evidence that was very much more eloquent and illuminating. I had the evidence of the 'triple bite'. In your uncle's case, Miss Cameron, and also in the case of the death of Hoad in the yard of the 'Red Stag', there occurred this 'triple bite'. Your uncle had the tiny marks in the flesh just under the ridge of the right lower maxillary and the poor devil of an inn-keeper had them on the left-hand side. I will explain the reason of this trifling difference a little later. When I came upon Hoad, that night, lying dead in the inn-yard, my mind had already commenced to toy with the idea of the leech and I attempted there and then by the science of deduction to strengthen what, after all, were only suspicions."

"How could you do that, there? In the inn-yard?"

"I will tell you. But before that, to help you to understand better, let me give you a little information respecting the habits and characteristics of the leech. In England, I believe I am correct in saying, there is only one kind that can be termed 'serviceable'. That is the large brown leech with a whitish belly. Although I employ the adjective 'large' the term is only relative, for the leech seldom attains a length of more than four inches. But it has a peculiar feature, our friend the leech. Using 'peculiar' in its literal sense, that is. A unique feature. It has been provided with a mouth of two lips and it has *three teeth*. These teeth are so sharp that they have actually been known to pierce the skin of an ox. When it is applied to flesh these three teeth suck very similarly to the action of a cupping-glass, and they inflict a 'triple bite'. Just such a bite as the marks on the two dead men suggested. I have been told that these marks have been known to remain on a person's body during a life-time and they resemble nothing so much as the pock-marks sometimes left by chicken-pox. In reference to. and in support of, this last statement of mine, I have an intimate friend who carries on his chest three old chicken-pox marks. When examined for the Army in 1914, one of the doctors mistook them for the bites of leeches which he conjectured had been applied to the man's heart at some time during infancy. So, you see, I was well on the 'leech' trail when I saw the puffy, pink marks underneath poor Hoad's jaw. Although I will admit that I was at a loss to know how the thing 'flew' and wondered if we had deduced the right verb after all." He turned and smiled to me. "But never mind that for the time being. Now I will tell Miss Cameron what she asked me. And I will, in the first place, carry her mind back to the occasion when we found her uncle's message. What can you remember particularly, Miss Cameron?"

I considered for a moment. "The smear of blood that you were able to trace along the grass and the—"

He intervened. "That will do, Miss Cameron. You have remembered the very thing I wanted you to remember. That was the bloody trail that the leech had made when he had dropped, saturated, from your uncle's body, and was making for—where? Any idea?"

I shook my head blankly. Bathurst turned to Baddeley as though demanding the answer he wanted from him.

"Search me," said the Inspector laconically.

"For water. For the little stream below," came Bathurst's dramatic reply to his own question. "The home of the leech, the true home that is in shallow, running water, and it was making for it. If you searched that particular stretch of stream it wouldn't be terrific odds against finding it still there somewhere. A leech will hold clotted blood inside itself for months at a time, and if plucked away from the body will leave a nasty wound." He paused. "Now for Hoad's death. When I flashed my torch over his face, saw the marks, and clung tighter, as a consequence, to my idea of the leech, I looked for any evidence of the running water clue. I argued to myself that it was just on the cards that the second leech, gorged, like its predecessor at the murder game, had also sought water." He paused again and leant over towards me intently. "Consider what I found, Miss Cameron. There was a tiny puddle in the inn-yard that had collected in a depression between two cobblestones, and on the larger of the two stones, which was also the stone nearer to the water itself, was a thin smear of blood. The blood of Hoad the inn-keeper. When I saw that, I can tell you that my heart began to beat pretty rapidly. Things were beginning to shape my way rather pointedly. I went a step farther. I tried an experiment. I felt certain that the leech that had been used to kill Hoad, had gone to that tiny pool as a natural attraction. So I baled out the little handful of water that was there in the hope of finding it. But I was unlucky."

"Lucky!" I cried involuntarily, "supposing it had—"

"Oh—it wasn't plucky, or courageous, or anything like that, Miss Cameron, I assure you. For one thing, I didn't know anything like as much as I know now, and secondly, I hadn't time to consider the risk, so no bouquets—please. The leech had gone, because there was too little water in the pool to keep it there. It had sought fresh pools and puddles new."

"How?" I cried, a second ahead of Inspector Baddeley.

Mr. Bathurst became dramatic. "As the Colonel had tried to tell us when he died. It had down! That was the secret of it all. Research tells me that the 'flying leech' is a native of the jungles of Ceylon. It springs, or 'flies', a considerable distance, by means of a filament that has been given to it by nature for that purpose, and in colour it is pinkish rather than our English brown. It is quite a common occurrence for it to attain a length of seven inches." He beckoned to me. "Come and have a look over here at our present capture, and you'll see what I mean."

I went across and he held up the net to me.

"This is a smaller specimen, probably. About five and a half inches, I fancy. Nice little chap, isn't he? As I said just now, blood will remain clotted inside a leech for months. You remember the stench from the pocket, don't you?" I shuddered and he put the loathsome creature on the floor again. "Let us get back, however, to the genesis of the crime—the repulsive death of Crosby the banker. I have looked the case up, through the kindness of Sir Austin Kemble, and I find that Crosby was killed by a red leech that had just previously been applied to a patient suffering from the coolie disease of Sumatra. This, as you probably know, kills without fail in about three days and the sufferer's death is an absolutely horrible one. Crosby took the disease in its most virulent form, from the 'red leech' that crawled over him and took his blood and died like an animal with rabies. The murderer was never brought to book, but it can be accepted as almost certainly true, from the marvellous accuracy of Holmes's investigations, that a doctor whom Crosby numbered amongst his acquaintances, was the guilty party. Holmes knew that there were many instances on record where syphilitic diseases, for example, had been communicated through the medium of leeches being used on patients, after they had been applied to other patients suffering from those diseases. The leech becomes impregnated, and the next time it 'sucks' the disease is passed on. I will return to Armstrong in this particular connection later. It's getting horribly late, I'm afraid, and Mr. Lampard here requires accommodation for the night—or, rather, morning. Come along, Baddeley." He turned to me. "You can sleep o' nights now, Miss Cameron, and Miss Fletcher can grow sleek-headed. I'll come over again to-morrow evening. I expect Mr. Strachan and Mr. Douglas Cameron will be keen to hear the rest of the story." I shook hands with him, and as I did so, breathed a fervent prayer of gratitude for the impulse that had prompted me to call him to my side.

"You can tell me the remainder of the story when you tell them, and thank you so much for all you have done for me."

"By the way, Lampard," I heard him say as they escorted their prisoner away a moment or so later, "I wouldn't waste any more time, if I were you, on the Trout cryptogram. It really isn't worth it. You may be interested to know that I removed the late Lady Strone's diamonds about twenty-four hours ago." He looked at his wrist-watch. "Twenty-two hours, Lampard, to be exact."

## Chapter XXIX

# THE READING OF THE RIDDLE

BATHURST leant back in his chair and lit a cigarette. Nigel and Douglas quickly followed his example. Major Neale sat with me, whilst Lois patted the hand of Aunt Elspeth, with a motherly solicitude that was rather charmingly absurd, and absolutely wasted on the recipient.

"What do you want to hear about first of all?" asked Anthony. "The cryptogram, or the inner details of the murders? As far as I am concerned I don't mind which I deal with first, because one may be said to—"

"Take the Trout cryptogram first, Mr. Bathurst, will you?" said Nigel Strachan. "That appeals to me as the logical order. If there hadn't been a cryptogram, there wouldn't have been the murders. Also, it's where I first came into it."

"Very well, Strachan. Have it your way. It will suit me as well as the other. We will go right back to the genesis of the whole matter." He crossed his legs and made his lithe, lean, athletic body quite comfortable. "I want you all to carry your minds back to the crashing of the Trans-Continental Airways passenger plane on the eighth of May last. If you remember, the plane carrying Lord and Lady Strone, Viscount Collingbourne, their son and heir, and five other passengers, broke in mid-air from an almost unaccountable cause and crashed, a few miles from Horsham, in the county of Sussex. Every one of the passengers was killed, together with the pilot, observer, and the mechanics. The case is doubtless still moderately fresh in your minds. Yes?" We assented as a company, and Bathurst proceeded. "That tragedy may be said to be the beginning of it all. For, of that tragedy, was born the Trout cryptogram as we have all learned to call it. On that eighth of May, let me tell you, Trout was 'wanted' by the police authorities, for a little matter of burglary, and he, being a lover of freedom, was doing his best to effect a 'get-away'. But, unfortunately, he had only a few hours' start, and he was very doubtful, I should say, in his own mind, as to whether he would reach the coast for which he was making, before feeling on his shoulder the irritating touch of the hand of Justice. I mention this, in order that you may be able to gauge accurately, Trout's mental conditions as he made his way to the Sussex coast line. Somewhere—I cannot tell you exactly where—his course touched on that of the ill-fated passenger plane. Somewhere, I should say, not very far from here. They were ships that passed in the day, and for the first time in his crooked career, our friend Trout had wealth, or the equivalent of wealth, rained upon him from the skies." Bathurst paused for a moment and both Nigel and Douglas took advantage of the pause to nod their confirmation. The former translated his into words.

"I know what you mean. You're referring, of course, to Lady Strone's jewel-case."

"I am. The late Lady Strone was carrying her jewels with her, on her way home from Aix-les-Bains, and when the plane broke in two, which is virtually what happened, and the poor creatures were hurled to their death, her jewels were scattered over the countryside. Many were found, but not all. For this reason. Our friend Trout, assisted by circumstances, and, perhaps the best eye-witness of the accident of all, salvaged sixteen of her famous Murranmore diamonds. They were, no doubt, part of the historic Murranmore necklace. You see now what he means by his line in the cryptogram 'from sky they came, on the Death Parade'. He valued them at fifty thousand pounds, but this was merely a guess on his part, and inquiries that I have made, have elicited the fact that his estimate was considerably under than over." Bathurst turned to Nigel Strachan. "What you thought might stand for 'sixteen paces' stood for 'sixteen diamonds'. Trout made a careless 'D' which could be easily mistaken for a 'P'. As a matter of fact, I was in doubt myself until I actually laid my hands on the stones themselves, whether I was going to find diamonds or pearls. The point was, that I couldn't trust Trout's valuation. In which decision I was right."

Nigel cocked his head in consideration. "Now you're approaching, I suppose, the point where I begin to come into the story?"

Bathurst smiled his corroboration. "Yes, I suppose I am. Consider friend Trout. There he is, with his pockets full of diamonds, some of the finest stones in the world, that he has only had to crawl over the earth to find. All the time, however, he knows, that with ordinary luck, he is unable to count on more than a few hours' liberty. So, with two eyes on the future, he looks round for a hiding-place. And, remember, he hadn't a tremendous variety of choice *and little time.* He had no tools with him with which to dig, even if he had wanted to, and I presume, that while turning and churning the problem over in his mind, he came to the empty bungalow, the same as in which you and I are now sitting, known, as he could see from the front gate, as Dallow Corner. Empty of inhabitants, as the board outside told him, but not empty of appointments. Now Trout was no fool and he knew something of the psychological value of hiding-places. He resolved to enter the bungalow somehow—no great task for a man of his professional skill—and look round for opportunity. What he found when he entered caused him to put into practice Dupin's principle as demonstrated in the story of the 'Purloined Letter'. The best place to hide jewels is in a jeweller's shop! That not being forthcoming, diamonds conceal themselves splendidly when placed side by side with cut-glass! And Trout had found the cut-glass ready to hand!" Bathurst rose from his chair and pointed about his head. "'Look ne'er for sun, But seek the shade.' This crystal shade or lustre arrangement round the electric-light belonged to the Christies—it's one of the old-fashioned type. In my father's time people were proud of their lustres. Look at these pieces, knobs, if you like, of cut-glass, that hang down all the way round. There are between thirty and forty of them. I know because I've counted them. By the time 'Salmon' Trout had very cleverly contrived to fix the late Lady Strone's diamonds there, there were sixteen more. And I defy anybody looking at the shade, in the ordinary way, and with no special knowledge, to have picked them out. It took me a matter of twenty minutes, the other night, to get them down, but it must be remembered that I had an advantage. I knew then what I was after. Sir Austin Kemble, to whom I have forwarded them, is in touch with the present Lord Strone and they will soon be back to Strone Towers. So don't build any castles, Strachan, out of your legacy."

"I am still in the dark, though, Bathurst," advanced Major Neale. "Trout, of course, was arrested after he'd constructed his cryptogram and—"

"Patience, Major," came Bathurst's interruption. "I'll clear up all your doubts and darknesses if you'll only give me time. You're wrong in your assumption of Trout's construction of the cryptogram. The chain of events was this. After Trout had finished up his little job in Dallow Corner, he resumed his journey to the coast, comforting himself with the thought that, even if he were arrested within a few hours, and rewarded with a term in 'stir', there was a land of promise flowing with milk and honey waiting for him directly he had served his sentence and had come out again. Passing the next house, I am of the opinion that, in some way, he encountered Armstrong. Here we travel, more or less, into the realm of conjecture, but it may be taken for granted, I think, that Armstrong succoured him in some way. Gave him food and drink in all probability. Trout asked for it, perhaps, and after all, there is much truth in the attraction of like for like. Each was a wrong 'un and birds of a feather will always flock together."

"I'm beginning to see light," I declared. "Trout was grateful to Armstrong for his hospitality. That's what you mean, isn't it?"

Anthony Bathurst smiled. "That's what I think happened, Miss Cameron, though we shall never know the exact nature of what did occur. Each of the actors is dead. But Trout, I think, after his arrest, after his trial, and after he had served his sentence, was on the point of sallying forth to recover his diamonds that were 'cached' in Dallow Corner when he was stricken with pneumonia. Now, as I told you previously, Trout was neither simpleton nor ignoramus, and he quickly summoned sufficient sense to realize that he had no chance of getting better. He had managed to crawl to a 'doss'-house in Stepney, that was kept by a certain Luke Morton. This Morton, some years before, had married Trout's only child, but the old man hated his son-in-law like poison. He knew that anything he left to his girl would inevitably get into Morton's clutches, and that one assuredly meant the other, so he sought, in his last conscious moments, clarified and sharpened by extremity, for fresh heirs. In this connection, he thought of two people. To employ the phrase that he used himself in his letter to you, Strachan, 'the only two people in the world who had ever lifted a finger to help him'. They were Nigel Strachan, the young barrister whom he had chosen to defend him at his trial, and who had fought for him tooth and nail, and Ralph Armstrong, the man who had given him hospitality, when he had been hunted by the police. His brain-power made a last, supreme effort, and on his death-bed, some day or so, probably, before he actually shuffled off this mortal coil, he produced the piece of doggerel which you and I have come to know as the Trout cryptogram. He sent one copy to you, Strachan, and one to Armstrong. As he stated therein, he gave you an equal chance. He declared that the prize would go to the candidate with the best brains."

"Just a minute," intervened Douglas. "Who posted these two letters? Could he trust Morton to—"

"Mrs. Morton posted them, in all probability. Mrs. Morton *née* Trout. He could trust her. She was bone of his bone. There was, I think, a very strong bond of affection between them."

"Yet she betrayed him—or rather his wishes," cried Nigel Strachan.

"How so?" demanded Anthony Bathurst quietly. He turned to the speaker with some surprise and continued. "I'm sorry, Strachan, but I don't think that I follow your statement. Please explain."

"I'm thinking of Lampard," returned Strachan. "If Mrs. Morton were the only occupant of the 'doss-house' that knew old Trout's secret, it must have been she who passed the information on to 'Flame' Lampard."

"I think you do her an injustice, Strachan. Although I cannot pretend to any degree of certainty, I think that Trout passed the knowledge on himself."

"Himself? How?"

*"In his delirium,"* returned Bathurst. "Morton heard it, saw that it might put his hands on to something big—he was well aware of his father-in-law's profession—and promptly sent for the brains of the party, Lampard, and his confederate, Allen. They listened to the dying man's incoherences and I suggest they gleaned such data as 'Dallow Corner', 'diamonds', 'hidden', etc., etc. We know that they learned enough to find the place. Happily for all concerned, they knew no more."

"Luckily also," put in Nigel, "I was a little bit in front of them. Only a short head, perhaps, but it counted, as heads and necks always do. I dug the 'Dallow Corner' significance from the cryptogram, discovered that a bungalow bearing the same name as the district was in the market, and induced Colonel Cameron, who was on the look-out for a place, to buy it." He looked at me as he spoke. "For that part of the business, Cecilia, I shall never forgive myself. I'm frightfully sorry I said 'luckily' just now." I made no reply and after a moment's hesitation he went on. "I did not, however, understand that the cryptogram referred to the bungalow itself. I don't know yet how that is explained. I thought it meant the district."

Bathurst raised his hand. "Just a moment, Strachan, and I'll tell you. The key to that fact lay in the first line of all of Trout's message. You remember what it was. 'No Dancers need Apply'. To you as you read it, it was apparently meaningless and purposeless. But Trout was an old 'lag' and the word 'dancer' meant a different thing to him and his kidney from what it means to us." Anthony Bathurst proceeded to explain and we all listened to the explanation eagerly.

"That is so," confirmed Major Neale. "I heard the expression constantly when I was Governor of the prison at Wandle I wonder it didn't strike me before. Still—go on!"

"We can say," proceeded Bathurst, "that the stage is now set for the big drama that was to follow. You are on the spot, Strachan, to all intents and purposes; Armstrong, whom we will call your co-heir, is in the wings, all ready for his cue, and Lampard and his men are about to descend after the manner of Sennacherib. Now, who among the contestants for the late Lady Strone's diamonds, or among those that may be termed the onlookers, has what Trout requires? The best brains?" He paused and looked round for a reply. None came. None of us saw where he had led us. "I will answer my question, then, myself. The man among you, who had the best brains, paid a heavy price for them. For they took him to his death!"

"You mean—" I cried wildly, seeing his allusion too late.

"Your uncle, Miss Cameron. Colonel Cameron solved the cryptogram the night that Major Neale dined with you and his reward was death."

"But how?" demanded Douglas.

Bathurst's voice became very quiet and very intense.

"Because, unsuspectingly, he told of his knowledge. Because he took his solution to the very last man on God's earth whom he should have taken into his confidence. Armstrong! Armstrong—Nigel Strachan's rival."

"I begin to see," muttered Neale. "When he heard the Colonel's story, he realized that his chance of the diamonds had gone."

"Almost," corroborated Bathurst, "but not quite. For the Colonel told him that night, that he *had not yet told Strachan or anybody else* that he had hit upon the solution. He let Armstrong see that the two of them held the secret. Now Armstrong was a complex creature. Most murderers are. He certainly was no exception to the rule. He loved the flesh-pots of Egypt. He liked good food, good wine, and the comfortable places of the earth. Old books, old pictures, old furniture, but not old women. And he was very nearly at the end of his financial tether. Trout's legacy, for I suppose that is the light in which he regarded it, spelled salvation for him, and when he heard of it, for the first time, in Trout's letter, he grasped at its possibilities even as a drowning man clutches at a straw. The Colonel's news made him desperate and he saw his prize being snatched from him. Directly the Colonel left him that evening to walk home he put one of his devilish pets in the breast pocket of his guest's overcoat, knowing that it could be only a question of a few minutes before the beastly thing struck."

"How was the poison transmitted?" questioned Major Neale.

Anthony Bathurst shrugged his shoulders. "That yet remains to be established. I've had a word or two with Dr. Elliott, and I'm afraid the question may prove too subtle for him to solve. My views on the matter are these. Armstrong was a much-travelled man who had spent several years in Ceylon. I've discovered that. On one occasion he journeyed from Colombo to Anaradhapura, the one-time capital of Ceylon and its 'Luxor' of buried cities, on a hunting expedition for elephant and red deer. It was this little jaunt, I fancy, that provided him with his colony of flying leeches. According to Dr. Elliott, the poison is an obscure vegetable poison, not unlike adenia, the new bulb poison of South Africa. Armstrong introduced it into his leeches and they passed it on with undiminished potency to their next patient as their fellows in the past have undoubtedly passed on syphilis and kindred diseases from one person to another. It was a much finer method of murder than the knife or the revolver because it was somewhere in the neighbourhood of a thousand to one against the crime ever being brought home to him."

"Admitting that, what made you suspect *him*, then?" demanded Douglas.

Bathurst hesitated. "I had wonderful help. Help at the right moment. At the very best moment of all. At the beginning of things. The criminal never knew that Colonel Cameron contrived to leave a message behind. He told us of what we were to beware, and he also told us something else—*that Armstrong would help*. Get the last fact well into your heads for a moment. I shall come back to it. Until after the death of Hoad the inn-keeper, I had no *definite* suspicions of anybody. I schooled and disciplined myself so that I shouldn't."

I interrupted him. "Not even 'Flame' Lampard, or one of his henchmen?"

"Not even of 'Flame' Lampard, Miss Cameron. I was tempted to suspect him and his confederates, and, perhaps, in a way, I did—but nothing like *definitely*. I managed to keep an open mind. I didn't eliminate Lampard, but I kept my suspicions of him, strictly within limits. When you, Miss Cameron, gave me direct evidence that Lampard was concerned in your cousin's disappearance, I was in a quandary. I reasoned this way, and that, and eventually came to the conclusion that there was a bigger brain in the business than Lampard's. Before I finished my brain-wringing I even considered the possibility of Lampard and Armstrong working together and actually was some time before I relinquished the idea. But I put Baddeley on to the Lampard end and you know how we finished up. As I said, however, the turning-point of the investigation was the murder of Hoad. *By the same agency, mind you!* It seemed to me, that, considering that Hoad was alive early in the evening and dead within an hour or so, and killed in his own inn-yard at that, the murderer must be somebody *near*. Somebody *intimate*. Somebody *whom Hoad knew*. Why had Hoad gone out? Whom had he gone to see? That, again, we shall never know, for his secret died with him. But he *knew something*. Either Armstrong had given something away to him in an unguarded moment, or he had seen something himself on the night Colonel Cameron was murdered. I incline to the former suggestion. I think Hoad had heard Armstrong talk of his life in Ceylon and he may have heard of some of his private pursuits. I know for a certainty that Hoad was troubled by the Colonel's death from what he had confided to me himself, and had he been blessed with a few more hours of life, I should have known what it was that troubled him. I think he showed his hand after he had spoken to me, went to Armstrong deliberately and asked certain awkward and pointed questions. But dead men tell no tales, either here or anywhere else, and Armstrong saw that Hoad qualified for that gallery. Now on the very night when I found Hoad dead, my mind had begun to toy with Armstrong. You remember, Major Neale, and you, Miss Cameron, the 'attack' that had been made upon him here in this bungalow some little time before Hoad was murdered, on the evening when we entertained Lampard?"

Neale nodded. "That business puzzled me considerably. How do you explain it?"

"Can you recall that he *volunteered* for the position in the room where the Colonel's body lay? That was his first real chance to bag the diamonds. They were what he was after. But he hadn't time to do the job. You and I were back too quickly for him. So he contrived to work one of the windows from the inside, so that he could get in again pretty easily and then fell from the table deliberately, shammed unconsciousness, and fabricated the attack'. But the extraordinary thing was, that what he told us coincided with the Colonel's last message. You didn't know that, but Miss Cameron and I did. 'A thing that flew.' Very illuminating that phrase, don't you think? He was either telling the truth, said I to myself, or *he knew a great deal more than was good for him.* Knowledge is double-edged and cuts both ways, you know. That's why it's dangerous, both in large and small quantities. I began to think, and to think hard."

"You've brought something back to me," I cried. "The very morning after my uncle's death, when he came here to me to offer his condolences, he came into this room on the pretext of looking at Uncle Ian's body. I remember now that he looked all round."

"With a purpose, Miss Cameron. With a definite purpose. He was measuring details and working out how he could manage to bring off his 'coup'. After the inquest, I visited him, and he began, ever so slightly, to give himself away. Despite what the Colonel, with perfect trust in Armstrong, had told us with his dying breath, as it were, *Armstrong couldn't help at all*! Couldn't *because he wouldn't*. There are none so deaf as those that won't hear. Instead of telling the truth with regard to your uncle's visit that night, and of the solving of the cryptogram, he deliberately went back to a previous conversation that Colonel Cameron had had with him. Talked about fishing, and 'salmon' fishing at that. I question very much if the Colonel had ever mentioned the word 'salmon' to him. Just imagine salmon fishing in Sussex! That came from his own knowledge again, and he thought it would serve to confuse the issue." Bathurst half-smiled and moved his long arm to reach for and grasp the box of cigarettes that was on the mantelpiece. "It did the very opposite, and my visit to Armstrong, on the morning of the inquest, gave me my strongest clue of all. A clue that gave me a lot of heart. From it, I received something very like corroboration of what, after all, up to then, was no more than pure theory. It seemed to join up two of the most awkward flats of the picture that I was endeavouring to assemble. My theories, based on inferential calculation, began to show signs of definite development. Armstrong wasn't expecting me to return home with him after the inquest that morning, and as a consequence, there was something on his table when I reached there that he would have preferred me not to have seen. For he had no time to remove it. You'll never guess, any of you, what it was."

We shook our heads unanimously. Neale's cold eyes were alight with interest. The semi-resentful attitude that he had been inclined to use towards Bathurst had evidently gone for ever. Anthony, comprehending this, was pleased. His crisp voice came again.

"My investigations regarding our friend, the flying leech, had told me, pretty generally, that their water in captivity is usually drawn off and replaced or changed by means of a small wooden or metal funnel. Imagine my inquisitorial delight when I saw such a thing actually lying on my host's table! His eyes followed mine as I caught sight of it. His own guilty knowledge thrust fear into his heart, and I was afraid that he would know that my brain was shaking hands with itself. He fell back for attempted safety on the first lie that his quick mind could parent. He used it, he explained to me, for decanting wine. But there is no silt or mud in wine, and clinging to the tip of this funnel there were tiny traces of wettish earth that had come from his wooden bowl, or perhaps deal box, of leeches." A film of smoke rose from Anthony Bathurst's cigarette. "All I had to do then was to arrange my battle-array. Not easy, I can assure you, for he was cunning incarnate. I knew from his tampering with the window that he was coming back for the diamonds, and that if I cleared, he would consider that the coast was all the clearer. I determined that A. L. Bathurst should win the toss and bat first. Also, that when his turn came to put on the pads, I should still be there to meet him with the good scout Baddeley in the offing. I should be fittingly armed, too, against his especial line in domestic pets. Your amazing presence, Miss Cameron, and the sudden reappearance of our mutual friend, Mr. Lampard, rather disturbed my field tactics, but all's well that ends well. . . . I'm rather sorry Lampard shot him . . . in a way, I'd have liked to have let loose his own devilish weapon against himself. Measure for measure, eh? I'm afraid I'm cultivating a strain of vindictiveness, Miss Cameron. But he was a nasty, messy piece of work, and I expect that hell was all a-flutter to receive him. They have their excitements there, no doubt, and possibly ran a special excursion on the Styx for his arrival."

He shrugged his shoulders and looked round interrogatively. "Any more flats require joining. Tell me if there are. I'm always pleased, you know, to . . . you, Strachan . . . you, Neale?"

Hesitation marked each of them.

"I think not," declared Nigel. "I'm clear on all that matters, anyhow. What say you, Douglas?"

"Yes," said my cousin. "One. Lampard got me away by means of a false phone call—I've told you that. But how did he know of Nigel's connection with the Yorke-Singleton case?"

Anthony Bathurst smiled.

"I fancy Mr. Strachan's clerk, Coleman, could supply the answer to that question. I don't know what the bribe was. . . ."

Then I stood up suddenly and sought the grey eyes of Anthony Bathurst. Those lazy eyes, the changing moods of which I had come to know so well during those last days. "I've one question to ask you," I said. "It doesn't matter half a bean really, but I'm just curious, you see, being a woman. . . ."

The grey eyes, a little tired from the strain of the days, regarded me gravely. When he spoke, he spoke gently. "It's been your show all through, Miss Cameron. Ask on. *'Ad Caesarem'* and all that, you know."

I smiled, and put my question. "What did you want a nurseryman for? Was it anything to do with the case or was it something that you . . . ?"

Another light danced in Anthony's eyes now, and made me doubly glad that I had remembered to ask the question. For I don't think I had ever seen it there before.

"That was a long shot, Miss Cameron. A very long shot. One from the bag to beat the book. Almost as good as finding the winner of the Grand National." He rubbed his hands in undoubted pleasure. "Our friend of the triple bite is always at his best when he has the roots of Florence Iris close to hand. He revels in it. I discovered this, and wondered if our murderous merchant knew it, too. So I took a chance. By a glittering fluke it came off. Croft, the nurseryman on the left of the Quoynings road, had actually sent him supplies. We will call that the crowning culmination of corroboration." He wrinkled his brow humorously as he looked at me. The question that came was quizzical. "Well—how many out of a hundred?"

"A hundred and one plus," I replied, warmly and promptly. "For your kindness, your sympathy, your marvellous—"

Anthony Bathurst put playful hands to his ears. "Spare me, Miss Cameron, please. What have I done to deserve it?"

"Everything," I answered smilingly, and thoroughly wound up. "I'm going to be utterly shameless and show you the extent of my maidenly adoration. I'm going to be perfectly oblivious to the fact that we are not alone. Here goes. I'm certain that you're flawless, that there's nothing that you don't know . . . that you're the really finished product . . . that you're above the angels. . . ."

He interrupted me with a quick wave of the hand. "You're hopelessly wrong, Miss Cameron. I'll tell you one thing at least about which I know nothing. Nothing whatever."

I smiled again and shook my head contradictorily. "I don't believe you. What is it, Mr. Bathurst?"

He smiled back. "The way to treat a woman."

"Good heavens! Why? With all your powers of . . ."

"I've forgotten it," said Mr. Bathurst. "I had to. There are some things, you see, that I would rather not remember."

THE END